The Applecross Saga

Amanda Giorgis

Book 3

Guy Pender

Other books by Amanda Giorgis

The Wideawake Hat

Shepherd's Delight

ISBN 9798653094651

To Bran and Zoe.
The first of the new generation.

CHAPTER ONE
Homesick

Zurich - February 1867

Guy Pender was feeling the aching pangs of homesickness. How he yearned to see his friends once more. The Mackenzies and their neighbours, who farmed sheep in the high country of New Zealand. To hear Sophia singing to herself as she swept the kitchen floor, or maybe to listen to Lucy chattering to her 'creatures' as they gathered around her to eat the seeds that she had scattered for them. To inhale the fresh aroma of the clear air and to listen to the cacophony of birdsong each morning as the sun rose into a clear blue sky. Memory tends to forget about the bad things and to dwell on the optimistic side of life, where the sun always shines. Guy chuckled as he thought to himself that there were also days when the north west wind blew relentlessly across the plains and where temperatures fell so low that even your hair would freeze solid, breaking off in your hand if you dared to push it back from your face. Even those kind of days would, he felt, be preferable to his current state.

As he took a sip of his bitter coffee, served in a tiny cup, the handle so small that his fingers could hardly hold it safely, it occurred to him that he was homesick, not for his real home, but for his adopted land. A land where he had found good friends and felt like part of a family for the first time in his life. Not for the first time in the last few days, he reached into his jacket pocket for the dog-eared photographs he kept there to cheer himself up. As he looked down at James standing on a wide verandah next to Sophia, baby John James in her arms, he felt the familiar feeling of sadness. And there was Freddie, dressed as if he was going exploring in the mountains in his tweed breeches and wearing a pith helmet, standing on the lake side, the tallest mountain of all behind him - the one the native New Zealand people called 'Cloud Piercer'. Then there was his favourite photograph of Friday, the collie dog. It had been his first photograph with the Mackenzie family and, though Friday had been gone some time now, buried on a hill overlooking the plains where sheep roamed in huge numbers, it was still his most treasured memory. That day, when everyone had gathered round to see the magic of developing a photograph from a glass plate, the day he truly never expected Friday to stay still long enough to make a good clear picture. But, of course, she did sit still. She would do whatever her master James told her to do without question. And what fun it had been to show young Freddie how the camera worked and how to turn a wet plate into a proper photograph. How disappointed Freddie had been at first, when he saw the negative, or 'inside out' as he had called it.

A few spots of afternoon rain began to fall around Guy, bringing him back to the present day with a rush. He quickly put the precious photographs back in his pocket before any raindrops hit the flimsy cards. Guy looked up from his outside table at the small restaurant, which had become his habitual lunch venue, to see people beginning to hurry towards shelter. Some stopped to put up an umbrella, while others ran as best they could on the cobbles towards the shelter of a shop doorway, or under the ordered row of trees alongside the small, central park, with its close-cropped lawn and formal flower borders. The ornate clock on the balcony of the town hall across the square sprang into action with a clunk and a whirr. A mechanical sort of a tune sounded out while wooden knights rode their wooden horses into a circular battle, culminating in them striking a bell with their jousting poles. Guy knew that he had

Amanda Giorgis

just enough time to hear the two bells strike before he must get back to the studio. As he left the table he threw a few coins down to pay for his lunch, making sure there was an extra tip for Luigi, the waiter. His wife was due to give them their first child any day now, and Guy knew that his job at the restaurant would not be well paid, by any means.

Oblivious of both the rain falling around him and the curious glances of those people who now sheltered in every doorway, Guy strode across the cobbled square, the brim of his hat tipped forward to protect his face from the sudden storm. His mind was preoccupied with thoughts of the people he was missing so much, so he failed to notice the adoring glances of the three young ladies who giggled under the cover of a shared umbrella. Guy was a handsome man, dressed well in an expensive tweed jacket, matching plus fours and ribbed argyle socks up to his knees. His well-made brogues would keep the damp from his feet and the latest fashion of a bowler hat to match his suit sat rakishly on his head. Dark, curly locks could be seen not quite fitting under the brim. But what the ladies noticed most were his piercing blue eyes, blue enough to make them think of the deep mountain pools they had seen in the nearby alpine valleys. It was enough to make the three young ladies swoon.

Guy paused as he reached the faded blue door next to the book shop and, with a shake of his shoulders, he shed his feeling of homesickness, just as if he was removing a wet overcoat and forced himself to focus on the job in hand. Opening the creaky wooden door, he found his next client waiting for him in the gloomy interior.

It was a necessity of being in Switzerland that one needed to be familiar with a variety of languages and he knew, because of the name he had written in his ledger, that he should use french to address this afternoon's first customer. "Mademoiselle Dupont?" he questioned, adding, "I will just be a moment while I prepare my equipment, so please do take a seat." He indicated a worn red leather couch, the only piece of furniture in the room, and leaving the lady and her chaperone to sit for a while, he slid behind the heavy curtain that separated his studio from the waiting room and set about rolling down a crudely painted sheet of mountain scenery, placing a heavy wooden chair at a slight angle in front of it and making sure there was a chair to one side for the client's companion. He had noted in their brief first meeting that Mademoiselle Dupont was a lady of significant bulk, not fat but rather big-boned, and it occurred to Guy that the prettiest part of her portrait would be the backdrop. Again he chuckled to himself as he remembered his Aunt Emmeline once saying that you couldn't make a silk purse out of a sow's ear, but he would do his best in this case, just as he always did.

Trying to dispel the image in his mind of a sow's ear, Guy put his head around the heavy curtain and invited his client into the studio.

"Ici ma chaperone, ma tante, Frau Muller," said Elise Dupont.

"Guten tag, Frau Muller," said Guy, with the merest nod of the head and kick of the heels. "Please do sit here." As Frau Muller sat in the chair Guy had indicated to one side of the fake scenery the sour-faced aunt allowed herself a tiny smile in gratitude for Guy's attempts at German. The truth was that Guy has almost exhausted his German vocabulary with a simple greeting, and he hoped that Frau Muller would not engage him in further conversation. Fortunately, she seemed to have turned into a grotesque statue at once, her beady eyes on her young charge, lest some dreadful ill befall her at the hands of this photographer fellow.

"She speaks no English," whispered the young lady with a twinkle in her eye, "so we may continue in that language if you wish."

"That is a relief to me in more ways than one," laughed Guy, and the ice was broken between them. Guy always like to make his clients feel at ease as he preferred the photograph to show them in their most natural pose. He had the ability to judge people very quickly, and he already knew that this young lady had a keen sense of humour and was willing to hoodwink her chaperone by speaking in a foreign language. He would do his best to capture that spirit in his photographs. Not for him the stuffy, formal shot with a stern face staring back at the world without giving away any secrets about the subject's personality. And that was why his reputation as a portrait photographer was beginning to grow in the city of Zurich and even further beyond around Switzerland.

For the next half hour he asked his young client to arrange herself in various attitudes in front of the painted mountains and lake. She stood, or sat, facing toward the camera, or to one side, as if gazing at the far peaks. She held a parasol or rested a lace-gloved hand on the back of the chair. Each time he talked to her to put her at her ease, only asking her to stay silent and still for the exposure of the photograph. He felt sure he had ended up with five or six good portraits by the end of the session.

"Thank you, Mademoiselle," he said, as he brought the session to an end. "Give me a little time to work on your portraits. Shall we say two days?"

"And Danke, Frau Muller," he added, thereby exhausting the remainder of his very limited German vocabulary.

With thanks in French and German, the two ladies made their farewells. Guy had just half an hour to process the photographs, it being a necessity to act quickly before the plates dried out. Then the whole rigmarole would begin again with his next clients. Sometimes a single lady, with a chaperone of course, or a young man standing proudly to attention in his new, ill-fitting military uniform. Sometimes a young couple, just married perhaps, and sometimes a family with a stern father attempting to rein in his family in order to record them for posterity through a photograph. Guy enjoyed the family sessions best, even though it was hard to keep the children still for a clear picture to emerge. He had a growing collection of photographs, which could not be delivered to the customer, because of a blurred movement of one of the youngsters. Although they were not suitable for selling, Guy quite liked the dynamism that could be created with such movement. He was keen to try the same technique outside the studio where subjects could not be stilled - a river running by, a tree bending in the wind or a waterfall flowing into a pool.

The afternoon continued in this way with three more customers who could each have been called

Elise Dupont for all he cared. Guy found his subjects merging into one another. They all dressed in similar layered dresses with no full crinoline skirt these days, but rather a small bustle to accentuate the shape. The hats, it seemed to Guy, were becoming more and more outrageous, there being a growing fashion for decorating your hat with what amounted to a fruit stall, or even with poor imitations of the birds that looked so much better on a real branch in a real tree. Nevertheless, Guy did all he could to bring out the best in each one of his clients. In forming some sort of a relationship with them it never occurred to him that he was building himself a reputation as an eligible bachelor. Little did Guy seem to realise the reason why most of his clients these days were the affluent young ladies of Zurich.

By the time he turned the sign in the small front window to closed, Guy was not in the mood for any more work. Now he had finished processing the plates, the printing of this afternoon's portraits could wait until tomorrow as his first appointment was not until eleven o'clock.

Not for the first time, Guy silently cursed his aunt for the layout of his studio and apartment. Although he lived upstairs in just one open room, there was no access from below without going outside first. Of course, Aunt Emmeline had let out the ground floor as a shop while living on the first floor herself. Now Guy used both levels he had to make the awkward journey home by leaving through the front door, heading all along the street to the corner, taking a small alley between two buildings and accessing his living room via a metal staircase. Or, just to make life interesting, he could walk to the other end of the line of buildings, take a similar, but wider passage and squeeze past his photographic cart, parked there for safety, before reaching the same staircase. It was a game he played with himself to make that decision only once the door of the studio had been locked. "Left or right?" he would mutter to himself, "left or right?"

Tonight was a night for going left. The advantage of this choice being that he passed Monsieur de Fevre's boulangerie where, no doubt, he could purchase the last of today's crusty loaves. The thought of breaking off a chunk of bread to add to the emmental cheese and german sausage he knew he had in his larder cupboard made Guy realise how he hungry was. Coming out into the fresh air, locking the door and turning left out of his studio, he realised that the rain had stopped. The cobbles glistened with water, but the late sun was casting long shadows and the birds, roosting in the trees in the centre of the square, were making a noisy job of telling everyone that the weather was improving and spring would be here soon. Leon de Fevre saw his favourite customer turn his way and had time to grab the last long stick of bread before meeting Guy on the front step of his baker's shop.

"Je suis glad you turned my way ce soir, Monsieur," said Leon in his heavily accented mix of French and English. "There is jusque thees one left pour tu. Please to take it before it is eaten by mon brother's peegs."

"Merci, Monsieur de Fevre," Guy said as he accepted the long stick of crusty bread with what he knew would be a white and fluffy centre. "Avec les saucissons et le fromage."

They both laughed out loud at their poor attempts to communicate, Leon slapping his English friend on the back while Guy waved his supper in the air like a sword. As Guy continued along the terrace of brick fronted houses it occurred to him that Leon was the nearest he could come to a friend in Zurich. Not that he knew anything about him, other than that he baked the best bread for miles around. So he supposed that made him an acquaintance rather than a friend.

Holding that thought as he turned left at the end, taking exactly twenty four paces to reach the little alleyway that would take him to the back of the very same building he had just left. That was the trouble with his life. He had acquaintances, but no friends. Even his favourite family at Applecross sheep station were but transitory friends. Their lives continued while he was not there, and he doubted they ever thought of him, but perhaps to wonder when he might call again. But it was all his fault that he had chosen to run away from the only true friend he had ever made.

"Ah, but then there is Albert," he thought to himself, as the tabby tomcat, who had made himself at home in the apartment lately, wound himself somewhat dangerously around Guy's legs as he climbed the metal stairs to his apartment.

Albert followed Guy into the untidy living room, hopping up onto the free standing kitchen bench and sitting down to await his share of supper. It was not long before Guy had put the dry corners of his cheese and the rounded end of a spicy sausage into a bowl, which he then set on the floor for the cat. Albert purred with satisfaction at this feast, his tail erect with just the very tip waving from side to side as he ate.

Guy cut off several chunks of cheese and meat for himself and laid his share on a wooden board. Taking the board and a sharp knife to his dining table he proceeded to tear off pieces of the delicious white bread and stab the other items with the point of the knife before popping them into his mouth. Guy sniffed it gingerly to see if it had gone sour before pouring a generous measure into the glass he had used last night and taking a good swig to wash down his dry supper. His aunt would have been appalled at his table manners, but he just couldn't see the point of 'dressing for dinner' these days.

He was still thinking about friendships as he poured himself another glass of the excellent red wine taken from his aunt's collection, and moved across to his favourite chair next to the window overlooking the square. Albert quickly jumped onto the table to finish the crumbs before another leap to curl up on Guy's lap where he knew he would get his fur stroked for a while. When he had had enough attention, he would go out again to hunt for a late night snack in the rubbish behind the bakery, but for now he purred contentedly in his favourite after-dinner spot. He sensed his master was distracted tonight, so he gently nudged his arm with his shiny black nose, as if to say, "stroke me, please."

It worked, as it always did, and Guy continued to tickle Albert behind the ear and smooth his tabby coat while thinking about his friend, Frewin. Or should he say ex-friend these days?

Guy Pender had, he realised now, grown up in an entirely masculine world. Apart from his nanny, whom he had never considered to be either male or female, just Nanny Bee, all the people that he had spent time with had been men or boys. He barely remembered his mother, who had died giving birth to his sister when he was only three years old. The tiny baby girl had lived but a few days longer, mother and baby being reunited in the family plot at the local church. Nanny Bee had arrived to take on the role that Ralph Pender could not fulfil for his son in his grief-stricken state, though it was not long before Guy had been shipped off to boarding school. He often wondered what Nanny Bee did during term time, but she was always there to greet him, to tut over his torn trousers and socks in need of darning and to wipe the dirty marks off his face with a lick of her fingers.

School had been a hard journey for Guy. Not the learning part, which he mopped up like a small sponge, but, partly because of being top of the class, and partly because he was a handsome boy with a girlish mop of chestnut curls, his classmates bullied him mercilessly. He accepted the pinches and punches that happened out of sight of the masters, but it was harder to learn to live with the verbal assaults. By the time he had reached puberty he couldn't wait to get away from the place. It felt like a prison where torture was meted out on a regular basis, the holidays all too brief a chance to be cared for by Nanny Bee. However, one September day at the start of the academic year, his luck changed. The older boys had the privilege of moving out of the stark, austere dormitories and into rooms for just two to share. No-one else wanted to share with the school swot, Pender, so his housemaster had put the new boy, Frewin in with Guy.

It wasn't long before the two boys were inseparable. They shared the same passion for learning, and as they grew into young men, they discussed the latest ideas in politics, in religion and in anything else they considered important. For the very first time in his school life, Guy didn't want the Michaelmas term to end. However, in line with his newfound change of fortune, the fates conspired to keep the two boys together over the Christmas holiday. Frewin received a letter from his parents informing him that they would be unable to get back to England for Christmas and that arrangements had been made for him to stay at school with the other boys from overseas. In the same post Guy received a long letter from his aunt in Switzerland. Aunt Emmeline was his mother's sister and had, over the years, corresponded with her nephew in order to keep in touch with her only remaining blood relative. To his knowledge, Guy had reached the age of fifteen without meeting his aunt, although he had grown to admire her through their letters. He had even received a regular parcel from her on his birthday, and it always contained just exactly what a small boy wanted at the time. Guy thought fondly of the box of coloured pencils, which had arrived at the very time he had developed a passion for drawing, the wooden carved bear holding a brass bowl that even now stood on his bedside table and the leather-bound set of Mr Charles Dickens' serialised stories.

It seemed that Aunt Emmeline was planning to visit England this Christmas and was looking forward to spending some time with her only nephew. Guy wondered if his father would be as happy about this arrangement as he was. When he had mentioned his aunt's letters to his father, he had noted the look of disapproval.

"Perhaps, my dear Frewin, you could come home with me too?" suggested Guy when they had shared the contents of their correspondence with each other. And so it was arranged. Their housemaster was glad to dispose of at least one more encumbrance over the holiday period, and Guy's father breathed a sigh of relief that he wouldn't have to entertain a son he hardly knew.

The boys had declared it the best Christmas ever. Aunt Emmeline had filled their time with games and entertainments, the pinnacle of which had been a riotous puppet show based on the story of the nativity with words written by Guy, puppets and scenery made by Frewin and an appreciative audience made up of Aunt Emmeline, Nanny Bee and the kitchen staff. Guy's father had preferred to keep to his study, thereby missing out on the three legged donkey, the dropping of baby Jesus by Mary and a crown rolling across the stage as one of the wise men bent to offer his gift to the manger.

In quieter moments Aunt Emmeline, who had never married and had little experience of young people, found a natural ability to relate to the two boys. She particularly enjoyed sharing her love of books and reading with her young nephew and his friend. As the relentless rain of an English winter fell outside, the three of them could be found in the library exploring dust-covered books that hadn't been taken from their position on the shelf since Guy's mother had died. In the evenings, in that magic hour after supper and before bedtime, Aunt Emmeline told Guy all about his mother. Guy had not even realised that his mother was Swiss, not English, but Emmeline told the boys all about their early lives as sisters living in the countryside near Geneva. Their father, Guy's grandfather, had been a schoolteacher and it was his desire to immerse his family in English that had brought them to a school in Surrey. It was here that Guy's mother met and married Ralph Pender. Emmeline had returned to Switzerland as soon as she was of age, living these days in an apartment in Zurich. The girls had grown up with a passion for books. They had even planned to open a bookshop together, but of course, their father soon pointed out that young ladies do not enter the world of commerce. It was a bitter disappointment to them both at the time.

Guy was happy that he had inherited a passion for reading from his mother. His aunt considered that Guy had inherited much more than that from her in the way of looks and mannerisms, and, thankfully in her opinion, very little from the odious man who was his father.

Over the last two years of their schooling Guy and Frewin made every effort to keep up with Aunt Emmeline's high expectations. They read as many of the classics as they could lay their hands on in the school library or from the library at Guy's home, as well as practicing conversational french between themselves. Guy really regretted his inability to pick up a language as it would have been so useful to him in Zurich. While it came naturally to Frewin, somehow Guy failed miserably to reach Aunt Emmeline's high standards, remembering only the odd french word or phrase these days.

It was as if Aunt Emmeline had adopted a second nephew in Frewin, a boy who had been shifted around from place to place all his life, never finding time to make any sort of a relationship with anyone. He revelled in his new found friend and adopted aunt.

Circumstances led to it being Frewin who visited Aunt Emmeline in Zurich in the weeks after they finished their schooling and before they were due to go up to Oxford. Frewin was to study languages while Guy had signed up for the classics, though neither boy looked forward with enthusiasm to even more formal studying.

Aunt Emmeline had invited them to Switzerland for the summer. However, on the last day of term Guy was summoned to the headmaster's study where he was given the dreadful news that his father had died tragically in a house fire. It seemed he had fallen asleep at his desk in the library and was unaware of a coal spilling from the grate. By the time Nanny Bee and the kitchen girl had become aware of smoke and run down from their top storey rooms, the flames were too fierce for them to even open the library door. They could do nothing but escape for their lives and call for help. But help came too late to save Ralph Pender.

Guy took the news without saying a word and left the headmaster's study in a state of numbness. His greatest loss was that of the books in the library, rather than of his father, though he had a strong sense of guilt in feeling that way. But it meant that his trip to Switzerland was postponed while he attended his father's funeral and helped Nanny Bee to rescue what they could from the fire damaged house. The only other people to attend Ralph Pender's funeral were a Mr and Mrs Paget and their two young daughters, good friends of Guy's mother, who had not been encouraged by Ralph Pender to continue the friendship after her death. Guy had happy memories of the Pagets, who had a son a year or two older, with whom he had played in the garden on the rare occasions that Noah and Dorcas Paget had called on them. He was really pleased to restore their acquaintance, but truly saddened to hear of the recent death of their only son in the Crimean conflict.

Ralph's estate was left entirely to Guy, with the proviso that he kept Nanny Bee in comfort for the rest of her life. After everything had been sorted out, he bought a small cottage in the village of Upton Barwood, with a tiny garden where Nanny Bee was more than happy to potter for the rest of her days. A small second bedroom was always ready with clean sheets and fresh water for a time when her precious charge needed a bed for the night.

After the death of his father Guy had no appetite for university study. He suddenly found himself to be a young man with some money, and he intended to use it in what he and Frewin called their university of life. Guy joined Frewin and Aunt Emmeline in Zurich, the two young men writing letters to their respective deans declining the places they had been offered at Oxford. Guy and Frewin shared a corner of Aunt Emmeline's living space in her small apartment, a curtain hung across for privacy's sake, while they planned what to do with the rest of their lives.

Frewin had not been idle while Guy was tidying up the loose ends of his father's affairs. He had become friends with the gentleman who leased the shop below Aunt Emmeline's apartment. Herr Greben was the first person in Zurich to open a photographic studio where he sought custom from the richer classes. It was becoming the fashion to have a portrait taken at moments of importance in life, a wedding perhaps, or the birth of a baby. And Fritz Gruben was one of the first to go into the new science of photography. He was beginning to make a decent living out of it too. Fritz was a regular guest upstairs for supper, and Frewin became fascinated by his descriptions of the equipment used and begged Fritz to let him learn how it all worked. By the time Guy got to Zurich, Frewin was determined to make a career out of photography too. It was not long before Guy became just as enthusiastic. Fritz was happy to work in his studio where he could have all his equipment laid out in readiness, it being a necessity to work fast to create a good image, but he knew a man who had imported a travelling studio taking photographs of the nearby alpine scenery. He wondered if the boys would like to spend some time with Monsieur Benne?

A camping trip with Monsieur Benne was quickly organised before the end of the hot summer of 1857. The seed of an idea began to form in Guy's mind. One that he shared enthusiastically with Frewin. Perhaps this was how he would spend his money, in buying a travelling studio and touring the world. He may not even need to eat into his capital if they found enough clients for portraits to subsidise their travels. And what perfect timing it turned out to be. Eugene Benne could no longer travel away from home for long periods now that his wife had given birth to twin boys. A deal was done, and Frewin and Pender became the proud owners of the contraption and all its equipment. All that was left to do was to hire a horse to draw the cart along.

Over the winter of 1857 and the start of 1858 they learned how to take good photographs under the tutelage of Eugene Benne and Fritz Gruben. Frewin became the expert at portraits while Guy preferred the landscapes, but between them they got used to judging light levels, setting up the perfect pose and using the chemicals effectively to bring out the detail in their glass plates. The only fly in the ointment was the cramped living conditions in Aunt Emmeline's tiny apartment. It was time for them to find somewhere else to live.

In the end, it was Aunt Emmeline herself who suggested New Zealand, although nobody ever knew quite why. Perhaps she had hankered to travel there herself one day, but it was too late to ask her now. The boys stayed with Aunt Emmeline for one last Christmas before returning to London for Frewin to say a grudging goodbye to his parents and for Guy to see Nanny Bee for the final time. Where Frewin was not worried at all that he may never see his parents again, Guy was sad to see his beloved nanny for one last time. The elderly lady, who had been, to all intents and purposes, Guy's mother, took him in one last hug, licked her finger and pushed back the curl that refused to stay out of Guy's eyes. To this day he wasn't sure if the moisture he felt on his face was Nanny Bee's spit, or his own tears beginning to fall. It would always be a matter of regret that he never saw her again after that.

The photographic cart was shipped, at great expense, to the port of Deal and stowed aboard the steamship 'Ambrosine' where Guy and Frewin joined as second cabin passengers, just in time to leave port at the end of February 1858. It was the beginning of June before they arrived in the town of Wellington, at the bottom of New Zealand's North Island, where they had originally planned to stay. But a chance encounter with a fellow passenger, who was heading further south to see the mountains, which he told them, were just like Switzerland, had encouraged them to take that route too. The cart was duly transferred to a smaller coastal craft for the journey to Port Chalmers.

The growing town of Dunedin was the perfect place for two young photographers at that time. The town was booming with settlers, many arriving from Scotland. And what better way to record your family's arrival in a new land than to have a portrait taken. Frewin was in his element. But, looking back now, Guy could see the first cracks in their relationship at that stage. Guy wanted to explore the countryside and take the cart to photograph the scenery, whereas Frewin was happy to stay in Dunedin. Guy stuck with Frewin for the first year or so, admitting to himself that the steady income gave them a good start in their venture. Dunedin was growing at an alarming rate, and they never seemed to be short of customers looking to record a special moment for posterity. Nevertheless, the countryside was a draw that Guy could not ignore forever, so with some reluctance Frewin was persuaded to follow him up the coast to Oamaru, where they leased a tiny studio for six months before heading even further north, across the wide Waitaki river to the new town of Rhodestown. It was here, much to his surprise and by sheer chance, that Guy came across the Pagets again. The two young men had spent a discouraging day looking for premises in which to set up their studio before Guy started his travels inland with the cart in search of mountain scenery. No suitable shop or office could be found, and Frewin was getting grumpier and grumpier as the day went on. Coming out of yet another unsuitable building Guy stepped into the street and collided with a gentleman, who was passing by with his head down. Turning to apologise, he found himself looking at a familiar face, last seen on the other side of the globe.

"Mr Paget!"

"Guy Pender!" both men exclaimed at once, taken by surprise at this most unexpected encounter.

Questions and answers were exchanged before Guy remembered his manners and paused to introduce Frewin, who had been standing to one side with a face like thunder. He cheered up a bit when Noah Paget suggested that they both join him and his wife for dinner at his new home, and wondered, perhaps, whether they were in need of a bed for the night?

Over supper that evening Guy and Frewin learned the reasons for the Pagets coming to New Zealand and listened to the sad story of their tragic journey. Noah and Dorcas had been so distraught at the loss of their son in the Crimean conflict that they had made a decision to leave England, joining a group from their local church who had been invited to assist in building a new town in New Zealand. Bringing their two daughters with them, they had embarked on the 'Strathallen' with great hope for a new start. A house had been commissioned for them in advance with room for a growing family, but tragedy prevented it from ever being filled with children. A dreadful sickness had spread throughout the ship, being especially prevalent amongst the youngest passengers. First it had taken young Emily, then her sister Edith. Both had, by necessity, been buried at sea and Noah was, in some ways, relieved that his wife was too ill to come up onto the deck to see their tiny bodies, wrapped in calico, sliding into oblivion. It was a memory he would never be able to erase from his mind. To add to the tragedy, Dorcas recovered from the sickness on board, but not before she had lost the child she was carrying, and she had now been told that she would be unlikely to conceive again. Meanwhile, the family home had been made ready for their arrival but now gave them far more space than the two of them required. Dorcas was thrilled to have two young men to stay for as long as they wanted, and their new cook, Mrs Bennett, was equally pleased to be able to provide hearty meals for two extra mouths.

The thought of Mrs Bennett's fine steak and kidney pudding brought Guy back to the present. Pushing the dozing cat off his lap, he went across to the table to tear off another piece of crusty bread. Albert stretched from nose to tail before returning to Guy's warm lap. He picked a crumb of bread from the folds of Guy's trousers and considered heading outside for a juicy mouse. "Maybe later," he thought to himself.

A sudden shiver ran through Guy as he continued to think back over the last year or so. He had indeed made his trip inland from Rhodestown, leaving Frewin behind. But he had done so on horseback, it being a rough journey for the cart to tackle. Frewin had been persuaded to meet him later by taking the cart by a flatter route. It was on that first trip that he had the pleasure of meeting the Mackenzie family at Applecross and their neighbours, the Lawtons at Combe station. All had been going along so well, and for the first time in his life, Guy had a circle of friends. Not only that, but he found himself to be a popular visitor, especially with the youngsters in the families. He thought fondly of Freddie. He should not have favourites, but Freddie was a very special boy indeed! The only ripple in things was Frewin's growing sulkiness. There were one or two disagreements between the two men, even one that had resulted in Guy spending Christmas away from Frewin, but the real battle had begun when

Guy received a letter informing him of Aunt Emmeline's death. Guy had no choice but to travel back to Zurich as soon as he could, as it seemed she had left him everything, including the apartment. But, in his mind, it was a temporary absence from New Zealand while he sorted out her affairs and sold the apartment. However, Frewin was keen for them both to go back to Switzerland permanently. Things came to a head one night after a day of constant bickering which had driven them both to drink heavily. Perhaps Guy had a need to drown his sorrows for the loss of his aunt, perhaps Frewin had his reasons too. Whatever it was that had made them down one drink after another, Guy could recall with horror every word spoken between them, every moment of that dreadful evening.

They were staying at Hither House with the Pagets, an almost permanent state of affairs these days. Noah and Dorcas had retired to bed soon after supper, leaving the two men to discuss their future. One glass of wine followed another, almost without realising how much they were drinking, as the conversation went one way, and then the other. Guy was determined that he did not want to leave New Zealand forever. It was his home, and he had good friends around him and a reasonable career. Frewin, on the other, had reasoned that they could make more money in Switzerland and have the advantage of a place to live too.

Perhaps it was the drink that made Guy bold enough to say out loud what had been festering in his mind for a long time. Looking back he regretted saying it in such a way, but perhaps it was better out in the open. "Frewin, it is MY money that you are spending, and MY apartment. She was MY aunt. So I will make the decision about what we do with it." With each 'MY' Guy banged his fist on the table.

To his horror Guy looked across to see a tear rolling down Frewin's cheek. Frewin wiped it away with a bony finger and, getting up from his chair he staggered drunkenly around the table until he was standing next to Guy. "But I thought you wanted to do things together," moaned Frewin, "I thought you loved me."

With that, he reached down to clasp Guy's face in his hands and turning it towards him, he placed his lips on those of Guy and attempted to kiss him fervently. Horrified by such intimacy, Guy pushed Frewin away with as much force as he could muster, sending him staggering backwards into an empty chair, before escaping to the fireplace, where he turned on his friend.

"What on earth are you doing?" he exclaimed, as he wiped the unpleasant wetness from his lips with the back of his hand.

"I thought you loved me," Frewin repeated. "I have always loved you from the day I met you. How can you not feel the same?"

There are, Guy thought, moments in your life when the world turns. One minute you are going along quite happily in one direction and the next second something happens that instantly sends you on a different path altogether. This was such a moment.

"But," Guy tried to put a coherent sentence together despite his befuddled mind, "but, you are a man!" was all he could think to say.

"I know," replied Frewin with his head cast down. "But I thought you understood me. I thought you had the same feelings. Can you not give me hope that we can be together in this way?"

"No I cannot," replied Guy, a feeling of revulsion coming over him. "It is wrong. It is a crime. And, while I am your friend, I can never be your lover." He almost spat the last words, so disgusted was he with the very idea.

"It may be a criminal act but it doesn't make me feel like I am committing a crime," replied Frewin softly. Aware of his defeat, Frewin's shoulders had slumped, and he now put his elbows on the table and hung his head in shame. Guy could see a wet pool spreading over the white tablecloth as tears fell freely from Frewin's eyes.

With all sorts of thoughts running through Guy's mind and the sudden realisation that he had done nothing to prevent the situation he now found himself in, Guy could think of nothing more to say. He just needed to get away from Frewin, otherwise he may well pick him up from his chair and throw him head first through the window. He downed the last dregs of his wine, flung the empty glass into the embers of the fire with a crash and left the room as fast as he dare. Later, lying sleepless in his bed, he came to the conclusion that he would prefer never to see Frewin again.

Rising early, still bleary eyed from a combination of the drink and a restless night, Guy found himself alone at the breakfast table. He had already apologised to the maid who he had found cleaning up the broken glass in the fireplace and was forming in his mind an apology for their hosts and the proper words to placate Frewin. In the light of day he realised that, if that was the way Frewin wanted to live, then who was he to judge it. But it was not to be with him as a lover. There would be, he was sure, other men who felt the same way as Frewin. He would tell him those things as soon as he could. They had been friends for some years, and he hoped they could stay that way.

But it was not to be. Noah Paget came into the breakfast room waving a piece of paper. "What's this I hear, Guy? Frewin tells me he has been called away. Thanks me for our hospitality and wishes me well. Packed his bags and gone to Dunedin already. Sounds a bit final, somehow. Have you two fallen out again?"

Guy had no choice but to admit to an argument, but he would not be drawn on what had caused it. Noah Paget, being a man of the world, suspected the truth, but held his tongue. When he read the letter to Dorcas she had replied that she thought their friendship was a bit 'unhealthy' and Guy would be better off without him.

Guy had put his New Zealand affairs on hold for a while and travelled alone to Switzerland. His letter to Frewin, apologising for his reaction and offering Frewin the use of the studio in Dunedin and assuring him that they could still continue to be friends, had gone unanswered. And perhaps that was for the best.

The quick trip to sort out his aunt's affairs had dragged on for longer than anticipated. Swiss legalities, it seemed, are more complicated than the English way. Guy had no choice but to await the outcome of his aunt's probate. In the meantime he had her apartment to live in and an empty studio below. Fritz Greben had used Aunt

Emmeline's death as a reason to retire, so the studio was vacant when Guy arrived. Opening it again was a way to pass the time for Guy, but he rather wished it was all sorted now, and he could go home to New Zealand.

A sudden flash of lightning, followed moments later by a loud rumble of thunder brought Guy back to the present day, not least because Albert's claws had worked like razors into the fabric of his trousers before the cat leapt in the air and retreated under the table in sheer terror. Rain was falling hard again. Between the rolls of thunder Guy heard the town clock strike ten. Time for bed, he supposed, wondering as he lay his head on the pillow, what tomorrow's clients would bring.

CHAPTER TWO
The Eligible Bachelor

The next morning Guy was still in a thoughtful mood as he made his way back down the metal staircase, each step making a musical clanking noise. It really was about time he considered finding a wife, but he couldn't seem to untangle that thought from the constant desire to return to New Zealand. And he couldn't do that until his aunt's estate had been finalised.

It was natural that the majority of his clients were women, but, with their frills and giggles, he couldn't conceive of any of them being his kind of wife. He found himself daydreaming about Lucy Cartwright once more. The image of her sitting in her beloved orchard, half a world away at Applecross, surrounded by her precious birds, was one which kept on coming into his mind these days. He had considered the implications of this vivid mental picture, and though he had to acknowledge that Lucy was a gentle soul and would make someone a wonderful wife, his feelings for her were no more than he would have felt for a sister. He remembered the dreadful day when that awful man Drummond had shot Lucy's precious pheasants. That day he had taken Lucy in his arms to comfort her, but as far as he could remember, he had felt no signs or stirrings of emotion, just a desire to comfort her. Not that he was really aware of how that should feel.

As all schoolboys do, he had picked up a certain level of knowledge about the relationship between a man and a woman at boarding school, although he suspected that would have been somewhat exaggerated by those boys who wanted to boast about their expertise in that area. The whole business of relationships between two men had always been there, in the school dormitories, only as an undertone, never overt. Perhaps, as a consequence of him spending most of his time at school alone, it was really only after the incident with Frewin, that he had been reminded of the occasions when he had suspected improper behaviour between two boys in his year. He really was naive in matters of the heart.

His father hadn't been any help at all, even though he had taken him on one side one day in the school holidays and, hesitatingly and with great embarrassment, explained the whole physical part of lying with a woman. Even Nanny Bee had not been able to add much to the conversation when Guy had asked her about it later.

"Well, young man, one day you will meet a girl, fall in love, and you will know exactly what to do then," she had told him. Looking back it was probably all that Nanny Bee knew, never having married herself.

On the voyage to New Zealand the two handsome young men had found themselves the focus of attention amongst the young, female passengers, and Frewin had even gone to one young lady's cabin on his own. When Guy asked him about it afterwards, Frewin had been coy about the detail, but had given the impression of it not quite living up to Frewin's expectations of the event. With the benefit of hindsight, Guy realised now that Frewin would have preferred such an encounter to be with a man instead.

Rather more out of curiosity than desire, Guy had sought out a lady of the street when the two men had arrived in Dunedin. Assuming that he would, one day, have to take the lead with a girl who was likely to have even less knowledge than himself, he just felt he needed a little first hand experience before any future wedding night. Fortunately, her painted lips and powdered cheeks belied a kind heart and the girl with a name Guy had, to his shame, now forgotten, was gentle and understanding with him and had guided him through the process without making any judgements about his prowess. The enjoyment he had felt was pleasant enough, but the overriding feeling afterwards was one of guilt in paying for something which should have been given as an act of love. He had been more than generous in his payment, so much so that the girl had offered her services to him whenever he desired, but he had not taken up her offer again after that one and only encounter.

"Come on, Pender," Guy said to himself as he took the keys out of his pocket to unlock the door to the studio. "Stop thinking about a wife and concentrate on today's customers."

As it happened, the first of Guy's clients was just about to leave her family home diagonally across the square from the studio. Number forty two was on the better side of the square. Rather than opening onto the street directly, the houses on the east side were set back by a few steps up to the painted front door with its polished brass handles. Enough room to set out a few pots of flowers, or closely sculptured bay trees standing erect like lollipops. Wrought iron railings, painted in glistening paint to match the colour of the front door, ran between the tiny, narrow garden and the street, giving the effect of some privacy. Three storeys high, plus a basement, the houses stood apart from each other, meaning that there was room for a narrow passageway between each one to the back and then down some steps for deliveries to the kitchen. Each brick built house gave the impression that one could open the whole front up to reveal a neat and tidy doll's house inside, furnished with all the latest interior fashions. It was easy to imagine tiny figures working in the basement kitchen to prepare meals delivered by footmen carrying silver salvers up to the candle lit dining room. A parlour would catch the best of the daylight from the tall windows overlooking the street below, for the ladies of the house to work on their embroidery, while next door, the patriarch of the family sat at his desk in the leather-clad and book-lined study. Above that were the bedrooms, the rooms at the back having a pleasant view across the river and beyond and at the very top the sparsely furnished box rooms where the servants slept for just a few hours between each arduous day's work.

The von Trubers had recently arrived at number forty two. Of Austrian aristocratic descent, Herr von Truber had, for some years, been acting as the Emporer Franz Joseph's viceroy in Lombardy, based in the beautiful city of Venice. Lombardy had been part of Austria's empire since the Congress of Vienna in 1815, but as a result of the recent defeat in the war with Prussia, it was in the process of being handed back to Italy. Finding themselves no longer welcome in the city that had been their home for twenty years or more, the von Trubers had been forced to leave with almost nothing but the clothes on their backs. With some forethought of what was to come, Frau von Truber had been wise enough to sew the family's jewels into the hem of her velvet cape, hiding the smaller items in a similar way in the outer clothing of her two daughters, Amelie and Augusta. The shortest and safest route out of Lombardy would take the family to Switzerland and thus to Zurich where a house, furnished to a suitable standard and with servants who were happy to stay on despite the step down in social status of their employers, was found in exchange for a proportion of the hidden jewels. Once he had settled his family in comfort, albeit temporarily, Herr von Truber planned to return alone to Austria to deal with his affairs and to seek recompense for the loss of his belongings from the Emperor himself. In the meantime, he considered the marrying of his two daughters into wealthy families the quickest way to restore his fortunes, and he set about the task with a good deal more enthusiasm than the aforementioned young ladies could muster.

Amelie and Augusta were considered by their governesses in Venice to be high-spirited girls. So much so that a series of governesses had come and gone over the years, unable to cope with their antics when they got together. Individually, the girls were charming, well-behaved young ladies. Amelie had been born in Salzburg and was now twenty two years old. She was the taller of the two and had inherited her mother's fine features and fair hair. Augusta had been born in Venice only eleven months after Amelie's arrival. Their closeness in age had meant that they behaved almost like twins, but Augusta certainly did not have the same good looks as her older sister. Taking after her father, who those of a kindly nature may call stout rather than overweight, Augusta had his wide shoulders and the same tendency to gain weight. Even the very best of corsets, tied as tight as could be borne, would not hide the portly figure beneath. Herr von Truber considered it an easy task to find a match for his eldest daughter, but wondered sometimes if the same could be said of his beloved Augusta.

The two sisters had recently been hatching a plot. Little did Guy Pender know that he was the object of so much discussion amongst the young ladies of Zurich. He was entirely unaware of his own good looks and oblivious to the reasons for his client list consisting of a high proportion of young, single ladies. But Mr Pender's name had been much on the wagging tongues of the young and unattached ladies of the city lately. Augusta and Amelie had often day-dreamed of meeting the eligible bachelor who lived across the square, talking in whispers, late into the night in the bedroom they shared. It was the two sisters and their friend Elisabet, who had been watching from beneath their umbrellas, as Guy dashed through the sudden rainstorm the previous day, giggling because the sisters had told Elisabet about their plans to meet the man of their dreams very soon.

It was Amelie who had come up with the idea in the first place of having their portraits taken. It would mean being physically close to their idol. He may even be required to arrange their outfit or push back a loose lock of hair. At such a thought the two sisters positively swooned! But how could they persuade their parents to allow them to visit the studio?

"Perhaps we can suggest that Papa keeps a portrait of each of us in his pocket," suggested Augusta. "Then, when he meets a gentleman whom he considers to be a suitable beau for you or me, he can show them how beautiful we are before we even meet."

"We will have to be chaperoned," said Amelie, "so we will need to ask Mama too."

Frau von Truber had considered it an excellent idea, particularly as her new friend Madame Martinez, Elisabet's mother, had already accompanied her daughter to Mr Pender's studio. The resulting portraits were delightful. Elisabet looked demure but radiant, surely suitable attributes for any prospective husband. She suggested that the sisters have their portraits taken alone, but that a photograph of the two girls together would make an excellent gift to be sent to their grandparents in Salzburg. Frau von Truber had visited Guy to make a booking for her daughters. It was a mark of his popularity that the first appointment available had been more than a week hence.

There had been much preparation for the day's appointment at number forty two. Amelie rued the fact that her best dresses had been left behind in Venice and there had been little spare money to allow for the purchase of new clothes recently. But she had been busy with her needlework and had made the best of a plain dark blue dress with long, narrow sleeves and a high neck. She had found some deep red material to add colour to the cuffs and yoke, as well as an extra flounce along the hemline. She had even embroidered a motif of the flower they called Edelweiss here on the yoke and at the waist. A bonnet had been found to match, and with the addition of a lace neckpiece, Amelie felt that she looked the part of an eligible young lady. Nothing too daring, but she rather hoped Mr Pender would be impressed by her attire.

Augusta had been squeezed tightly into her corsets by Lizzy, their English maid. "Breathe in, Miss," she had pleaded, "or you won't never fit into your dress."

It was a good thing they had tried their outfits on the previous day because Lizzy had time to let out a seam or two of Augusta's pale cream dress, which could be hidden by a wide pale yellow belt tied in a bow at the back, sitting neatly to accentuate the bustle. "Not that the bow will show up in any photographs," she complained to her sister, while turning round as much as she could to look at her back in the long mirror.

"You look lovely, dear sister," said Amelie.

"Not as lovely as you," came the reply.

Lizzy had her faults as a lady's maid, having worked her way up from the very bottom of the servant hierarchy, cleaning fireplaces and emptying water closets and chamber pots, before being offered the role of maid to the ladies of the von Truber household. But she had magic fingers with a brush and comb. On the morning of the appointment it took her no time at all to pin the sisters' hair up from their faces before placing their hats at exactly the right angle with even more pins. "They need to see your face proper in them photographs," she said, as Augusta complained about her hair feeling like it was coming out at the roots.

Their mother was waiting for them at the bottom of the stairs. "You both look lovely, my dears," she exclaimed. Although she knew that her older daughter had been blessed with the better looks, she remained scrupulously fair in her praise. "And," she thought to herself, "Lizzy has done the best she can for Augusta with that sash at the waist."

"Now, let's not be late for our appointment," she said out loud as she led her daughters down the steps to the street below.

Guy had arrived at his studio this morning with enough time to work on all of the previous day's portraits. He was just in the process of placing them carefully into the right envelopes for collection when he heard the sound of the town clock striking the hour, the volume increasing as the front door opened. Assuming from the name in his appointment book that the ladies would be German, he pushed back the heavy curtain and greeted them with, "Guten Tag, Frau von Truber, und zu deinen tochtern." He was glad he had taken the opportunity to consult his German dictionary beforehand, but he need not have worried.

"You are welcome to speak English, Mr Pender," said Frau von Truber, realising from his accent that it would be hard to continue in German. "We are from Austria, though the girls are used to speaking in Italian. They are proficient in English too."

"For that I am most grateful," replied Guy. "Now, ladies, perhaps you would like to come through to the studio, and we can decide who goes first."

With their mother in front, the sisters had a chance to hang back, exchanging excited smiles. For just a moment, Amelie clasped Augusta's hands in a shared frisson of excitement. As Guy held back the curtain he took stock of his two clients. The shorter and presumably younger girl was much like the majority of his clients. A figure confined by corsets, but failing to hide the tightness of the outfit. But she had a pretty face, a long, slender neck and a look of impudence and humour in her eyes. He was already thinking of placing her behind the chair where the waist would not be so obvious, and he had a few more tricks up his sleeve to ensure the slimmest of effects.

None of these devices would be required for her older sister. Guy thought to himself that she could be dressed in an old bedsheet, and she would still be stunningly beautiful. Amelie would have been somewhat disappointed if she had realised that her sewing efforts to enhance her outfit were wasted on Guy, who was entirely distracted by her face. To an outsider it would seem that Guy was looking into a mirror. Amelie had the same blue eyes, deep as pools of crystal clear water. For a long moment the two of them stared at each other, an emotion with which they were both unfamiliar caused the two of them to shiver slightly.

"May I be first, Mama?" asked Augusta, breaking the silence, "I am so excited!"

"Indeed you may," replied Guy, dragging himself away from those eyes. "Now ladies, perhaps you would care to sit to one side for a while." He indicated the two chairs he had already put in place for the mother and older daughter.

With some difficulty, Guy managed to concentrate on putting Augusta at her ease, but it was hard to avoid the watchful eyes of her sister. By asking his subject to stand at a slight angle, with one foot in front of the other, he hoped that the resulting photographs would hide the worst of her plump figure. He failed to see the glance that the sisters exchanged with each other as he instinctively reached out to adjust the folds of her skirt. It was all Augusta could do to stop herself from crying out with excitement, turning it, as best she could, into a sort of strangled gulp.

"Would you care for a glass of water, Miss von Truber?" asked Guy solicitously. Augusta waved a hand and shook her head, as it seemed she was incapable of speaking out loud.

Once the two young ladies had swapped places, Guy found it a good deal easier. It really didn't seem to matter how Amelie stood or sat, she made a perfect pose. At one point a single curl of blond hair escaped from under one of Lizzy's pins. Guy resisted a dreadful urge to push it back himself and wondered what on earth was coming over him. Instead he handed her a small tortoiseshell hand mirror which he kept for such occasions and discreetly turned away while she remedied the situation.

As he had been requested, he then took several portraits of the sisters together, even suggesting that they finish with a photograph of all three ladies. Mother sitting primly in the high backed chair with Augusta standing behind, in order to hide her waist, while Amelie stood tall beside the chair, with a gloved hand on her mother's arm. It was an enchanting group. Having then agreed that the photographs would be ready in two day's time, Guy, for a reason he couldn't quite fathom, offered to deliver them by hand.

"We will look forward to that," said Amelie, with a smile towards her sister. Guy assumed that she meant that she was looking forward to seeing the photographs, but the two young ladies were secretly anticipating the deliverer, rather than the delivery.

As Guy closed the door behind his latest clients, he paused by the shop window to watch them step across the street. He was pleased to see the two young ladies linking arms and giggling like giddy schoolgirls. They made a pretty family group, and he had enjoyed taking their photographs. A shiver ran through Guy as he turned away. He spent the rest of the day being distracted from his other clients by images of Amelie's deep blue eyes following him around the room.

Rather than leave the processing of the von Truber's portraits until the morning, Guy decided to stay on in his studio, even as darkness fell outside. Not that he would notice in the corner of the room surrounded by heavy black curtains to keep out the light entirely. He just couldn't wait until the morning to see Amelie's portraits. As he suspected, the von Truber family were definitely the stars of today's assignments. Even Augusta would be pleased with the outcome, he was sure. And the family group photograph was one of the best he had produced. He made two copies of that, intending to keep one in his portfolio. Sometimes clients would ask to see samples of his work before deciding to book an appointment, and he had no hesitation in adding the photograph of this charming family to the album, which he displayed on the counter at the front of the shop.

Guy had once shared a box of beautiful Swiss chocolates with his aunt many years ago. Delicious dark chocolates shaped into hearts, or drops, or squares, some plain, some mixed with hazelnuts and some topped with a cherry or a parma violet. He remembered taking his time to decide which was his favourite, but then choosing something else first. His aunt had laughed at him, saying, "Leaving the best until last?"

He felt just the same way this evening. Amelie von Truber's photographs were to be savoured, the anticipation growing as he worked his way through the lesser flavours first. Eventually, the time came to reveal each delicious photograph. Guy never ceased to be amazed at the magic that happened as the chemicals turned plain shiny paper into a portrait, the image appearing slowly from nothing, piece by piece. As Amelie's image began to appear, it was her eyes that came first, almost as if they were the strongest part of the image. Guy, who had gone through this process many hundreds of times over the last few years, suddenly found himself holding his breath. With expert hands, he knew just when to remove the paper, making sure the chemicals didn't run, and placing it to dry for a few minutes. Only then did he take a breath, gasping at the sheer beauty of the image before him. Each time he repeated the process, Amelie's eyes came first, followed by the rest of her face and beautiful body.

This time Guy made second copies of Amelie's portraits, but not for his portfolio. He knew it was improper and unprofessional, but he just could not resist the urge to keep her image as his own, to be treasured. It took all his inner strength to avoid clutching the thin card to his chest before the chemicals had dried. Not for the first time today, he wondered what on earth had come over him. Never before had he felt this way about any of his clients.

The town clock once more brought him back to reality. "Seven, eight, nine," he counted under his breath. "Goodness, nine o'clock," he added out loud. Nine o'clock and Monsieur de Fevre would have closed his bakery hours ago, so no supper tonight. With a new and unexpected feeling of hopefulness, Guy decided he could manage without food tonight, perhaps he would treat himself to a fresh croissant on his way to the studio in the morning. He cleared away his chemicals and equipment, made a final check on all the photographs he had created today and headed for the door. But not before tucking a photograph of Amelie von Truber in his jacket pocket, next to his heart.

For the first time in many months Guy paused on the doorstep to appreciate the stars above him and the almost full moon rising above the buildings across the square directly over the roof of number forty two. He wished Amelie a silent goodnight, and without pausing to consider his direction, he turned to the left. As he passed de Fevre's bakery the moonlight lit up a package wrapped in paper and placed on a wooden stool outside the door. On it was written in neat handwriting, "Mr Pender, bon chance." As he picked up the package, he felt the warmth of a fresh, crusty loaf inside. He silently blessed his friend the baker for providing him with supper after all and set off for home with a newfound spring in his step. Good luck had indeed come his way today.

CHAPTER THREE
Visiting

The improvement in Guy's spirits continued the following day. Albert, aroused from his sleep by the sound of his master whistling a tune, wondered what had changed to make the man so much happier. He rather hoped it would turn into a better supper tonight than the dry crusts he had been getting lately. Perhaps his master was inclined to stop at the butcher's shop for a little liver for his tea. The cat carried that thought with him as he sidled past Guy and out onto the metal stairs, before bounding down to the ground in two agile leaps.

Guy had taken a time to fall asleep the previous night, his head full of thoughts of Amelie von Truber. Once asleep, she was there in his dreams too. Rather annoyingly, now he was awake, he could not remember the details of those dreams, though he knew they were of a pleasant nature. He continued to whistle a tune as he descended to street level, turning right so that he could pass the bakery on his way to the studio. Leon de Fevre looked up from setting out his wares to see who was so cheerful this morning and was somewhat surprised to see the tune belonged to Guy Pender's lips.

"Monsieur de Fevre, thank you for my supper last night," said Guy. "You saved me from starvation after a busy day."

"You are most welcome," replied Leon. "You had many customers and I saw your light still lit as I was shutting up the shop." Clapping a floury hand on Guy's shoulder, he added, "The young lady, she is attractive, n'est pas?"

"I had several young clients yesterday. I wonder to which of them you refer?" questioned Guy, as he brushed the fine white powder handprint from his jacket, giving himself the chance to avert his eyes from his friend's piercing look.

"Why, the young lady from across the street, of course," replied de Fevre with a knowing wink. "The taller of the two sisters. Her young sister is, how you say...., full of lard, but the older one would have made a fine portrait."

"Indeed she did my friend, indeed she did," said Guy, tapping his pocket where the precious copy of Amelie's portrait had been placed and thinking that Augusta would be most offended at the unflattering description of her stout figure.

"Now, Leon," said Guy, "I am in need of a good breakfast today, despite last night's gift. What have you to offer?"

Guy left the boulangerie with a warm croissant and a sweet pastry curled up into a spiral containing juicy currants and cinnamon with icing sugar paste on top. He had not been able to choose between them, so had decided to buy them both. With a wave of thanks, Guy continued along the street to his studio, resuming his whistling along the way. Balancing his sticky breakfast in one hand, he opened the door with the other and set about beginning his day. Having done all the work last night, he had enough free time to savour both breakfast items and to wash his pastry-covered hands in water poured from a china jug into a tiny basin in his dark room. He certainly didn't want greasy finger marks on the precious portraits he now needed to put into envelopes for collection, or in one case, for delivery.

Somehow his clients seemed easier today. Perhaps they sensed his raised spirits, but whatever the reason, they were happy people today. Guy was sure the portraits would show this. Even the sombre German man, his stern-faced wife and their two small sons, who spoke not a word during the whole sitting. Even they had come across as happy and gay. Perhaps it was the tiny puppet that he dangled next to the camera to catch the gaze of the children. The two boys had stared at it open-mouthed, their mother smiling at their obvious joy. And, much to his amazement, father smiled benignly at the camera too.

To be honest, Guy could hardly remember the rest of his clients that day. He held the image of Amelie's eyes in his head throughout. He even managed to sneak a look at her portrait in between sessions, though he needed no reminder of her beauty. By the middle of the afternoon he found himself free for the rest of the day. At first, he thought he may take a walk along the river while the late winter sun was still giving out some warmth. But then, he thought he would deliver the photographs to the von Trubers, even though it was a day earlier than he had promised. Perhaps Amelie would come to the door when he knocked, perhaps she would be watching for him as he came across the square. Guy gave himself a silent telling-off. How stupid he was. Of course, they would have servants to answer the door, and Amelie would be busy with her embroidery, or whatever it was that young ladies of her class did with their afternoons.

He checked the contents of the envelope, turned the sign on his door to 'closed' and set off across the street, walking around the tree-lined central park and crossing the cobbled road right in front of number forty two. With his long legs, he managed the four or five steep steps to the door with ease and raised the brass knocker. It did not cross his mind for a moment to consider taking the side passage to the tradesman's entrance.

It seemed to Guy that it was an eternity before he heard slow and heavy footsteps on the tiled hallway floor, followed by the door being opened just a narrow crack. "Good afternoon," said Guy. "I have a delivery for Frau von Truber."

"Deliveries round the back," came the surly, heavily accented reply from the diminutive footman who seemed to be holding the door with long, bony fingers and sticking his equally long, narrow nose around it without revealing the rest of his body to the stranger. He reminded Guy of a scary pencil drawing of a gremlin in one of his childhood books of fairytales.

"Oh no, I mean I need to give this envelope to Frau von Truber herself," continued Guy. "May I come in?" he said, stepping forward on the presumption the door would open for him.

Indeed, the door was opened a little wider, the

gremlin standing back to allow Guy into the hall. Having shut it firmly behind him, the footman, who seemed to do everything in slow motion, turned to Guy and said, "I see. You have zee photographs. We deed not expect you until den morgen. Frau von Truber eez out. I speak to her daughter."

Before Guy had time to say anything in reply, the dwarf footman hobbled slowly towards the door Guy took to be the separation between the world of the 'family' and that of the 'staff'. After a wait of several minutes, while Guy paced back and forth across the black and white tiled hall, he heard the sound of someone coming down the stairs from above. Looking up with the expectation of seeing Amelie rushing down to meet him, he was instead greeted by a young girl in the uniform of a maid. Sensible black boots came down the stairs first, followed by a plain grey dress, with a white pinafore with frilled edging over the top. Finally, Lizzy's cheerful face arrived too, having been sent down by the footman to deal with Mr Pender.

"I'm sorry, sir," said the lady's maid. Guy was quite surprised to hear a familiar English accent. "The mistress is not at home. Neither is the master, nor one of the misses. But Miss Augusta reckons she will see you, if I stay with her too."

Not quite what Guy had hoped for, he would have preferred to have seen Amelie again, of course. Nevertheless, he gratefully accepted the offer to go up the stairs to the drawing room where Lizzy opened the door and announced, "It's Mr Pender, Miss Augusta, come to see us about them photographs."

Augusta had been standing at the window, and it was only as she approached Guy that he could see her flushed cheeks. He wondered if she was not well, hence being left at home alone. In fact, she had almost been overcome with emotion at the idea of meeting Mr Pender on her own, but for propriety's sake Lizzy had insisted that she stay too.

"Please do sit down, Mr Pender. I have taken the liberty of ordering coffee. I take it you prefer coffee to tea, as they seem incapable of making tea correctly here in Zurich," Augusta realised she was babbling and forced herself to stop.

"That is most kind," said Guy as he eased himself into an ornate upright chair, upholstered in the same material as the heavily striped wallpaper, giving the impression of the room being somewhat overdone, in his opinion. He passed the brown manilla envelope across the small table to Augusta, who went to take it, but then thought better of it.

"I think I will await Mama's return to see our portraits, Mr Pender," she said, "but thank you for bringing them to us. We understood you would be here tomorrow."

"I do apologise, Miss von Truber," replied Guy. "It was presumptuous of me to arrive a day early, but it is good to see you again. I hope you will be pleased with my work."

Augusta's further blushes were hidden from Guy as she turned to acknowledge the arrival of the tray. Yet another member of staff carried it in and placed it on the low table where Lizzy took over the role of serving tiny coffee cups to Augusta and Guy in turn.

"Thank you, Billy, you can go now," said Lizzy to the young servant before she poured cream from an ornate china jug. Billy gave the maid a scowling look that seemed to say, "Who are you to order me about?" before turning for the door.

There followed a long and awkward silence. It was obvious to Guy that Augusta had not yet acquired the skills of a good hostess, although she was doing her best. In order to break the silence, he chose the normal topic of conversation on such occasions by saying, "The winter is coming to an end, is it not?"

"Oh yes," replied Augusta, grateful for his lead. "But we must make haste to the mountains before all the snow melts in the spring sun. My sister and I are so excited because we go to St Moritz next week. Although it is mainly English people who stay there in the winter, we are to be guests of some Swiss friends. We will try to ski. Have you been skiing, Mr Pender?"

The idea of throwing himself down a snowy slope with two narrow strips of wood attached to his feet did not appeal to Mr Pender at all, but he could see that Augusta was excited by the idea. "No, I have not, but I am sure it will be enjoyable," he replied. "Perhaps you will meet a handsome Englishman while you are there," he added with a twinkle in his eye. He guessed that Augusta was of an age to enjoy the thought of a holiday romance.

"Oh, I rather think we have already met a handsome Englishman," Augusta replied before she had time to stop herself. She glanced across at Lizzy, who, behind Guy's back, slapped a hand to her mouth to stop herself from uttering, "Goodness, what have you said to this gentleman!"

Guy had the presence of mind not to react to this statement, which would, no doubt, cause further embarrassment. Oh, how he wished it was Amelie with whom he was having such a conversation. In which case he may have responded with a compliment too. Realising it may be time to take his leave, he put his cup and saucer down and rose from his chair. Both Augusta and Lizzy followed suit.

"Well, thank you, Miss von Truber, for your hospitality. I look forward to hearing from your mother after you have taken a look at the portraits together. But now, I must get back to work." As was the style of a Swiss gentleman, he stood to attention, bowed his head slightly and clicked his heels before leaving the room. Augusta had rather hoped that, by holding out a hand, Guy would take it and kiss it gently, but, as her hands were without gloves, he would have considered this far too risqué. Though, had it been Amelie who had offered a hand, he would have been seriously tempted regardless of her bare skin.

The fact that he had failed to see Amelie this afternoon could not entirely dampen Guy's high spirits. As he walked past his lunchtime cafe, even Luigi noticed a definite spring in his favourite customer's step. Just last evening he had shared a glass of absinthe at the bar with Leon de Fevre. The baker had mentioned that the beautiful and eligible daughter of Herr von Truber had been a visitor at Guy's studio, and he suspected that Guy's upturn in humour had something to do with that visit. He was pleased for Mr Pender, though he doubted that Herr von Truber would share his pleasure if he knew that his daughter had attracted the attention of a simple photographer.

As Guy disappeared through the door of his studio, Amelie and her mother, arms linked, came around the corner and into the square, walking directly to their front door. Luigi, pausing as he flicked the crumbs from an outside table with the cloth that usually lay neatly across his arm, looked up as they passed by. Amelie von Truber was hard to ignore. Tall, beautiful and elegantly dressed, Luigi could imagine her walking with Guy, instead of her mother. They would make a pretty pair indeed.

What Luigi could not tell was that Amelie was doing her best to hide her anger from her mother. She was pleased that her father had left them to make their own way home, because she was angry with him too - really angry.

The day had started well. The sisters had spent the first part of the morning telling Lizzy all about their visit to Mr Pender's studio. In other circumstances, the two girls would, perhaps, not have been so close to their servant, but in Lizzy's case they made an exception. Lizzy had been a housemaid at their beautiful and luxurious residence in Venice. Nobody really knew how a girl from the streets of London had come to be in service on the other side of the continent, and Lizzy herself would never speak of it. When the time came for the household to leave Venice in a hurry, most of the staff had families nearby and were not in a position to join their employers, but Lizzy had been called to Frau von Truber's salon to be asked to join them in Switzerland.

"Well, ma'am, I may as well, if you please," Lizzy had said at the time. "There's nothing to keep me here, after all."

Frau von Truber was pleased to see Lizzy nodding her head in acceptance. She found it hard to understand Lizzy's thick English accent sometimes, although the girl had done well to improve herself since they had taken her on.

So Lizzy found herself suddenly a lady's maid. Not only that, but being of a similar age to the two daughters, a special bond had been formed during their traumatic escape to Zurich. It was as if the three young ladies were friends, but only when they were alone. Lizzy reverted to servitude whenever anyone else, either family or fellow servant, was within earshot.

Lizzy was excited to hear all about the photographs while she brushed the sisters' hair and piled it up with her seemingly endless supply of pins. She reached into the pin box, took two pins out, put one in her mouth and stuck the other firmly into Amelie's thick, blond locks. Talking with the pin still in her mouth, she said, "Lordy, Miss Amelie, this Mr Pender chap sounds handsome as pie to me."

Used to Lizzy's comparisons making no sense at all - how could someone be as handsome as a pie? - Amelie tried to nod her head without being stabbed viciously with a hairpin.

"He is, Lizzy," she sighed as she replied, "but I doubt he will even notice me. He has so many other clients."

"Oh, I think he noticed you, Amelie," replied Augusta, "but I wish it was me," she added, clutching her hairbrush to her chest, arms crossed in front of her heart.

At that moment there was a gentle knock on the bedroom door. "Can I come in, girls?" asked their mother, not waiting for a response before pushing the door open.

Lizzy, instantly transformed from friend to servant, bounced with a tiny curtsy towards her mistress and silently withdrew from the room, leaving mother and daughters alone.

"Now, Amelie dear, I want you to put on the dress you wore yesterday. Your father and I have an invitation to lunch, and we would like you to accompany us," said Frau von Truber.

"Where are we going?" asked Amelie.

"You remember your father has made an acquaintance with Herr Linburg? He is the gentleman who has invited us to his lodge at St Moritz. He wishes us to see his factory where chocolate is made, followed by lunch at his home with his wife," said Amelie's mother, neglecting to add that another member of the family would also be present.

"Can I come too?" asked Augusta. Amelie had already guessed the reason for only her being invited, not Augusta. So too, it seemed had Augusta, and she could not resist adding, with a twinkle in her eye, "and what is the name of their son, Mama?"

"No, you may not," replied Frau von Truber. "And Tobias will join us for lunch, I am sure. I understand he runs the factory. He must be a little older than you, Amelie, and very handsome, I am told."

Amelie's heart sank, but she knew she had no choice but to obey her parents' wishes. Her father had made it plain to both the girls that a good marriage needed to be made for each of them for the sake of the family. "Ah well," she said to Augusta after their mother had left them to continue dressing, "at least Mr Pender is not visiting until tomorrow. I had hoped to keep busy today while we awaited his visit, although this was not at all what I was hoping to do with the day."

Later that morning, Herr von Truber, accompanied by his wife and oldest daughter, set out to walk the short distance to Linburg's chocolate factory by the river. As they got nearer to the building it was hard to ignore the bitter sweet smell of rich, dark chocolate. A pleasant aroma in small amounts, but quite overpowering on an industrial scale. Amelie felt her throat and lungs fill with the acrid smell and wondered if she would embarrass herself by coughing. She felt for her silk handkerchief tucked discreetly into her left sleeve and was reassured by its presence.

A fierce looking woman, who Amelie presumed to be Herr Linburg's secretary, greeted them at the door and showed them through to a comfortable and opulent office, furnished with leather couches and lined with dark oak panelling. From behind a huge desk, piled high with handwritten ledgers, Herr Linburg rose to greet them. He reached for a stick before limping towards them. Amelie realised that he must be quite old and looked very frail indeed.

Despite this, he led the way to the factory floor where he looked around for his only son. "Tobias," he called, seeing him leaning over a table where various samples of chocolate were laid out.

Tobias Linburg looked up from the tray of chocolates he was studying in great detail. Recognising his father, he came towards the party. "Father," he said in German. "And we have visitors, I see."

Amelie took stock of the man her father had contrived to bring into her life. Tobias Linburg was not quite what she had been expecting after meeting his father. She had assumed he would be a good deal older than her, but it seemed not. He was a handsome man, fresh faced with a mop of unruly dark hair and brown eyes that seemed to dart around from side to side all the time. His nose had a roman quality to it, not surprising as Amelie knew the Linburgs were originally from the Ticino, so more Italian than Swiss. Had she not already given herself, in her mind at least, to Guy Pender, she could well have been quite taken with the looks of young Herr Linburg.

"Fräulein von Truber," said Tobias, "it is good to

make your acquaintance." He clicked his heels and bowed his head in a formal greeting. Amelie was more used to the Italian habit of taking an offered hand to kiss the fingers gently, and she found the German way rather formal. Apart from anything else, she was not sure how to respond. She gave the merest nod of her head, although it seemed that Tobias Linburg had already set off on his tour of the factory, expecting the two women to follow him. She gained the impression he was an impatient man, always thinking about the next thing and failing to concentrate on current business. How she knew all this in the short time they had known each other, she could not tell, but first impressions often turn out to be true. Her father and Herr Linburg had already returned to the office to talk of business matters, promising to meet with Tobias' mother for lunch in an hour.

Had anyone asked Amelie to explain the process of making chocolate after her visit, she would have been unable to do so. On the outside she displayed a look of fascination into the mixing of ingredients and the shaping into items which could be placed in ornate boxes tied with wide ribbons. But inside she could not stop herself imagining it was Mr Pender showing them around, or at the very least drawing comparisons between the two men. It was a long and tedious hour which ended, at last, back at the table where they had first seen the young Herr Linburg.

"These are for you, Fraulein von Truber," said Tobias, picking up a heart-shaped box made of card containing a dozen chocolates of different shapes and flavours. The lid of the box was painted with a design of red roses. Tobias fitted it over the box and tied a red ribbon deftly over the top with a practised hand before holding the gift out for Amelie to take.

"Why thank you, Herr Linburg," replied Amelie. "I will look forward to sharing these with my sister, Augusta."

As the party moved back to the office where Tobias' parents were waiting for them, their son contrived to fall behind, next to Amelie. He leaned towards her and whispered, "I hope you will consider addressing me as Tobias, Fraulein von Truber, and perhaps in time I can call you Amelie?" Amelie, shuddering at the feeling of Tobias' warm breath on her face, forced herself to smile but could not go so far as to reply one way or the other. A sudden realisation that Tobias was also fully aware of the reasons for this meeting made her feel quite faint. She reached out to steady herself with a hand against the door frame, but Tobias was already striding ahead to greet his mother.

Luncheon was excruciating, although the food was superb. Amelie normally had a healthy appetite, but today she merely picked at the array of cold meats and cheeses on her plate. The Linburgs had made every effort to force the two young people together by placing them at the end of the table facing each other, but conversation was stilted with long, awkward silences in between. It seemed that Tobias and Amelie had little in common and it didn't help that Tobias spoke German, a language that did not come naturally to Amelie, although she did her best. It was exhausting to listen to his words, translate them into the Italian which was her natural tongue and form a reply which then needed to be translated back to German. She suspected that Tobias would have some Italian, considering his birthplace, but he made no attempts to use it in conversation.

After lunch the two families took a walk around the delightfully laid out gardens surrounding the Linburgs' home. The beautiful gardens had been designed in the formal style and Amelie's mother was keen to hear from Frau Linburg about plant choices, colours and seasonal differences. Amelie knew little about the names of plants, but she certainly could appreciate the beauty of the formally laid out beds and neatly cut grassy pathways between them. She paused to take a heavy pink rose bloom gently in her hands, raising it to her nose to inhale the sweet scent. A moment broken by the realisation that Tobias had appeared by her side once more. Amelie was beginning to feel some annoyance at his regular interruptions to her silent thoughts, but Tobias didn't even seem to notice the beauty of the flower that Amelie held between her fingers as he said, "I look forward very much to you and your family joining us at St Moritz. We have a house there in the mountains. I will teach you to ski."

Amelie had forgotten about the proposed holiday, which had sounded like an enjoyable diversion when her mother had first mentioned it. But now she saw it for what it was. Another way of pushing the two of them together. Perhaps she was being overly sensitive, but she would have preferred Tobias to have offered her the opportunity to learn how to ski, rather than stating the fact that he was going to teach her. Tobias, she was already beginning to realise, was used to things happening the way he wanted, and without question. A vision of a bleak future where she was married to a man who made all the decisions for her flashed through her mind before she replied, "Thank you, Herr Linburg, my sister and I will enjoy it, I am sure." Once more Tobias had turned away before she replied and Amelie was left talking to the rose that she held in her hand.

"Thank you Frau Linburg for your hospitality and for an excellent lunch," said Amelie's mother when they reached the house again, having made a circuit of the formal gardens. "Now we must take our leave."

Frau von Truber looked across at Amelie, expecting her to add her own thanks. "Thank you, Frau Linburg, for a most pleasant visit," she said before turning to give her thanks to Tobias for the box of chocolates.

"Tobias, come and say adieu to our guests," ordered Frau Linburg. Her son had already started up the steps into the house and had to turn and come back to make his goodbyes. In one final act of defiance to play down any romantic intentions in his gift, Amelie said, "Thank you, Herr von Truber. My sister Augusta will enjoy the chocolates, I am sure. I do not care for them much myself."

Once the von Trubers were out of earshot of their hosts on their way home Amelie's mother said, "Really, Amelie, what were you thinking? How ungracious you were concerning Tobias' gift."

"But Mama, he did not even notice what I said. He doesn't listen to anything I say. He is just so - so, superior," retorted Amelie, stamping her foot as she said the last word. "Please, please can we not go to St Moritz? It will be just awful." Amelie pulled the handkerchief from her sleeve and patted away a tear from the corner of her eye.

"We are going to St Moritz, young lady, regardless of your bad manners," ordered Amelie's father. "The Linburgs are a good family and Tobias would make an excellent husband for you."

"You mean he would make our family rich again, father," replied Amelie, before she could stop herself. But inside she knew she could not fight with her father. He was determined to marry her off to the first person he could find with money and class.

"I would rather be in a position to choose my own husband, thank you. And I would like to do so for love, not for your convenience," she added.

Her father stopped and turned to his daughter with a face like thunder. To avoid causing a spectacle in the street, he restrained himself from wagging a finger at her while hissing, "Well, Amelie von Truber, you will go home and go straight to your room where you will consider your position. You can join us for dinner if you have come to realise how fortunate you are to be the object of Tobias Linburg's affections. Now I have business to attend to, so will leave your mother to ensure you follow my instructions." With the merest nod of the head, Amelie's father turned to walk along the street towards his usual drinking venue where, no doubt, he would stay until dinner time.

Amelie knew it was pointless to argue with her father, and that her mother would support him regardless. A feeling of helplessness descended on her soul, along with a deep anger growing inside her. For the rest of the journey home she kept silent, reluctantly accepting her mother's arm through hers, in a small gesture of motherly love.

CHAPTER FOUR
St Moritz

Amelie took to her room, as she had been bidden by her father. A third emotion had been added to that of dread and anger when Augusta told her of Guy's visit. Such disappointment! And Augusta so pleased to see him and keen to tell her sister all about it. She simply couldn't bear it, throwing herself face down on her bed, tears dampening her pillow.

"Go away," she sobbed at her sister. "Just leave me alone."

Some hours later, Augusta, with Lizzy accompanying her to help her to dress for dinner, found Amelie still face down, still in the crumpled dress she had worn all day and still unwilling to talk.

"Mama says you may come down to dinner. Papa is not home yet," said Augusta. "What has happened, Amelie? Surely it is more than just Mr Pender visiting while you were out."

Reluctantly, Amelie sat up, wiped her eyes with her damp handkerchief, and in between sobs, recounted the whole story of the day's meeting with Tobias. "It is just so unfair. He is awful, and Papa will make me marry him, I am sure," she finished as Lizzy gently unbuttoned Amelie's dress and laid out another from the wardrobe on her bed.

"Come here, Miss Amelie. Let's tidy you up a bit, eh?" said Lizzy, sympathetically. "I'm sure this Tobias fella ain't that bad or your pa wouldn't be pushing him at you."

"Oh Lizzy, he just seems so, well, so arrogant," Amelie replied.

"But is he handsome?" questioned her younger sister.

"Well, yes, he is tall with chestnut hair, but I didn't dare look into his eyes, and he turned away before there was time to see more," said Amelie. "I just can't imagine spending the rest of my life with him."

"Come now, Miss," said Lizzy. While the sisters were talking she had been wringing out a cloth in the water basin which she now used to wipe away the tear stains on Amelie's face. "That's better. Just your hair to put right now, Miss Amelie."

By the time Lizzy had finished with her, Amelie gave a reasonable appearance at the dinner table. Her mother, sensing that there was more to Amelie's outburst than it seemed, gave her hand a gentle squeeze as she sat next to her at the table. Herr von Truber had not arrived home yet and it occurred to Amelie that perhaps her father found Tobias to be a suitable husband because he was very much like him. Living in his own world, with only a passing interest in his wife and family. For the very first time in her life she wondered whether her mother was happy, or whether she had just become accustomed to being a mere distraction, an attractive status symbol to be presented in public while being ignored at home.

Amelie hardly ate a thing, picking at each course while Augusta cleared her plate in no time at all. She couldn't wait to excuse herself from the table and did so as soon as her mother put down her spoon after an excellent creme caramel. Amelie's remained intact on her plate and even Augusta sensed it was not the moment to ask to finish it for her sister.

As Amelie stood and went towards the door, again her mother took her hand. "You will find a way to make it work, my dear, just as I have done with your father," she said with sympathy. "And when children come along, and they surely will, they will be as much of a joy to you as you two girls have been for me."

Amelie started up the stairs, and she was glad that she hadn't eaten a lot of food when a wave of nausea passed over her as she considered the necessity of closeness that would be required to ensure that she did indeed have a family. Falling into bed almost immediately, she turned her head away from Augusta when her sister retired a little later. But sleep wouldn't come to her for several hours as she counted the strokes of the clock as each hour passed. When it did come, it was filled with dreams of Tobias holding her, tearing off her clothes and doing whatever it was he had to do to make sure he created an heir to the family's fortune. All this while turning away from her, his attention drawn by a table of incongruous chocolates that seemed to be calling her name, "Amelie, Amelie….."

"Wake up, Amelie." It was Augusta shaking her shoulder. "You have missed breakfast, but Mama wants us to look at the photographs together."

A while later, after Lizzy had once more tidied

Amelie's tear-stained face and tamed her hair into order, Frau von Truber and her daughters sat together in the drawing room, the brown envelope still unopened on the table in front of them. Augusta could hardly sit still in anticipation of seeing their portraits. Her mother opened the package and tipped the contents out in a heap allowing Amelie and Augusta to pick up each one in turn. They were, in Frau von Truber's opinion, the best portraits she had ever seen. Her daughters looked beautiful, even Augusta. That man Pender had a very special talent in bringing out the personality of the subject. Every single portrait was just perfect.

Amelie found herself incapable of speech. She merely held her favourite portrait in her hand, wondering what was to become of the person she was looking at. It was like looking into a mirror, but a special mirror that made her look even more beautiful, with an aura of serenity and grace which she hardly knew she possessed. A tiny shiver of dread ran through her as she considered Tobias carrying her portrait in his pocket, showing it to his friends and saying proudly, "This is my wife." An opposing thought came to mind too, although she tried to push it away. She wondered if Mr Pender had made himself a copy of her portrait and carried it now in the pocket of his jacket. "No," she thought to herself miserably, "no, it will be Augusta's picture that lays there next to his heart, not mine."

During the night, in those hours punctuated by the striking of the clock, a feeling of resignation had come over her. Seeing her mother in a new light had helped her to see that a marriage had to be about more than love. It was her duty to marry well, for the sake of her family, and she imagined there were worse men in the world who her father could have chosen than Tobias Linburg. Apart from anything else, it was obvious to Amelie that Mr Pender had chosen her sister as the object of his affection. She presumed he had been watching her leave the house yesterday, and it was because he realised that Augusta was at home on her own that he had chosen to deliver the portraits a day early.

Over the next few days, the von Truber household was busier than ever. Preparations were underway for the journey to St Moritz, a mountain resort to the south east of Zurich, a journey that would take a good two days of travelling. They would be staying one night at a hotel in Chur before the climb into the mountains to St Moritz, where they would be the guests of the Linburgs in their alpine lodge, situated on the edge of the town. Though money was tight, Herr von Truber had given the sisters and their mother an allowance for appropriate clothing to be purchased. He considered it an investment into a more lucrative future where his family would be associated by marriage to one of the richest families in Switzerland. Lined cloaks with fox fur collars, warm woollen skirts, leather boots with high sides and fur hats had all been found for the three women, as well as new outfits for the evening. Frau Linburg had assured her friend that the house was kept warm by wood burned in huge fireplaces, so the usual evening wear would be appropriate, and that fires burned in each bedroom too, to keep the guests warm in their beds at night.

On one of her shopping expeditions, Frau von Truber had called on Guy Pender to pay the bill. Seeing only Amelie's mother at the door had caused Guy a deal of sadness. He had been waiting in anticipation for Amelie to visit, but it was not to be. He wanted to tell her something important. An idea that had been growing in his mind ever since he had seen Augusta. She had mentioned their visit to St Moritz and, although Guy had no intention of taking to a pair of skis, he liked the idea of getting some fresh mountain air and setting up his equipment to take some landscape photographs. He had returned to his studio after seeing Augusta and immediately checked his appointment book for the next few weeks. He had the odd session booked in for this week, but nothing in the following fortnight so far. He took this as a sign that the fates wanted him to go to St Moritz, so he picked up his pen and drew diagonal lines across the dates for the next two weeks. If anyone came into the studio to book a sitting, he would now tell them that he was away on business, but that they were welcome to select a date after he returned.

That evening, with Albert purring on his lap, Guy wrote a letter to the proprietor of the Kulm Hotel in St Moritz requesting a room for fourteen nights, and further asking if he could store his photographic equipment and cart at the hotel for the same period. He was surprised and pleased when a reply came back to him swiftly, informing him that a room had been booked in his name and that, not only were they pleased to accommodate his photographic equipment, but that they would also be happy to allow him to take portraits of their clients for a small commission, of course.

The Linburgs had set out for St Moritz the day after Amelie and her parents had taken lunch with them. So they were already in residence when the von Trubers arrived three days later. As they stepped from their carriage they all stood in awe of the mountains around them. Of course, they had seen mountainous scenery from afar, but to be so close to the massive, snow-covered slopes around them was incredible. After the comparative warmth of the covered carriage, the cold air hit them and Amelie pulled her new warm cloak around her, pleased that her father had allowed them to purchase suitable clothing for the alpine climate.

Frau Linburg met them on the balustraded balcony that ran all along the front of their mountain lodge. The building was painted white and had a steep roof with wooden eaves, which Amelie learned later was designed to let the snow slide down to the ground, rather than weigh heavily upon it. Despite its somewhat rustic appearance from the outside, the visitors were surprised to find a luxurious interior with a full height open room for day to day living. An archway led through to a formal dining room at the rear. A blazing fire already burned in the huge fireplace, making the whole room very warm indeed. The visitors were pleased to hand their cloaks to a servant before being shown to a wooden staircase.

Upstairs they could walk the length of a landing which stretched out on three sides of the living space. At any point one could look down on the space below. It reminded Amelie of the gallery in a church. Frau Linberg indicated each room as they passed along the corridor. Amelie was not altogether pleased to see that her room was the last of the guest bedrooms, presuming that the Linburgs occupied the remaining rooms. Tobias, it would seem, would be a little too close for comfort. She wondered if the arrangement of their rooms had been made especially for this purpose by Tobias' mother.

As Frau Linburg was showing her guests to their rooms, Amelie looked around for Tobias. She was dreading meeting him again, but had steeled herself to accept his advances and make the best of it. He was, after all, handsome and rich, and she forced herself to think that she could grow to love him over time. The object of her thoughts, however, was nowhere to be seen.

"Frau Linburg, may I ask if Tobias is here?" said Amelie.

Frau Linburg smiled to herself, pleased that Amelie was keen to see her son. "He is skiing with some friends this afternoon," she replied, "but he knows you are due to arrive before dinner, and I am sure he will be here soon."

Amelie was not surprised that Tobias preferred the company of his friends to the opportunity to welcome her, but she couldn't help feeling annoyed with him for not being there when they arrived. It was not until everyone had gathered in the huge living space for a warming drink before dinner that Amelie, standing at the window, saw three young men approaching with skis balanced over their shoulders. It was hard to work out which one was Tobias because they were all wrapped up against the cold, but as they reached the steps to the house, the group split up. Two of the men turned to the right to head back to the hotel which dominated the landscape. A huge edifice of a building with four storeys, a crenellated tower at each corner and many smoking chimney stacks.

Tobias bounded up the steps, swinging his skis from his shoulder and handing them to a waiting footman, who waited to collect his master's headgear, gloves and coat. It was some time before Tobias joined the rest of the party, once he had changed for dinner. Amelie was standing by the tall windows admiring the magical view of the lights being lit, one by one, at the hotel. Turning to find herself alone she was not surprised to see Tobias striding straight across the room towards her.

"Ah, you are here. And you look lovely tonight, my dear," said Tobias.

Amelie, irritated by his lack of an apology for missing their arrival and by the intimacy of his words, took a moment to form a suitable reply in German. She opened her mouth to say, "Yes, we arrived early and were sorry to miss you."

But her words were wasted. Tobias had already moved on to greet her parents and to be introduced to Augusta, who was gazing in awe at this man who would likely be her brother-in-law one day soon. He was indeed tall and handsome, and she wondered why Amelie had been so upset by their initial meeting. She would be pleased to be made to marry a man half as handsome as Tobias Linburg, for sure.

Another awkward meal followed with Amelie sitting next to Tobias. She did her very best to enjoy the food and the company, but it was not easy to do either. She was only thankful that Augusta was sitting opposite her, and Tobias seemed happy to talk across the table to her, in fact, she thought he was flirting with her sister rather too much, if truth be told. The two young Englishmen, who turned out to be recent acquaintances of Tobias, had joined the party too. Augusta was excited by the two men being seated on either side of her, and Amelie could see how much her sister was enjoying all the attention. Augusta's face was quite flushed, and not just from the heat of the huge fire, which was almost overwhelmingly hot. Amelie felt left out of the conversation and, when attempts to speak directly to Tobias failed to draw her in, she turned to her neighbour on the other side instead. He was English too. St Moritz, he told her, was fast becoming the place to visit in the miserable English winter and the Kulm Hotel the place to stay in the weeks after Christmas.

"Do you ski?" Amelie asked this gentleman, who she learned was a Doctor Corbett.

"Oh no, my dear, I am far too old for that," he replied with a laugh. "It is a young person's pastime. Perhaps your host Herr Linburg will teach you. I am here to walk in the hills and to make sketches of the flowers and plants."

"I think, Doctor Corbett," answered Amelie, "I would prefer you to teach me about the flowers, rather than be taught to ski by my host."

"Well, Miss von Truber, you have time for both activities while you are here. Perhaps we will await a fine day to take a walk, with a suitable chaperone, into one of the alpine valleys," suggested the doctor. "But before that, you will become proficient on your skis, no doubt."

Later that evening Augusta joined Amelie in her room. It was a novelty for the sisters to be sleeping in separate bedrooms, but that didn't stop them wanting to compare notes on their impressions of the day before they went to sleep. Lizzy was there too. She had been given a bed in a room in a building adjoining the lodge, sharing a room with three other maids. She was full of stories of the other staff, who, it had to be said, were none too keen on having extra staff in the way and extra mouths to feed at the kitchen table.

However, her room mates had made Lizzy very welcome and had promised to have a kettle of hot water ready for her to wash her face when she had finished her evening duties.

"Tobias and Edward and Wilfred are so nice," Augusta cooed, as she twirled around Amelie's room in sheer excitement, her skirts swinging. "I will leave Tobias to you, dear sister, but shall I choose Teddy or Wilf to be my beau?" She put a finger to her lips as if considering an important question.

"Well, thank you, sister," answered Amelie with a smile, caught up in her sister's enthusiasm for a moment. "But I rather think it is your father who will make the choice for you, and it may not be Edward or Wilfred he chooses."

"Ah, but they are both very rich, and Edward's father is the Earl of somewhere," replied Augusta. "Wilfred's family has made heaps of money building steam ships. Oh, who shall I choose?" she repeated.

"Stand still, Miss Augusta, while I unbutton your dress," ordered Lizzy.

"Ah, but I can't, Lizzy," said Augusta, "I am just so excited. And tomorrow we have our first lesson in skiing."

Amelie did not entirely share her sister's enthusiasm for the company of the three men, nor for the act of skiing. She had been serious about preferring a walk in the mountains with Doctor Corbett, but she kept that very much to herself as she wished her sister and Lizzy a good night and shooed them both out of her room. She hoped the fresh mountain air and the long journey would help her to fall asleep quickly, but there came one more interruption to her slumber with a discreet tapping at the door. Realising that everyone else would be in their beds by now, she hissed, "Who's there?"

She realised it was Tobias' voice replying in a whisper, "Don't worry, my dear Amelie. I only wished to bid you a good night, and to tell you that I look forward to tomorrow's lessons."

She heard his footsteps tiptoeing along the corridor and could not resist the urge to jump out of bed and open the door a crack. She was just in time to see the door close at the end of the corridor. By the light of the dwindling fire downstairs she could also see a small package placed on the floor outside her door. Checking that nobody else was up and about, she opened the door a bit wider so that she could reach the parcel. Back in her room, with the door firmly closed again, she pulled on the red ribbon around a cube shaped box. Inside she found four heart-shaped chocolates on a bed of tissue paper. "Is he determined to make me as plump as Augusta with his gifts?" she thought to herself, before putting the box on her bedside table and returning to her warm bed to fall asleep almost at once.

Back in the town of Chur, half way between Zurich and St Moritz, Guy was attempting to sleep as well. Wearing almost all the clothing he had packed into his travelling chest, and wrapped in an old blanket, he shivered himself to a restless sleep in the cart, surrounded by his chemicals in blue glass bottles and the paraphernalia of his cameras and photographic equipment. He had even wrapped the painted sheet of mountain scenery around him as an extra layer of warmth. It had not occurred to him to book a room in Chur and none could be found on his arrival. It was just as well that Leon de Fevre had suggested that he take a blanket in case he couldn't find a bed at Chur. It was not the first time Guy had been forced to sleep in the cart, but it was certainly the first time he had felt so cold overnight.

It was his own fault really. It wasn't until he called into the bakery to ask Leon de Fevre to keep an eye on his studio that Guy had even considered the fact that it took more than a day to get to the resort of St Moritz. Leon had said, "I hope, monsieur, that you have a room at the hotel in Chur. It is a busy place these days with the skiing.

It was just a quiet town when St Moritz was known only for its mineral waters."

Guy knew none of this. He realised he had rushed into going away just for the sake of seeing Amelie again, without much thought to the practicalities of such a journey. "I can sleep in my cart, my friend," he replied. "I have done so many times before."

"Ah, then make sure you take a warm blanket," Leon advised, "and at least get that horse into stables somehow, or the poor creature will freeze to death overnight."

After thanking Leon for his advice and the good stock of bread and pastries now packed into a wooden box, Guy climbed up onto the cart, flicked the reins, clicked his tongue to get the horse started and set off into the unknown. He had hired a horse, just as he and Frewin had done several times before, but they had never ventured out in the winter season, and always to the south west, where the mountains were more gentle and the tracks easy to navigate as they meandered along beside the river.

It had been an easy ride to begin with. The track was well worn and only muddy in parts where the winter rain left water lying in the ruts. The horse plodded along with a rhythmical jangle of bridle and reins. It was a sound Guy loved, like the percussion section of an orchestra providing a steady beat. He lunched on sweet pastries beside the river, the sun warm on his back as he sat by a babbling stream. As he packed things away he noticed the clouds were gathering and it wasn't long before rain started falling steadily. His misery increased as the horse started slipping and sliding on the stony track. It took all his efforts to keep the cart in a straight line and to avoid the other traffic heading the same way as him. Chur was a busy town indeed.

It came as no surprise that a bed could not be found that night. The rain had turned to sleet and then snow over the last mile or so of the journey, and Guy looked enviously into the windows of the hotels where he could see warm fires burning and food and ale being served to the customers. At the third hotel he tried, the manager took pity on his bedraggled appearance and offered him a stable for the horse and a sheltered spot to place his cart under the cover of an open fronted barn. Not only that, but a serving maid appeared a while later with a bowl of thick soup and a mug of ale for his supper.

He woke to the sound of bells jangling from the town's church tower. He would never get used to the continental habit of jangling bells in a discordant fashion, and he much preferred the ordered sound of English church bells which reminded him so much of his childhood. He lay there thinking of Nanny Bee putting on her Sunday hat and heading off to the tiny church just across the lane from her little cottage.

Despite the shelter of the barn, a considerable amount of snow had built up overnight and it took Guy a fair time to clear it from the cart and from the ground around him. At least this manual work warmed him up a bit, helped by the morning being bright and sunny, although the mountain air was still colder than he was used to.

Not waiting to eat breakfast, he was on the road again before most other travellers, and he made good progress. He was thankful that the horse, though something of a plodder, was agile and strong, having no trouble at all in climbing up the ever increasingly steep tracks. He took lunch within sight of the town of St Moritz. What a view it was! From the vantage point of a rocky outcrop he looked down into a wide valley, a sparkling blue lake, and all surrounded by the most impressive snow-covered mountains. The town of St Moritz was dominated by the huge Kulm Hotel, a citadel against the encroaching snow. It was not a pretty building, but it certainly was impressive. Guy knew that it was only in the last year or so that visitors had wanted to come here in the winter. Prior to that it had been a summer resort, renowned for its mineral baths which were said to provide medicinal qualities. He imagined it would be beautiful in summer too, with green pastures and a host of alpine flowers and plants, but no wonder people wanted to come here in winter too, especially English folk who were used to such dreary winter months back home. There was something special about the sparkling white light of all that snow. And, to cap it all, the beautiful Amelie von Truber was there already. Perhaps she was one of the tiny dots he could see walking slowly up the slopes, or rushing down again leaving the twin tracks of their skis behind them. The cold and damp of the previous night forgotten, Guy jumped onto his seat and urged his horse onwards with renewed enthusiasm.

Guy's hotel room on the second floor had a window overlooking the lake. His photographer's eye was already analysing the light and working out the best places to set up his tripod. Although the hotel manager had welcomed him enthusiastically and told him that there was already a lot of interest amongst the other guests in having portraits taken, Guy was keen to get outside to capture the scenery. And maybe, just maybe, come across Amelie too. But first, he would go down to the dining room for a drink before dinner, which he hoped would be a good deal more luxurious than last night's supper.

As tends to happen in hotels the world over, it was not long before Guy was joined in a corner of the bar by a fellow guest. Guy had taken a leather seat next to the window, where he could watch the mass of people returning from the slopes. Everyone seemed happy, with smiling faces flushed after a day in the mountain air, as Guy scanned each one to see if he could recognise Amelie passing by. With some irritation Guy realised that someone was speaking to him.

"Good evening, may I join you?" Guy turned away from the window to see a smartly dressed gentleman indicating the seat opposite him. From his words, Guy realised he must be English.

"Please do," replied Guy, adding, "I did not expect to see so many people here."

"Word has spread quickly throughout England of the beauty of this place in the winter," said the gentleman, easing himself into the leather armchair. "Only two or three years ago people came here only in summer for the mineral waters and the beautiful walks, but now they prefer, in the main, to come after Christmas for the skiing."

"You are English?" questioned Guy, already knowing it to be true. With a nod of the head, by way of introduction, he added, "Guy Pender, another Englishman, living in Zurich at present."

"Doctor Dudley Corbett at your service, sir," replied the doctor. "Though these days my interests are more botanical than medicinal. I am here to study the early flowering plants of the alpine valleys, and I will stay until the snow retreats in spring and early summer. By that time the meadows are covered in blooms of every colour. It is indeed a splendid feast for the eyes."

The two men found themselves engrossed in conversation, with much in common. The doctor was fascinated to hear of Guy's photographic work while Guy was eager to see Doctor Corbett's sketch books where he recorded every species of plant he found here in minute detail. In the end they shared a table for dinner and arranged to meet the following morning, before taking a well-worn track up to a vantage point, where the doctor thought Guy would find the most spectacular view of the town and surrounding mountains.

They had been so engrossed in conversation over dinner that Guy had forgotten all about Amelie, and now finding it dark outside, he had no hope of catching a glimpse of her passing by. He retired to his room where the high mountain air and the warm, comfortable bed helped him to fall asleep almost at once.

CHAPTER FIVE
Avalanche

That same day, while Guy was making his way to St Moritz, Amelie and Augusta were being given their first skiing lesson. After breakfast Tobias and his two English friends Wilfred and Edward met the sisters on the balcony of the lodge before setting off for the slopes. The men were well used to walking on the slippery ground but the two young ladies found that they needed to take tiny steps to keep themselves upright. Amelie thought to herself that she was hardly likely to be able to stand up on the ski slope if she couldn't even walk on a flat path, but she kept going bravely, hanging on tightly to Augusta's arm for balance.

Rather to her surprise, Tobias walked beside her too, even putting out a hand to steady her as she stumbled on the icy path. She wondered if his attentiveness was merely for the benefit of his friends, in the same way that her father behaved like the perfect husband in public places. Pushing such cynical thoughts away, she forced herself to concentrate on enjoying the day. Looking across at her sister she could see by her sparkling eyes and happy smile that Augusta had no need to feign enjoyment. It was obvious to anyone that she was loving every moment of the attention of Wilfred Dannay and Edward Wingfield. And the two men were plainly having a wonderful time vying for her attention.

The morning passed quickly, though it seemed to Amelie that it took most of the time to cover oneself up against the cold. This involved putting on warm gauntlet gloves and oddly close-fitting woollen hats, finally wrapping a fox fur stole around the neck. Then there was the long and complicated job of fitting the skis to her boots with leather straps and buckles. Tobias was enjoying the necessity to hold onto her waist while he showed her how to slowly edge sideways up the slope, before turning to push herself down again with the single pole she carried for support. Even though they only took a few steps at first, the whole process was exhausting and the moment she turned at the top, the wooden skis had a habit of getting tied in knots resulting in an undignified landing in the cold and wet snow. Tobias was being as patient as possible with her, but she was conscious of Augusta climbing higher each time she tried, and with the assistance of two instructors holding onto her, she was soon becoming proficient at sliding gracefully downhill before digging the skis into the snow at an angle at the bottom to bring herself to a halt while still remaining upright. She hardly seemed to need support from her wooden pole, whereas Amelie clung to hers tightly throughout the whole process.

When it was time to stop for luncheon Amelie suggested that she and her sister return to the lodge for the afternoon. She saw a look of relief in Tobias' face, but Augusta opened her mouth to protest. "I am having such a good time," she complained, "and I am getting to be quite an expert now."

"Yes, sister, you have done very well," replied Amelie, "but our tutors would like the chance to climb higher without us holding them back, I am sure." She could see the three men exchange relieved glances behind Augusta's back, and she knew she had made the right decision.

Leaving the men to climb the slopes once more, Augusta and Amelie slipped and slid their way back to the lodge, the track made worse by the number of people using it as the day went by. By the time Guy had arrived at the hotel, the sisters were already back in their rooms changing into dry clothing before Lizzy brushed out their damp hair and pinned it back into shape again. Unknown to him, Guy may well have seen Tobias and his friends walking past the hotel later that afternoon. He was still blissfully unaware of the intentions of Tobias Linburg towards the beautiful woman whose photograph he carried in his pocket.

The following morning Augusta was keen to continue her lessons on the slopes, but Amelie had decided the previous night that she would not join the party. It was with some relief that she found a handwritten note from Doctor Corbett awaiting her at the breakfast table, in which he suggested that it was a fine day for a walk into the valley to look for plants, and that she was welcome to join him accompanied, for decency's sake, by her sister as a chaperone.

Amelie knew all too well that Augusta would stubbornly refuse to give up her day on the slopes, especially as Edward had persuaded his sister to join them too. But who could she ask to come with her? Her mother would not approve at all of her going out alone with Doctor Corbett, even though he was a respectable old gentleman.

Back in Augusta's room, Amelie was sitting on her sister's bed holding Doctor Corbett's note in her hand. "I do understand why you would rather not come with me, Augusta," said Amelie, "but who can accompany me? I don't think Mama would wish to walk that far."

"Miss Amelie, can I come, please?" Lizzy begged. "I love flowers, and I would like to see them growing here in the snow."

"Why, that's the perfect solution," said Augusta enthusiastically. "We both have our chaperones for the day now."

What Doctor Corbett had not felt the need to tell Amelie in his letter was that someone else would be joining their walk too.

Edward's sister Charlotte was of a similar age to Augusta and the two young ladies were soon arm-in-arm, chattering and giggling on their way up the icy path to the ski slopes. The three men swaggered along in front of them with their skis balanced over their shoulders. This happy group garnered many an admiring glance from the other people heading the same way. Amelie watched them go from the balcony outside the lodge, wondering whether she and Tobias would ever find any common interests between them. With a sigh of resignation to a life stretching ahead of her in loneliness, she turned back to see if Lizzy had brought their coats downstairs yet. Lizzy was indeed coming towards her with both their coats and a wicker picnic basket, but it was neither of these things that caught Amelie's attention. Lizzy had stopped dead in her tracks with her mouth open, the colour draining from her cheeks, as if she had seen a ghost.

Wondering what it could possibly be that had caused Lizzy to display such a shocked expression, Amelie turned to find Doctor Corbett climbing the steps, dressed in a tweed suit, a matching deerstalker hat and a short cape over his shoulders. Behind him was another gentleman in similar dress. A man she recognised immediately, but could not believe to be here in St Moritz. Catching her eye, Guy Pender, from behind Doctor Corbett, held a finger to his lips just in time to stop her greeting him out loud. As the two gentlemen approached the lodge his heart had almost leapt out of his chest when he saw Amelie waving to her sister and realised that the good doctor had inadvertently brought them together. Fortunately for him, Augusta had been far too busy with her friends to recognise him as he passed them.

Amelie's eyes sparkled with joy at seeing him again, and that was all he needed to know. What he could not tell from her look was that Amelie was in turmoil. She was indeed overjoyed to see him, despite the fact that she thought he preferred her sister's company, and that since their last meeting, she now had Tobias to consider too.

"My dear Miss von Truber, how lovely to see you again," said Doctor Corbett, as he reached the top step. "And may I introduce you to Mr Guy Pender? He is joining us today to set up his equipment to take photographs of the scenery."

Guy stepped forward to make a formal bow towards Amelie. "Fraulein von Truber, it is a pleasure to be reacquainted with you," he said, before winking at Lizzy and adding, "and to meet your ladies' maid again too. Miss Lizzy, I believe?"

Lizzy, blushing a deep scarlet at being addressed in person, bobbed a flustered curtsy towards the doctor and said, "Pleased to make your acquaintance, doctor," and turning to Guy, "and pleased, I'm sure, to meet you again, sir."

Amelie, feeling the need to explain added, "This is my maid, Lizzy, who is to be my chaperone today, Doctor Corbett. She is looking forward to seeing some flowers as much as I am. And you will have realised by our introductions that we have both previously met Mr Pender, although on separate occasions. Why, we are almost neighbours back in Zurich, but we did not expect at all to be here in St Moritz at the same time."

"What a pleasant coincidence!" said the doctor. "Now come, we must make haste into the valley. The sun is shining this morning, but I fear we have a storm brewing later this evening. The clouds are gathering in the west."

The sun indeed shone warmly upon them all, and in Guy's heart in particular. Unfortunately, the narrow path allowed only for single traffic as they followed the winding route around the lake. Doctor Corbett went first to lead the way. He walked with a stick, but not by necessity as he took long strides and set a fast pace for his fellow walkers. So much so that he occasionally found himself waiting for the other three. Not that he minded at all. The view across the lake was magnificent from almost any viewpoint.

Amelie came next, able to keep up with the doctor most of the time, except where the path lay constantly in shadow in the low winter sun and became muddy. This necessitated a lifting of the skirts and careful steps through the slippery mess. Lizzy walked behind her carrying the picnic basket, the two of them exchanging the odd word of admiration for the view and the freshness of the mountain air. The last person in this little cavalcade was Guy Pender. Inhibited somewhat by having to carry his equipment, which consisted of the wooden camera box slung by a strap over one shoulder, the long wooden legs of the tripod on which he would set his camera and a square-shaped leather basket holding as much equipment as he could fit in. The strap for this box sat on the other shoulder, a rolled up blanket bobbing along on top. He too was admiring the view, although not entirely that of the mountains, but rather more of one of the members of the party in front of him.

Doctor Corbett paused occasionally to show Amelie and Lizzy a patch of tiny flowers displaying their colour midst the melting snow. By the lake the climate was a little milder than higher up the slopes, so plants could find their way out from under the blanket of snow as it melted. The doctor was particularly pleased to find a vivid blue flower clinging to a mossy rock. "It is a gentian," he explained. "It is often used for complaints of the stomach and to brew ales. But I prefer to see it growing in the wild in all its beauty."

Turning gently away from the lake, the path became more rocky as they climbed higher. In places, Doctor Corbett strode ahead up a steep step and then turned to hold out a hand to Amelie, and then to Lizzy to pull them up over the rocks. Guy found he needed to pass his equipment up to the doctor before clambering up himself. It was hard work, but with every rise in the path the magnificent view improved behind them.

Amelie was quite relieved when they reached a grassy platform surrounded by moss-covered rocks to shelter them from the cold breeze. Beautiful white daisy-like flowers grew in patches all around the edge. All in all it was the perfect picnic spot. Guy was already picking the best place to set up his tripod to capture the view back towards St Moritz. The view was glorious indeed. The placid waters of the lake perfectly reflected the thin spire of the church of St Moritz and the snow-covered peaks of the surrounding mountains. Looking in the other direction, the valley lay like a perfect V-shape between the peaks. With an artist's eye, Guy was already framing his picture in his mind, the little wooden hut he could see not far away making the perfect foreground interest for his landscape. A deep sense of contentment descended gently over Guy as he mounted his camera onto the tripod while the ladies unpacked the picnic basket onto the tartan blanket Guy had unrolled for them. Doctor Corbett, sleepy from the warmth of the sun and the exertions of the climb, had propped himself against a rock to soak in the beauty of his surroundings, his pipe held unlit in his hand. Amelie and Lizzy chattered with excitement about the flowers they had seen and the view before them now.

"Come and eat, Doctor Corbett," ordered Amelie, "and you too, Mr Pender, before Lizzy steals all the potted meat sandwiches."

"Oh, Miss that ain't true," complained Lizzy, "although they are very nice indeed," she added, picking up another tiny crustless triangle from the plate before offering it to Guy as he joined the ladies.

Amelie, not wanting her feelings for Guy to show, stood up immediately to offer a platter of cheese slices to Doctor Corbett. Guy felt a pang of regret as he sensed that Amelie had moved away on purpose. "Does she not care for me, as I do for her?" he asked himself.

But it was hard not to be cheerful in the presence of the ever-bubbly Lizzy, who chattered endlessly about the weather, the view and the flowers around them. Once or twice Amelie and Guy caught each other's eyes, but it concerned Guy that Amelie's shy smile was a fleeting thing, those beautiful eyes hardening before she turned away. "What is going on here?" Guy posed the question to himself. "Come on fellow," he thought, "just enjoy Amelie's company and stop worrying about anything else."

He was still deep in thought while Lizzy cleared the food away into the basket. "Jump up, sir," she ordered. "The doctor says we should start back with them clouds gathering."

Looking up with a start, Guy could see that the lake was no longer the flat, mirror-like surface it had been before their picnic lunch. Instead, the rippled surface was growing angrier by the moment. Perhaps he would not be able to take any photographs today, after all. What a shame! Realising that it may take a while for him to pack his camera equipment away, he said, "Doctor, perhaps you should go on ahead with the ladies while I put things away here."

"A good idea, sir," replied Doctor Corbett. "I am so sorry for misjudging the bad weather which seems to be arriving sooner than expected. I fear we may get a soaking before we reach the lodge. How careless of me to bring you this far up the valley."

"No matter, Doctor," said Amelie, "the beauty of this place is well worth a spot or two of rain. Thank you for bringing us here, dear Doctor Corbett."

Guy watched with some concern as the doctor and the two ladies retraced their steps. Fortunately, he had finished packing things away in his leather case before he felt the first spot of rain on his shoulders. He thought he would probably catch the rest of the group up before they got back to the lake now. But looking up, he saw that Amelie had become separated from the other two. She seemed to be climbing above them towards a patch of meadow flowers that had managed to burst into glorious colours in a sheltered spot on the hillside. Guy guessed correctly that Amelie wanted to pick a selection of the flowers to take back to the lodge. In no time at all the doctor and Lizzy were well ahead of Amelie, reaching the flat path by the lake where Guy hoped they would wait for Amelie. He hoisted his bags over his shoulders and picked the tripod up, with the intention of catching her up.

Before he could make a start, a sudden bright flash of lightning crackled around him, making him duck down instinctively. It was followed almost immediately by a loud roll of thunder, echoing ominously through the mountains. Seeing Amelie frightened by the lightning, causing her to slip back down the slope, he broke into a run, as much as he could with his heavy baggage. He could see Amelie pick herself up and hear Doctor Corbett's voice calling her to get down to them as soon as she could.

But then another noise overtook that of the thunder. A similar sound, but growing into a deafening roar. Above the point where Amelie stood, oblivious to the danger, the deep snow appeared to be moving. Cracks appeared in the white surface as the avalanche, set off by the vibration of the thunder, began to make its way downhill, gathering speed and pushing rocks before it. The wave of snow and debris was heading straight for Amelie while the onlookers below were powerless to help her. Throwing his bags to the ground, Guy sprinted as fast as the rough ground would let him in a direct line towards Amelie. Now she had realised the danger from above and Guy could hear her plaintive cries for help.

"Run," he shouted, though he doubted she could hear him, and she remained rooted to the spot like a startled rabbit. How he made it in time to grab her before the snow hit, he would never know, but grab her he did, dragging her back the way he had come. Thankfully, they were on the very edge of the flow of snow, ice and rocks. Guy pushed Amelie behind the nearest rock that looked like it was big enough to withstand the onslaught and threw himself on top of her to protect her. The noise was immense, and the air filled with tiny crystals of ice as well as rocks and mud. Guy said a silent prayer in the hope that his chosen rock was strongly rooted to the mountainside, or they would be crushed to death in moments. The two of them could do no more than see out the minutes, which seemed like hours to them both, while the avalanche continued on its journey downhill.

And then there was silence. Occasional trickles of tiny stones punctuated the quietness, and the rain was beginning to fall harder now, but it was the sudden cessation of the deafening noise that hit them both.

From below, Doctor Corbett and Lizzy watched in absolute horror as they saw the wall of snow come tumbling down between them and Amelie. They couldn't tell if Amelie had been swept into the avalanche or had escaped from it on the far side. Neither could they see Mr Pender.

"I must go to my mistress," said Lizzy. But the doctor pulled her back to the path saying, "No, my dear, we cannot rescue them on our own. We need to go back to the village for help."

On the way back towards the town Doctor Corbett was forced to physically guide Lizzy along in the right direction. The poor girl could not help herself from stopping often to turn and look for her mistress. "Come along, Lizzy," ordered the doctor, "We would be best to keep going as fast as we can to raise the alarm."

Indeed, help was already on its way and coming towards the doctor and Lizzy at a fast pace. The sound of the avalanche had been heard back in St Moritz. The alarm sounding by the ringing of the church bell, and several groups of people were already on their way along the lakeside, some holding long poles to be used for searching through deep snow. Tobias and his two friends were there too, leaving Charlotte to comfort Augusta, who was fully aware that her sister may have been caught up in the tragedy. When Tobias and his friends reached Lizzy, and discovered that Amelie was indeed missing, he ordered her to go to Augusta, while the doctor turned back with the rescue party to give advice on the possible location of the two people who could be buried in the snow.

But the doctor was finding it hard to recognise the scene now. It was as if the whole hillside had changed shape and landmarks like trees and rocks had been swept away entirely to be buried under a huge white blanket. He was exhausted too and getting cold and wet from the continuing heavy rain. Young Edward Wingfield broke away from his small group of would-be rescuers when he saw the doctor sink down to the ground, holding his head in despair. "Come on, Doctor," said Edward gently, "let me take you back to the hotel. You can do no more here today and we need to get you dry and warmed up." The doctor did not complain as Edward hooked an arm around him and virtually carried him back along the side of the lake. As they reached the town Edward was able to transfer the doctor into the care of Augusta and Charlotte, who were standing amongst a group of ladies watching and hoping for good news to reach them. Edward told them that there was nothing to report so far and then turned back once more to join the search while the young ladies helped Doctor Corbett back to his hotel room where a warm bath awaited him.

The rescue efforts had so far been fruitless, despite the systematic search by those with long poles pushed into the snow at regular intervals. Visibility was poor and getting worse as the rain turned to sleet which, if it became snow, would make the search even more difficult. It soon became obvious to everyone that nothing could be done before darkness fell. Once word spread that the rescuers were retreating, Tobias, pushing himself forward through the crowd of people, had to be physically restrained from going after Amelie.

"No, laddy," ordered a dour Scot who seemed to have taken charge of things. "There's no point in further injuries. We will just have to wait for daylight." Had Amelie been aware of what appeared to be Tobias' grief, she would perhaps not have been so happy with the way things would turn out on the other side of the mountain of snow blocking the path between them.

Unaware of the frantic activity on the far side of the avalanche, Guy and Amelie found themselves clinging onto each other for longer than perhaps was necessary. Amelie, still shivering from fright and the cold, was only too glad to have Guy's warm body close to hers. And Guy, still feeling warm from his run across the hillside, had no need to hold onto Amelie, but had no reason to let her go either. In fact, despite the adversity of the situation, he was rather enjoying the moment.

Realising that the danger had passed without either of them being injured, Guy sat upright and brushed the debris from his shoulders in a spray of ice and stones. Amelie uncurled herself from the crouched position she had found herself in and turned her body to lean against the damp rock which had been their saviour.

"Why, Mr Pender, thank you for coming to my rescue. Now perhaps we should head home," said Amelie. She went to stand up but found, to her horror, that her legs seemed incapable of bearing her weight. For the second time today Guy came to her rescue, catching her by the waist to hold her upright.

"I rather think we may find that impossible for now," Guy replied, "but we must find some better shelter from this rain before we catch our death of cold."

Once more, Amelie extracted herself from Guy's arms to stand stiffly with her head turned away from him. Guy was beginning to wonder what on earth had possessed him to travel to St Moritz in pursuit of a woman who now appeared to be uncomfortable in his very presence. Pushing such thoughts to one side in order to concentrate on the issue in hand, Guy said, as gently as he could, "Amelie, the avalanche has made our journey back impossible without assistance from the other side. I am sure that help is on the way, but we must be patient and await our rescue somewhere safer and more comfortable than this rock."

Guy remembered the shepherd's hut he had seen earlier and wondered if Amelie was strong enough to reach it. He could, he thought, try to carry her, something he would enjoy no doubt, but find very difficult to do over rough ground. And he doubted that she would allow it, anyway. The hut was well away from the avalanche, though he would need to ensure its safety from further slips, but it was the nearest reasonable shelter. He suspected that they would be there overnight, at the very least.

"Come, Amelie," he said, "we must go back up the hill a little way. Would you be able to walk, or can I take your arm?"

"You will do no such thing, Mr Pender!" replied Amelie, distancing herself even further from her saviour. "This is most improper. If you wish to take refuge elsewhere, then please do so. I will stay here until rescue arrives." With that Amelie sat down once more, her back against the rock and a determined look on her face.

"Amelie, please call me Guy. And, if I have to, I will carry you kicking and screaming to the safety of that shepherd's hut," he replied sternly. "You will die of the cold and wet if you stay here, merely for the sake of propriety."

Amelie realised she was beaten. The rain was now making its way down the back of her neck, and she felt shaky from the shock of recent events. Guy was right. They both needed shelter. But she would not allow him to get close again. She stood, waiting a moment to stop herself from swaying from side to side. "This way, Mr Pender?" she asked, indicating the route back to the platform where they had shared a picnic only an hour or so ago. Guy nodded and pointed in that same direction. "Come along then," she added as she set off as fast as her jelly-like legs would allow. Guy could do no more than follow her, wondering what kind of night they were likely to have if Amelie continued to be so obstinate.

Guy came across the pile of bags he had abandoned in such a hurry and managed to rescue his leather case and camera, deciding to leave the wooden tripod to its fate in the snow. Amelie stopped when she reached the grassy platform and waited for Guy to tell her where to go next. Guy could barely see the outline of the shepherd's hut through the teeming rain, but he pointed in that direction and Amelie set off in front of him at a fast pace. However, when she reached the door, she hesitated, unsure about what they may find inside.

More concerned with reaching shelter than about what lay beyond the door, Guy had no hesitation in lifting the roughly-hewn wooden latch. It moved easily, although the heavy door was less willing. Guy had to put a shoulder to it to ease it open to a point where Amelie could squeeze through first, with Guy close behind. He pushed the door shut against the wind and rain before turning to peer through the gloom to see what lay inside. There was only one small window, entirely covered by cobwebs, so it was almost completely dark. Amelie couldn't immediately find anywhere to sit down and was leaning on a rickety wooden table for support. She was so exhausted by the events of the afternoon that she didn't have the energy to pull away from Guy when he put his arm around her shoulders and guided her to sit on the edge of a narrow wooden bed taking up nearly all of the back wall of the hut. As Amelie sat down a cloud of dust rose up from the rough woollen blanket covering the bed.

It was obvious that there had been no human visitors here for some time. Guy guessed that it was only used in the summer months when sheep could climb higher up into the valleys, and even then he suspected it was just one shepherd and his dogs who slept here. There was a small fireplace with a stone chimney and across the hearth was an iron bar, at the right height for a cast iron pot to be suspended from it. Fortunately, there was a neat stack of wood in the corner of the room. Now all he needed was a means of making a spark and some water for the pot. There may be nothing to eat for the night, but he was sure that Amelie would like to wash the grey streaks of mud and dust from her face.

Amelie sat motionless on the edge of the bed, her hands in her lap, watching Guy go about the job of getting a fire burning. He raised a silent prayer of thanks to the usual occupant of the hut for being so well organised in providing kindling and logs for the fire, and on the mantel shelf he found a small tin containing a battered but dry box of lucifers. Building a stack of the smaller pieces of kindling, he struck a match against the stone fireplace before setting the flame into the centre of the stack. Thankfully, the wood was dry and the flames caught quickly, sending smoke up the chimney almost at once. While the fire got itself going, Guy lifted the pot off its hook and pushed the door open again to go looking for some water. The rain was still pouring down, although more like sleet now, but it enabled Guy to fill the pot easily from the water pouring off the roof. Because it was fresh water, straight from the roof, Guy hoped he could at least make a hot drink once the pot boiled.

When Guy opened the door again, he found Amelie had removed her gloves and hat and was pacing backwards and forwards in a state of distress. He quickly hooked the pot over the fire before once more taking her elbow and leading her to sit on the bed.

"I thought you had gone," sobbed Amelie. "I don't want to be left here alone." Her shoulders heaved with sobs and her dirty face was now streaked with tears coursing down her cheeks.

Guy sat down beside her on the edge of the bed, reached into his pocket for his handkerchief and handed it to Amelie. As he held it out, she clasped his wrist tightly with both hands, saying, "Mr Pender, why did you come to St Moritz? Why did you save me from the avalanche?"

Dropping Guy's arm, she once again stood up, turning to him and saying, "It would be better for everyone if I had been swept away."

"What do you mean, Amelie my dear?" asked a shocked Guy, jumping to his feet too. "Of course, I came to see you. I have wanted to be with you ever since the day you came to my studio."

"But, I thought…..," replied Amelie. They now stood facing each other, the only sound the crackling of the fire. Guy waited for her to continue, but Amelie seemed incapable of any further words.

"What was it you thought?" coaxed Guy, gently.

"I thought it was my sister you….., you wanted," explained Amelie. "I thought you had seen me leave with my parents that day and had purposely visited Augusta on her own."

"My dear Amelie," responded Guy, "I did nothing of the sort. I was deeply disappointed to find only your sister at home that day. Surely you must know that it was you I wanted to see again, and I couldn't wait another day to do so. Now come, sit again, while I put more wood on the fire and see if I can find a means to make a hot drink."

While Guy tended to the fire Amelie sat down, dabbing at her face with Guy's handkerchief. A cloud had lifted from her soul when she heard that it was her Guy had wanted to see again, not her sister. But it was not the only cloud getting in the way of the sun on her soul, of course.

Guy, meanwhile, had found another airtight tin on a shelf beside the fire. It contained tea, or at least what Guy took to be tea leaves. Gingerly, Guy sniffed at the contents and it certainly smelt like tea. Next to it on the shelf was a small metal teapot but only one battered metal mug, so they would have to share their drink. He tipped a good pile of the tea leaves into the pot and scooped a ladle full of the now boiling water on top. Leaving it to brew, he was pleased when he turned round to see Amelie looking a lot more composed. The sobs had ceased, although fresh tears were still coursing down her face, while she wrung Guy's handkerchief nervously round and round in her hands.

"But, Guy….," he noticed with pleasure that she had used his name for the first time, "I cannot be with you. My family want me to marry another man."

This time it was Guy who put a hand out to the table to steady himself. He needed a moment to gather his thoughts, so took his time pouring hot tea into the only mug, though he found his hand shaking as he did so. He was in desperate want of a drink too, but his needs would have to wait a while.

"No milk or lemon, I'm afraid," he said, as he handed Amelie the mug. For the first time in her life, rather than sipping from a delicate porcelain cup, she felt the warmth of wrapping both hands around a hot mug of tea and, at last, she stopped shivering. The tea tasted bitter and musty, it reminded her of the garden on a wet autumn day, but she felt the warmth of it coursing through her whole body. Having taken another gulp, she held the mug out for Guy.

"Here, you need some warmth too," she said, without understanding that the warmth Guy really wanted was not from a cup of tea.

He turned the mug around so that he was drinking from the opposite side and took a gulp of the hot liquid. It tasted as good as nectar from the gods as far as he was concerned, despite being made from some very stale tea leaves. The shared drink seemed to calm them both and they sat next to each other on the very edge of the bed passing the mug between them until Amelie offered Guy the last dregs. He made an effort to strain out the liquid between his teeth, nevertheless receiving an unwelcome mouthful of wet leaves. For the first time since the avalanche, Amelie smiled as he screwed up his face and started picking the dark leaves from between his teeth.

"Goodness," laughed Amelie, "just look at the two of us. My mother would be appalled."

"And I daresay your father would chase me down the mountain with a gun," added Guy, and they both laughed.

The ice broken, the two young people continued to talk. At one point Guy got up to light a rusty old lantern that stood on the shelf, but Amelie pulled him back. She rather liked the semi darkness, lit only by the glow of the fire. It helped her to relax and it was good that Guy could not see her face clearly in the gloom.

Slowly and with lots of hesitations, Amelie told Guy about the day she met Tobias and the need for her father to find suitable husbands for Augusta and herself after their hurried exit from Venice. She told him how Tobias was a very suitable husband but she didn't love him, and explained how she had come to realise that her mother's relationship with her father was one of convenience rather than of love, and that it was her destiny to follow in her mother's path with a life as Tobias Linburg's dutiful wife.

Guy could hardly believe what he was hearing. When Amelie reached a part of the sorry tale where she had to stop and form the next sentence in her mind he got up to put a fresh log on the fire. It gave him time to think clearly too. As the sparks flew from the fire, so did his mind go in a million directions. It had all seemed so simple when he had decided to join Amelie in St Moritz. He would just sweep her off her feet and they would live happily ever after. How stupid of him to imagine life would be so straightforward!

There was very little that Guy could do about the future, as it was obvious that Amelie's mind was made up. Duty over love. But the avalanche had given them a tiny chance to spend some time together, free from the interference of parents and prospective husbands. They both knew that fate had brought them together, but neither of them knew quite how to take advantage of the opportunity without destroying the feelings they had for each other.

The fire was down to glowing embers, the room almost entirely dark, although Amelie and Guy had grown accustomed to the gloom. They had no idea of the time of day but there was one pressing reminder of time passing for Amelie.

It took a great deal of courage for her to say, "Guy, I am afraid to say that I need to use the lavatory."

Now he came to think of it, so did Guy. When he had been filling the pot with water he had noticed an open shed attached to the back wall of the hut. It had shown signs of being a shelter for a cow or a horse. At the far end Guy had looked around a screened off section where he found a privy seat. It was certainly not what Amelie would be accustomed to using, but as he said to himself, "needs must when the devil drives."

Amelie didn't like the sound of it at all, but bravely nodded her head when Guy explained what she needed to do. To make it easier for her, he offered to light the lantern and visit the privy first himself. Once he had made use of it and checked for creeping insects and cobwebs, Amelie was happy to follow his lead, although she asked him to carry the lantern until she reached the other side of the screen. He discreetly removed himself, leaving the lantern where she could pick it up easily on the way back.

While she was out of the room Guy set about arranging somewhere for them to sleep. He took the dusty blanket off the bed and lay it on the hard floor in front of the fire. The sheets on the bed looked reasonably fresh and the feather pillow perfectly acceptable in the circumstances. He had previously unrolled the picnic blanket from his shoulder bag and lain it over the back of a chair near the fire. It was now warm and dry, so he lay it over the bed for Amelie.

By the time Amelie returned with the lantern, Guy had turned back the sheets for her and prepared his own bed on the floor. He took the lantern from Amelie and told her he would be outside until she called him when she had made herself ready for bed.

The sleet had briefly turned to snow, leaving a

sparkling white blanket in front of him, but the night was now clear and cold. So cold that Guy could see his breath like smoke curling into the clear air. It reminded him of a winter's night with his friends at Applecross, where temperatures could plummet making icy white sculptures out of trees and bushes. Looking up, he could see the stars above as if they were close enough to touch. It was a beautiful sight, and he wondered if it would be possible one day to take a photograph of the night sky.

"Mr Pender, Guy," he heard Amelie call. "Come in out of the cold."

He did as she suggested and found Amelie already under the covers, her outer clothing lay over the back of a chair, but Guy smiled to himself when he realised she must have retained her skirt and long-sleeve blouse for the sake of modesty. He merely removed his boots, blew out the lantern and went to lay on the floor in front of the fire. It took him a few minutes to roll the blanket around his body, and to find a reasonably comfortable position on the cold, hard flagstones. Even so, he found he just couldn't stop shivering. It was going to be a miserable night.

A little while later, still wide awake with little hope of sleep, Guy heard Amelie turning over in her bed. "Guy, you cannot possibly sleep on the hard floor, you must be even colder than I am, and a lot less comfortable than me," said Amelie softly. "Why don't you lay next to me here? Why should we not keep each other warm tonight?"

Guy certainly would not be sorry to give up his hard, cold bed, but he needed to be certain. "Are you sure, Amelie?" he questioned her. "It is a small bed and we will necessarily be close to each other."

"And we will gain warmth from each other and have the benefit of an extra blanket," she replied bravely, patting the narrow space beside her to encourage him to join her. He smiled as he tossed the blanket he had expected to be his only bedcover over the top of the picnic blanket. "Avert your eyes for a moment, Amelie, as I remove my jacket," he said.

Amelie turned over once more to face the wall, but Guy had failed to see a glass-framed picture hung on the wall above the bed. By the dim light of the fire's embers Amelie watched a mirror image of the man she was about to share a bed with, as he removed his jacket, finally sliding gently into bed in his tweed trousers and cotton shirt. With their backs to each other, Guy said, "Good night, dear Amelie, and thank you. This bed is a good deal more comfortable than the floor."

Amelie took a deep breath and made a momentous decision. She realised that they had only one chance for happiness together, a chance given to them unexpectedly. And she wasn't going to miss the opportunity to make the most of it.

Turning over she whispered, "Guy, would you hold me? Just to keep me warm, perhaps?"

He hesitated but a moment, before turning over himself and taking her into his arms. Amelie tucked her head under his chin, and he could smell her hair and feel her breath on his chest through the cotton of his shirt. He wondered briefly if the avalanche had carried him away after all, and he had reached heaven, especially as Amelie relaxed against him. It did not cross his mind to do anything more than hold onto her as they gave each other comfort and warmth. He dozed, and so did Amelie. Neither of them could say afterwards that they had slept at all, but they must have done so because at some point a ray of sunshine worked its way across the pillow as the sun rose. It woke them both with a start.

"Oh, goodness," cried Amelie sitting upright in bed with one of the blankets clutched to her chest to cover her crumpled white blouse underneath. "What if the rescuers come soon?"

"It is still early," Guy replied as he swung himself onto the edge of the bed, immediately grabbing the topmost blanket. It was icily cold. The fire had gone out and the frost had made intricate patterns on the glass window.

"It will be a while before we see anyone else. Stay there a moment while I set the fire once more," he continued. Using the blanket as a warm cape, he knelt down to lay new wood on the fire and struck another lucifer to get it going. The small room warmed quickly, assisted by the sunlight now streaming through the window. "I'll go and fill the pot with fresh water," he said, politely leaving Amelie to get out of bed on her own.

In daylight Guy could see a mountain stream nearby, running over the rocks on its way down to the lake. It was an easy task to fill the pot under an overhanging rock, and Guy used the opportunity to splash water on his face. It was so cold that it made him gasp for breath. He truly did not expect any rescue until later in the morning, but for Amelie's sake there was something he needed to do. Before he went back inside he took the blanket from around his shoulders and lay it on the straw under the roof of the open stable behind the hut. It would look, for all intents and purposes, as if he had slept there overnight.

Guy knocked gently on the wooden door asking, "Can I come in, Amelie?"

"Yes, yes," came the reply. As Guy went inside and hooked the water pot over the warm fire, he found Amelie standing facing the door. She had done her best to restore her dress and arrange her hair, and had put her coat back on over her blouse. Her gloves, hat and scarf lay ready on the bed. To Guy she looked as beautiful as ever, and somehow changed by her experiences yesterday and overnight. More mature, and more determined.

Without a word Amelie reached out for Guy, pulling him towards her. It took every bit of his self control not to take her face in his hands and kiss her lips.

"Thank you, Guy," she said, looking directly at him with those piercing blue eyes. "Thank you for coming after me to St Moritz, thank you for rescuing me from the avalanche, and thank you most of all for giving me the respect of sharing my bed without, you know…., without taking advantage," she finished awkwardly.

Before Guy had a chance to reply that it had been a pleasure to do all of those things, a huge brown and white dog appeared at the open door, panting from the run uphill. The dog issued a single deep bark before sitting to attention, his huge eyes fixed on Amelie and Guy. Moments later they both heard a familiar voice calling their names. It was Doctor Corbett and the rescue party approaching.

CHAPTER SIX
Rescue

Tobias had not slept. He was angry that he had not been allowed to continue the search for Amelie and angry with Doctor Corbett for seemingly allowing her to spend the day with another man, with only a maid as chaperone. What was the doctor thinking? And what was this Pender fellow up to?

Amelie had told Tobias about the portraits taken at Pender's studio, and when he mentioned it to Wilfred, his friend had raised his eyebrows and said, "Better watch out, old fellow. I hear he's one for the ladies, that Guy Pender." That didn't help at all now. So the woman he was expecting to be his wife was either lying buried under an avalanche, or spending the night in the company of a man with a reputation for womanising.

When Tobias had begged to carry on the search that evening despite the darkness, those around him thought it was because of his love for Amelie von Truber. And if anyone had asked him about it, he would have agreed that it was to find the woman he was to marry, of course. But it was not for love. Tobias Linburg, it seemed, was not capable of loving anything but himself. Back at the lodge Tobias had spent the long evening pacing to and fro in front of the blazing fire, deep in thought and with a look of anguish on his face. His mother tried to comfort him, but he pushed her away roughly, and his friends received a similar response when they tried to help too. Needing an early night to enable them to be out again at daybreak for the search, those around him left him to his thoughts. Amelie's mother had taken to her room before dinner, accompanied by Augusta and Lizzy, both of whom were in a state of shock. Herr von Truber had remained downstairs with Tobias' family and friends, but he too felt the need to get some sleep before joining the search party in the morning. Edward and Wilfred returned to their hotel rooms, but not before finding Doctor Corbett sitting alone in the hotel lounge. The poor man was beside himself with worry and feeling responsible for the events of the day. The two young men comforted him as best they could before accompanying him to his door with instructions to get some sleep.

Tobias continued to pace up and down, muttering to himself and occasionally stopping to consider a particular thought before stepping forward once more. In his mind, it all came down to two outcomes. In the first scenario, Amelie lay dead or dying beneath the weight of an avalanche. Tobias was not considering her possible pain, or her loneliness in such a situation, rather more he was considering the implications of her loss to himself.

Tobias Linburg did not like losing something that was his. Once, as a small child while they still lived on the shores of Lake Lugarno, he had lost a tiny wooden soldier. It was a special toy, and he had insisted on taking it when his nanny took him for a walk in the garden. Somehow it had slipped out of his pocket, and despite hours of searching by nanny and the other staff, it could not be found. Most children would have cried about its loss, but Tobias just became angry. He stamped his feet and sulked. And he blamed his nanny for making him lose it. In fact, his anger was so fierce that he refused to speak to Nanny ever again. But even worse than that, he had found a way to retaliate. He had taken hold of his left arm with the fingers of his right hand and squeezed and squeezed, so hard that it really hurt and hard enough to make two finger-shaped bruises. Then he had gone to his mother, tears streaming down his face and blamed Nanny for the bruises. She had been dismissed at once, of course.

With this one act of deceit, Tobias realised that he could always find a way to blame someone else if things did not go according to his plans. As he grew older he grew more devious and more jealous of his possessions. It accounted for his failure to have a real relationship with anyone prior to Amelie. Things would start off fine, girls enjoyed his attention and were keen to be seen with the heir to a prosperous business. But Tobias was so jealous that, as soon as one of his conquests even dared to look at another man, or made herself unavailable to him for the smallest reason, he would discard them immediately. That in itself was bad enough, but retribution was always necessary. The man who had been the object of the girl's glances would find himself suddenly out of favour in Zurich society, or perhaps the young lady would find herself the unwitting subject of a tawdry scandal. Tobias could always find ways to cast the blame elsewhere.

If he lost Amelie now he would be very angry indeed. Like the wooden soldier, she had become a prized possession, even in the short time they had known each other. If she was lost, then in Tobias' mind, someone was to blame. And there was only one person who could be said to have caused the day's events, and that was Doctor Corbett. Tobias paused in his walking backwards and forwards to tuck away that thought. If Amelie

is dead, then he would find a way to deal with
Doctor Corbett.

On the other hand, if Amelie is not buried under
the snow, then Tobias' logical conclusion was that
this Pender fellow had rescued her. Who knew
what they were doing now on the other side of
that mountain of snow? This scenario was even
worse than the first, in Tobias' devious mind. And,
of course, the object of his retribution, in this case,
would be Mr Guy Pender. Tobias would claim
Amelie back, but not before he had destroyed
Pender's reputation and livelihood.

If Amelie was found alive in the morning, then it
seemed to Tobias that there was one urgent matter
that must be dealt with. One that he had intended
to keep until they returned to Zurich, but that
could now be put in train as soon as she was
found. Happy that he had every likely eventuality
accounted for in his head now, Tobias smiled
quietly to himself and set off upstairs to take a few
hours of sleep before joining the rescue mission.

Most of the rescue party were up and ready to
resume their search before daybreak, and they set
out carrying lanterns as well as shovels and picks
to continue clearing the path of snow and fallen
rocks. It was a grim task, especially after the
plummeting temperature overnight. The locals in
particular were expecting the worst as they knew

that surviving under the snow for such a time was almost impossible. There was very little conversation as they made their way alongside the lake, and the first group of men set about the manual labour of digging as soon as they reached the blocked path. They made good progress and found that their job was made easier by the rain of the previous evening washing some of the snow away. Edward and Wilfred were in the midst of all the action and by the time they were relieved by another group of young men, they estimated they had almost reached the point where Amelie had last been seen. No trace of her, or of Guy Pender, had been found under the snow, even though a few people continued to climb above the path to probe the ground with long wooden poles, feeling for something soft beneath them.

A sudden bright finger of sunrise spread up the valley behind them, and it was not long before daylight gave them enough light that the lanterns could be extinguished. At least they had no need to contend with rain or snow. The day looked like it was going to be fine and warm, with not a breath of wind. Suddenly there was a shout from Doctor Corbett. "Smoke!" he shouted, pointing in the direction of the old shepherd's hut further up the valley.

Indeed, there was a wisp of wood smoke going straight up in the air from the chimney of the hut.

Guy Pender

The search party fell silent for a moment while the implications of a fire being lit in the hut sunk in. A small cheer rose up from the gathering crowd and those with picks and shovels at the front line set to with renewed enthusiasm. Doctor Corbett removed his hat and, with some relief, wiped a tear from his eyes. An elderly man wearing a green alpine hat with a pheasant's feather in the band and carrying a long shepherd's crook came up beside him and said in German, "They will be warm and dry in there. I leave it ready to be used in case of such a need."

"Danke," replied Doctor Corbett, not understanding every word said by the shepherd, but realising by his hat and stick that this man was the usual summer occupant of the hut where he now hoped to find Amelie and Guy.

"I'll send the dog on ahead," added the man, and with just a single whistle Doctor Corbett could see a big brown and white dog with huge paws taking giant leaps through the deep snow in the direction his master was pointing with his shepherd's crook. Adler was one of a rare breed of short coated St Bernard dogs these days. The current trend was for crossbreeding with the American Newfoundland dog, but Hans could see no purpose in encumbering the dog with long fur that attracted the snow and ice. He had seen many a dog weighed down by it. Adler, proudly named

137

after the mountain eagle, was by far and away his best dog and had sired a good few litters over the years of similarly short haired pups with huge paws and a head as big as a lion. There was no doubt in Hans' mind that Adler would reach the hut first, and he hoped the people inside it would realise, when they saw him, that the rescue party was close behind.

While the dog cut a sure-footed path through the snow, the diggers were working at breakneck speed and had all but reached the far side of the slip. Doctor Corbett could see the flat plateau where only yesterday they had enjoyed their picnic, and the path to the hut beyond was clear of debris. Not wishing to wait a moment longer, he stepped forward to climb over the last heap of snow. The front line of rescuers put hands out to help him, and he made it safely to the other side before breaking into as much of a running pace as he could manage uphill. He paused briefly when he saw Guy's wooden tripod on the ground and then positively sprinted the last few yards to the hut. As he ran he called out, "Amelie, Guy." The dog reached the door of the hut first. His training as a rescue dog meant that he simply issued a single deep bark before sitting to attention, his nose pointing in the direction of the people he had found, his short, docked tail wagging with excitement at the treat that always followed such an exercise.

Doctor Corbett could hear people coming up behind him now. He turned briefly and recognised Tobias Linburg and the two men who had been so kind to him last night, as well as the shepherd. Looking back to the hut, he could see that the door was open and that there were two people inside in an embrace. It took a bit of quick thinking on his part, but he realised that Tobias must not see what was happening inside the hut. He knew about Tobias' intentions for Amelie, and he knew Tobias well enough to be aware of his jealous nature too. He stepped onto the path and blocked the way as best he could before calling out again, "Guy, Amelie, we are all here to rescue you. Tobias is here too."

His delaying tactics continued as the three young men pushed their way past him. He grabbed Tobias' sleeve and said, "Thank God, Amelie has been found."

"Get out the way, you stupid man," replied Tobias, pushing the doctor to one side. "This is all your fault, you know."

Doctor Corbett had achieved a moment or two of time in which Amelie and Guy could put things straight. By the time Tobias reached the door, a couple of paces behind Edward and Wilfred, Amelie was standing next to the bed pushing a loose lock of hair behind her ear, while Guy had picked up the first thing that came to hand. He held the empty teapot, as if he was in the middle of pouring tea into an equally empty mug. Nobody would have guessed that, only moments before, they were in each other's arms.

Tobias strode past everyone to take Amelie by the shoulders, the poor girl casting a wistful glance at Guy before submitting to Tobias' firm grasp. "Amelie, I….I couldn't lose you, you are mine," he said. Guy thought it a rather strange thing to say to a person who had just been rescued from an avalanche, although he had no choice but to keep quiet. As Tobias held her, Amelie looked longingly over his shoulder at Guy. She felt as if she had been tossed from the calm and gentle world of Guy Pender into the tumultuous seas of belonging to Tobias Linburg.

Then there seemed to be such a crowd of people in the small hut, all talking at once. The doctor was trying to ask Amelie if she was alright, but Tobias still held her so tightly that she could hardly respond with anything more than a nod of the head. Edward and Wilfred were there too, clapping each other on the back. It was all a bit overwhelming for Guy, who managed to squeeze past everyone and through the door, much in need of some fresh air.

He took a couple of deep breaths of icy mountain

air and then felt Adler's cold, wet nose nudging his hand as if he was asking for attention. Guy turned to pat him on the head. He didn't have far to bend down as Adler's head came up to Guy's waist, even when the dog was sitting down. "Thank you," he said to the dog.

"He speaks only German," said the shepherd with a laugh, his accent heavy.

"Danke," Guy replied instead, aiming it at both the dog and the man.

In a mixture of German and English Guy was able to thank Hans for the use of his hut for the night and for providing wood for the fire. Guy promised to replenish the stocks as soon as he could and reminded himself to top up the tea and maybe find an extra mug, should there be two occupants next time a refuge was required.

Hans had one more favour to perform, albeit without realising its significance. The crowd indoors had started to stream out into the open, Tobias walking straight towards Guy, a belligerent expression on his face. But just as Tobias opened his mouth to speak, the shepherd said in German, "You will have been cold last night, sir, with only that blanket to keep you warm under the shelter of the stable."

Guy silently blessed the shepherd for saying exactly the right thing at the right moment. He could see Amelie standing behind Tobias with a look of relief on her face, and to add to it, Doctor Corbett pushed past Tobias asking, "Guy, are you well after your cold night outdoors? Should I examine you for signs of exposure?"

The wind had been taken out of Tobias' sails entirely. So it seemed the Pender fellow had done the decent thing and left Amelie to sleep alone inside the hut. Nevertheless, they were inside together when the rescue party arrived and there was something between them, something he could sense, something he didn't like at all. He resolved to continue with his plans with some urgency, as soon as they got away from this abominable mountain.

Once the party got back to town, Amelie was led away to her room with her mother and sister fussing around her like mother hens. Lizzy was dispatched to the kitchen to arrange for a tray of hot food to be delivered while Amelie took a most welcome bath. Guy, meanwhile, was more in need of a hot meal than a change of clothes and was happy to sit in the hotel lounge while Doctor Corbett fussed over his health, quite unnecessarily in Guy's opinion. Though he was happy to admit that he felt a lot more himself after he had tucked into a steaming bowl of soup, mopped up with chunks of fresh, warm bread. Once the doctor had been reassured that he was not suffering from frostbite and would most definitely survive from his overnight experience, Guy managed to get away to his room.

He lay down in the crumpled clothes he was wearing, sinking into a much more comfortable bed than the one he had shared last night with Amelie, his mind full of the dilemma in which he now found himself. How stupid he felt! His first encounter of a romantic nature had been with Frewin, and he couldn't help but shudder to think of that awful moment. And now there was Amelie. Love at first sight, but it was to be unrequited love. As a gentleman, he had no choice but to give her up, to leave her in the grasp of Tobias Linburg. It was obvious that Amelie was a dutiful daughter, and that she understood the need for her family to make a good marriage, and Tobias had so much more to offer her than his meagre fortune. Even if his aunt's legacy was sorted out soon, he could not compete with a whole chocolate empire! But he did not like the way Tobias had looked at him, nor did he like the way the man had talked to Amelie earlier, as if she was a possession. She deserved to be treated gently, talked to as an equal, credited with some intelligence and a will of her own.

Resigned to his fate, Guy decided he would pack his bags at once and return to Zurich with his tail between his legs. As soon as possible, he would do his best to hurry along the process of sorting out his aunt's will, and then move on from Zurich. He drifted off to sleep with thoughts of finding the quickest passage to New Zealand in his head, but Amelie seemed to be in his dreams too. Amelie and his friends at Applecross, all together. Amelie laughing with Nancy and Sophia, Amelie walking in the orchard, Amelie standing on the ridge and admiring the view of the plain with the mountains beyond......

Some hours later, Guy awoke to the sound of a gentle knocking at his door. He recognised the voice of Doctor Corbett saying, "Mr Pender, are you awake?"

"Come in," said Guy, sitting himself upright, flattening his hair and rubbing his stubbly face. He realised he was in desperate need of a shave.

"How are you feeling?" asked the doctor, as he entered the room.

"Better for a good sleep, thank you," replied Guy. "But in need of a wash and a change of clothes before I venture out of this room."

"Well, you will need to look your best this evening," said Doctor Corbett. "That's what I came to tell you. There is to be a dinner party tonight at the lodge to celebrate your rescue. Tobias has organised it all, and he made a point of telling me to invite you personally. Now, I'll leave you to get ready, and we can meet downstairs at five o'clock to walk down to the lodge together." With that, he left Guy to ponder on the reason for Tobias Linburg inviting him especially to a dinner party. He suspected it had nothing to do with thanking him for protecting Amelie, and rather more about making sure Guy knew who Amelie really belonged to.

Nevertheless, he would accept the invitation, if only for the one last chance of speaking to Amelie before he went home. Glancing at his pocket watch he realised he had slept for most of the day and now had barely an hour to get himself tidied up and ready. He had better get on with it!

CHAPTER SEVEN
Proposal

Once Amelie had gone to her room to be cosseted and comforted by her mother and sister, Tobias was keen to put his plans for the day into action.

First he spoke to his mother saying, "Mother, I would like to celebrate Amelie's rescue with a dinner party tonight. May I invite those involved? And would you talk to cook, please?"

"Why, that is a lovely idea, Tobias," replied Frau Linburg. "I will go and see cook immediately as she will need some time to prepare a menu. Something simple but hearty, perhaps?"

"Whatever you think best, Mother," said Tobias. "I have drawn up a list of guests." With that, he pulled a piece of paper from his pocket and gave it to his mother.

"My goodness, you are very organised my dear aren't you?" replied his mother, taking the list and heading straight for the kitchen where cook was none too pleased to be interrupted by the mistress in the midst of luncheon preparations, but happy to consider a suitable menu while she put her feet up in front of the kitchen range that afternoon. She then sent for a footman to fetch the necessary supplies from the butcher and greengrocer, before setting her team of kitchen maids to prepare the accompaniments.

In the meantime, Tobias made the rounds of people he wished to invite to the dinner party, including Edward and Wilfred, of course, and the doctor. Doctor Corbett was also instructed to make sure that the shepherd Hans and Guy Pender were both invited, along with any of the rescue party who Doctor Corbett considered necessary.

The rescue party had dispersed soon after their return, some to the hotel, some back to their usual jobs in the town. Before returning to his hotel, Doctor Corbett had instructed Amelie to stay in her room with a tray sent up for luncheon. This left the Linburgs and the remainder of Amelie's family to take luncheon at the lodge. Everyone was ready to eat after their early start to the day, but Tobias had time to sidle up beside Amelie's father on their way to the dining table.

"Sir, may I speak with you on an urgent matter this afternoon?" asked Tobias.

Suspecting the reason for such a conversation, Herr von Truber smiled to himself before replying, "Why, yes of course, Herr Linburg, perhaps you have somewhere quiet in mind where we could talk without interruption?"

Although the main part of the lodge consisted of one large space, a small room had been set aside as a quiet area. It was lined with bookshelves and had room for a desk and some comfortable chairs where Herr Linburg or his son could work quietly, or the ladies could retire for some reading or sewing. Tobias suggested that they meet in the library straight after lunch had been eaten.

Tobias enjoyed a hearty lunch. Everything was going to plan. Even the invitation to Pender to be in attendance had worked well. He really did want that man to be there, not as the doctor thought, to thank him for rescuing Amelie, but rather more to rub his nose in it all. He was looking forward to that part of the evening very much indeed. He really didn't care one bit who else turned up, he would leave that to the doctor, but if it gave everyone the impression it was an occasion to thank the rescuers, then all well and good.

As soon as the ladies left the table, Tobias moved

towards the library, to be joined by Herr von Truber. Tobias' mother, sensing what was to be discussed, took her husband's arm and guided him away from his attempt to join the other men. Herr Linburg was to find himself taking a walk to the lakeside with his wife, even though this was something they rarely did together.

In the library, the two men stood facing each other, neither of them knowing quite who should sit where.

"Herr von Truber," began Tobias. "I will come straight to the point. I have not known your daughter Amelie for long, but the events of the last day and night have made me realise how much she means to me. I have come to see that I cannot live without her. You know, also, that I have a considerable fortune at my disposal and have the prospect of inheriting the business empire set up by my father. I have no doubt that I will be able to offer Amelie a life where she will want for nothing. So I wish to ask your permission to take your daughter's hand in marriage and to do so as soon as possible."

It was a long speech, but one for which Herr von Truber had been ready. "Well, Tobias, that is wonderful news, and of course you have my permission," he said, trying hard to hide his elation at restoring his family's fortunes at last.

"Frau von Truber and I had hoped for such an outcome, though we perhaps did not expect it so soon. But in the circumstances, I can quite understand your haste. It sometimes takes an event like this to make us realise what is important to us."

Herr von Truber continued, "Now, I presume you wish to speak to Amelie alone. I will call for Lizzy and ask her to see if Amelie feels well enough to come downstairs. And then I will leave you two young people to talk."

Tobias had thought through the way in which he would propose to Amelie, and he did not want to leave her any opportunity to decline him. He rather suspected that, given the choice, she would turn him down, but equally he was certain that she would act dutifully in front of her family. So Tobias said, "Oh no, Herr von Truber, I am sure Amelie is already aware of my intentions, so it is but a formality to confirm your agreement to it. Perhaps we could ask both Amelie and her mother to join us here, and I can make my proposal in front of my new family."

In the end, Frau von Truber, made aware of the conversation in the library, went upstairs to prepare Amelie for what was to come. Amelie, still a little dazed from the events of the past twenty four hours, could barely believe what her mother was telling her. But it seemed her fate had been sealed. She had resolved to be the dutiful daughter, to accept a life with Tobias, but that was before spending such a pleasant time with Guy Pender. As she walked down the stairs with her mother, she felt as if she was walking to the gallows, but there was no choice, particularly as the proposal was to be made in front of her parents. This alone told her that it was more of a business arrangement than one built out of love.

Afterwards, she could hardly remember what was said, nor how she had reacted. All she knew was that a dinner party had already been arranged for that evening to celebrate their engagement, on the assumption that she would agree to the proposal, and that everyone around her was pleased for the happy couple. It had also been agreed between them that nothing would be said about the proposal outside the immediate family until Tobias stood up to make a speech. Amelie's new fiancé had briefly taken her hand and kissed it gently, but no other physical contact had been made, neither did she want anything further between them.

The rest of the afternoon was spent in preparing for the dinner party. Augusta seemed more excited about the whole thing than did her sister. In the end, Lizzy sent Augusta off to her own room for a while so that she could concentrate on helping

Amelie to dress. Lizzy knew her two girls very well indeed and was all too aware that Amelie's veneer of happiness covered up other feelings.

"What's the matter, Miss Amelie?" asked Lizzy with a great deal of sympathy in her voice. "You should be the happiest girl in the world."

A single tear rolled down Amelie's cheek. Lizzy reached out and wiped it away with her thumb, which only made more tears fall. Poor Amelie sobbed, "Oh Lizzy, I think I am the saddest girl in the world. I know that I must marry him, but I don't love him one little bit. And….., and there is someone else."

This came as no surprise to Lizzy. She had seen the way Amelie and Guy Pender had looked at each other before the avalanche, and she suspected that their relationship had blossomed before they were both rescued. "I know, my dear, I know," she reassured Amelie, patting at her cheeks with a handkerchief. "But you must see that Tobias is a good catch. You will want for nothing."

"I will want for love," was the simple reply from Amelie.

"Now, come along, let's mop up those tears and get you looking your best," answered Lizzy, "and perhaps you will grow to love Tobias in time. And there will be children to love soon, I am sure."

This thought just made Amelie's tears flow even more. She could only think of the tenderness of Guy's embrace compared with the formal coldness of Tobias' proposal. She had no choice but to allow Lizzy to fuss over her while she put on her ball gown and prepared her hair. By the time her mother knocked on the bedroom door, Amelie was looking calmer and resigned to her fate. She found herself being guided downstairs to join the other guests milling around the entrance hall, where drinks were being served prior to going in to dinner.

In a show of attentiveness, Tobias pushed his way through the crowd of people to meet her at the bottom step. Taking her arm, he accompanied her towards the table. "We are sitting at the top," he whispered to her, "Where everyone can see us."

Tobias began the move towards the dining room. The tables had been set out in a U shape to accommodate the unusually large number of people. Tobias and Amelie were seated across the top of the U, their respective parents on either side. On one side of the U sat Augusta and Charlotte with Edward and Wilfred while Doctor Corbett, Guy and the shepherd sat opposite them. The remaining diners were made up of a variety of townsfolk who had all taken part in the rescue. Some looked uncomfortable in such auspicious company, but were looking forward to a meal provided as a thank you, or so they thought.

Amelie had not dared to look in Guy's direction, although she had seen him on her way down the stairs. They had exchanged but a brief glance before Tobias whisked Amelie away. Guy's mind was in turmoil, but he had made his decision to return to Zurich, and he would get away from this party as soon as he could politely make his excuses.

At the top table, Tobias was feeling very pleased with himself. All his plans had come together. He had just one thing left to do with the day and the time for that arrived as everyone finished their dessert. He stood up and tapped his glass with the spoon he had just used to eat his syllabub. The chatter around the room came slowly to a halt as people realised that Tobias Linburg was about to make a speech.

"I have called you all together tonight, not entirely for the purpose of thanking you for rescuing Frau von Truber from the avalanche," he began. Guy's heart sank into his boots as he realised what was to come next. "Of course," continued Tobias, "I am thankful for your contribution to a successful rescue, and my family and I are more than pleased to provide this meal for you all." He waved an arm in the general direction of the lower end of the tables, pointedly ignoring the doctor and Guy in his praise. "But the main reason I have asked you here tonight is to celebrate the announcement of my engagement to Amelie von Truber, who has graciously agreed to be my wife."

With that, he raised a glass and offered a toast to Amelie, which was met with heartfelt cheers from around the room. Did Guy get the feeling that Tobias had held his glass out towards him for a little longer than was necessary? Did he sense a look of triumph on Tobias' face? A shiver ran down his spine. Throughout the whole speech, Amelie had kept her eyes on the half-eaten dessert in front of her and even as the toast was made, and Tobias offered a hand to help her up to stand next to him, she just couldn't bear to look in Guy's direction.

There followed an endless round of questions as people mingled around the happy couple, asking about a date for the ceremony, or if Amelie was happy, or how long they had known each other. Fortunately for Amelie, Tobias was happy to provide answers, although she was somewhat disconcerted to hear him answer that the marriage would take place as soon as it was possible for it to be arranged once they returned to Zurich.

Eventually, Amelie managed to whisper to Tobias that she was very tired and really needed to retire to her room. With a show of attentiveness, he immediately called for her maid to take her upstairs. As Lizzy came from the kitchen she almost bumped into Guy Pender on his way out of the door. "Oops, Mr Pender, I'm sorry," she said, and Guy realised it was more than an apology for their near accident.

"So Lizzy knows about Amelie and me," thought Guy to himself. Somehow that was a comforting thought, but it didn't stop him from the need to get away from this household as quickly as he could.

Amelie almost fell into Lizzy's arms as she left the dining room, but not before she noticed the empty chair where Guy had been sitting next to the doctor. More tears were falling before she reached her room, and it was all that Lizzy could do to calm her down before putting her to bed while the party continued downstairs. It was very late indeed by the time Tobias retired, after a night of heavy drinking with his friends Edward and Wilfred. They would all three wake with sore heads the following morning.

Long before that, Guy had his bags packed into the wagon and the horse hitched up for the journey home. The hotel proprietor had been alarmed at his early departure, but Guy assured him it was a purely personal matter that had forced him to leave so soon, and nothing to do with the excellent service provided by the hotel. With assurances to return once the snow had melted, Guy set off and was out of the town before Amelie was awake. Despite his promises to the hotel proprietor, Guy doubted he would ever return here. After all, he had a longer journey to organise to get back to his friends in New Zealand. This final thought offered him a small shred of comfort in an otherwise bleak future.

CHAPTER EIGHT
Charity

March 1867

Leon, the baker, and his friend Luigi from across the square were worried about Guy Pender. Luigi had time to spare before he started work at the cafe, so he decided to see what Leon thought about Guy's early return from St Moritz. He was leaning on the counter while Leon took the warm bread from its metal baking tray and placed it on wooden shelves behind him. The air was full of the smell of fresh bread, and Luigi thought he would be happy to stay here all day instead of running backwards and forwards at the cafe with drinks and food.

"What are we to do with him?" asked Luigi.

"Monsieur Pender, I presume?" replied Leon de Fevre. "Aye, aye, I had hopes for him and the beautiful mademoiselle. But it seems there has been a falling out. Why else would he return so soon?"

"Unless Herr von Truber has decided Herr Pender is not worthy of the attentions of his daughter," replied Luigi. Only in Switzerland could a man speak in his native tongue so naturally while still making perfect sense to his companion. The conversation continued in a mixture of French, Italian and German.

Luigi had overheard Madame Martinez whispering to a friend over their morning coffee that Frau von Truber had hopes for Amelie and Tobias Linburg, the heir to the Linburg chocolate empire.

"Good lord, I hope not!" exclaimed Leon, "Amelie von Truber is far too good for that evil young man. I hear rumours of his behaviour being beyond the law at times. I suspect that would be nothing but a marriage of convenience to Herr von Truber's pocket."

Leon de Fevre had his back to the counter as he spoke and had not noticed a customer come into the shop. Luigi spoke quickly, "Herr Pender, how was your trip to St Moritz?"

As it happened, Guy had heard most of the conversation, pausing outside the shop when he heard Amelie's name. So now it was apparent that everyone knew about his thwarted relationship with Amelie.

"Pleasant, thank you," replied Guy, not wishing to give anything away, even to his friends. "But there was an avalanche, after which I felt it best to return home as I could not go into the mountains to take landscape photographs."

All three men knew that this was not the full story, but Luigi and Leon respected their friend enough to keep silent. Guy pulled some coins out of his pocket to pay for his usual crusty loaf and left without saying anything more.

Luigi, realising he was now running late for work, followed Guy out of the door, but not before turning to Monsier de Fevre and saying quietly, "We must see what we can do to help our friend."

Leon considered this thought for the rest of the day while wrapping a loaf in soft, white paper or while popping two cream-covered choux pastries into a box. By the time he turned the sign to 'closed' on his door, he had made a decision, but his actions would need to wait until the von Trubers returned from St Moritz. He smiled quietly to himself as he took the last loaf upstairs for his supper before retiring in order to start the cycle of bread making once more in the early hours of the morning.

It was almost a week later when Monsieur de Fevre saw the von Truber's maid approaching the shop, an empty wicker basket hanging over her arm. He knew she would be calling into the shop soon after their return for her regular order of bread and pastries for the von Truber household. Now he could begin the first stage of his plan to bring Guy Pender and Amelie von Truber together again.

It just so happened that Leon de Fevre, being a kind and generous man, had an arrangement with the sisters of the convent of St Brigitte to provide bread for the poor of the area. It was an arrangement that had been made several years ago after Leon received a neatly written request from Mother Monica. Theirs was a closed order, which meant that, although the recipients of the charity donation were selected by the order, the distribution of those gifts had to be made by volunteers from the community. It was common for the young daughters of the richer families hereabout to offer their services on a weekly basis, and Leon's first step was to suggest to Lizzy that Amelie take up such a position. He rather suspected that Lizzy would know about Amelie and Guy and this proved to be correct.

In the end, Leon explained the whole idea to Lizzy, who naturally went along with it. She had taken a dislike to Herr Linburg from the start, and she knew very well how much Guy meant to Amelie. There was no doubt she could see the benefit in Amelie having a reason to leave the house on a regular basis without need for a chaperone. It was the perfect plan, and she couldn't wait to get it started. Leon was disconcerted to hear that Amelie's marriage to Tobias Linburg was to be arranged with some haste, but it made his resolve even stronger. Things would need to be set in motion immediately.

It was an easy thing for Lizzy to persuade Amelie to volunteer her services to the sisters of St Brigitte. To be honest, Amelie was glad to have something other than wedding preparations to do with her time. Lizzy explained that Monsieur de Fevre had suggested it, and that he would be pleased to introduce Amelie to the sisters. He was expecting her to call into the shop as soon as she was able.

Since the announcement of her betrothal to Tobias, Amelie had barely had time to think. There was a constant stream of visitors to deal with, all full of congratulations and admiration for catching such a handsome and wealthy young man. Then there were visits from Tobias, or suggestions of a walk by the lake or another day of skiing. She barely seemed to have any time alone. But then, she was glad of it in some ways. She had no time to dwell on Guy. It was only at night, when she tossed and turned, unable to get to sleep and plagued by dreams when she did eventually fall asleep. In the darkness of the night she could think of nothing else but Guy. How he had protected her from the avalanche, how he had saved her from being buried in it, how he had courteously and gently looked after her overnight, and how he had held her for those few precious hours together.

She had not been sad to leave St Moritz behind, with its mixed memories. However, she also knew that things would get even more serious once they returned home. No doubt Tobias would be keen to set a date, and no doubt her parents would want to start planning the event, and there would be dresses to choose, bridesmaids to select and all the things a bride should find exciting, but that she was dreading so much.

Tobias had originally wondered if they could get the ceremony done over Easter, but as that was barely three weeks hence, the practicalities made such haste impossible. A summer wedding had the advantage of the breakfast being taken outdoors, and Amelie's mother had made it clear that it would take time to make all the arrangements. In the end, the last Friday in July was selected as being time enough for everything to be arranged.

Amelie had agreed to it, just as she had meekly agreed to almost everything else to do with the marriage, and there was so much to do. Within the first day or so of their return her mother had arranged for a dressmaker to call, and a meeting had been booked with the priest who would conduct the service. Amelie had been summoned to meet the rest of Tobias' family of aunts, uncles and cousins and a trip to the jeweller to ensure that Tobias' grandmother's diamond-encrusted engagement ring would fit her delicate finger had been arranged. It was a whirl of activity from which Amelie was happy to have been given a reason to escape.

Amelie's mother was pleased to grant permission for her to visit the poor under the guidance of the convent sisters. After all, she was soon to be a married woman, and a wealthy enough woman to be expected to do charity work. She saw no reason to insist on a chaperone in this case, and it would be a good lesson for her in dealing with people less fortunate than herself. It was arranged for Amelie to meet Monsieur de Fevre at the bakery where they would take a basket of bread rolls and loaves to the people on the list provided by the convent. Little did Amelie realise that an extra address had been added to the end of the list by

Leon de Fevre's fair hand.

They began by knocking on the door of the convent. Leon de Fevre had warned Amelie that the nuns could not leave the convent, but it still came as something of a shock to her when a small flap in the door was opened and a face surrounded by the blue material of the order's robes appeared at the tiny window. Leon introduced Amelie to Sister Marthe, who raised a finger to the window, made the sign of the cross and whispered, "Bless you, my child," to Amelie.

From the convent they took a circuitous route along the river bank and into the poor part of the city. Amelie was shocked at the run down apartment buildings with no gardens or green spaces for the children to play. And there were so many children, most of them clad in nothing more than rags while they played in twos and threes in the dirty street. It was obvious that Monsieur de Fevre was a welcome visitor. The children crowded around them both, clamouring for a crust to eat. Amelie held her basket high enough up to avoid the grubby fingers clutching at her rolls and pastries while they waited for the mothers to appear. They came quickly down the stairs or from the narrow passages between the buildings, gratefully accepting their share of the gifts. Amelie had been fearful of approaching such a notorious part of town, but she left with a new understanding of the women who, despite their circumstances, seemed defiantly proud, doing their best to survive and to feed their families.

Returning to the corner of the square in which they both lived, Leon took his list from his pocket and ticked off all but the final address.

"Now, Mademoiselle," said Leon, "there is just one address left for you to visit. I must get back to the bakery, so you can take the one remaining loaf to this address without my help." With that he showed Amelie the address, explained how to reach it and swapped her empty basket for the last loaf, wrapped in paper, before heading along the street to his shop.

It took a moment or two for Amelie to find the narrow passageway, which she realised ran behind the shops in the square. She lived close by, but had never noticed that the building could be approached from the rear too. Finding the metal ladder, just as Leon had explained, she climbed up one storey to a small landing on which lay a fat tabby cat taking in the last of the spring sun. Before she could reach over to tap on the door, it was opened from within.

"Who's that I hear on the steps, Albert?" asked a familiar voice, as Guy Pender put his head out of the door into the daylight.

Both together, they exclaimed, "Oh!" and then neither knew quite what else to say. Albert, with a cat's sense of human emotion, stood up and wound himself around Amelie's skirts. He could tell that Guy liked this person, so he would like her too.

"I didn't know you lived here, Mr Pender," said Amelie, "Monsieur de Fevre sent me to deliver this." She held out the bread for Guy to take.

"I think perhaps my friend, de Fevre, has been making plans for us to meet," replied Guy with a laugh. "So, you had better come inside before the neighbours see us together in public."

"I….I am not sure that I should," said Amelie.

"My dear Amelie, we have spent the night together. Do you think one visit to my apartment will ruin your reputation further?" was Guy's response. He stepped back to encourage her through the door, but not before accepting the loaf from her.

She hesitated for only a moment before stepping over the threshold. It was a dark room and it took her a moment to accustom herself to the lack of light. She saw a simple space with simple furnishings. It appeared Guy Pender lived in one room, there being nothing but a kitchen cabinet with a table and two chairs, a washstand and a bed. It was the bed that dominated the room, or was it just that Amelie was reminded of the last time they had shared a room? Albert, who had followed them inside, was winding his body through the iron rails of the bedstead, his tail erect. He purred softly as Amelie held out a gloved hand to stroke him. He liked this human a lot.

They stood awkwardly facing each other, both suddenly aware of the moment, and that circumstances had indeed changed significantly since their last encounter. After several moments of silence, Guy said, "Come, Amelie, sit. The day is warm, so perhaps I can offer you a glass of cordial. It will perhaps taste better than the tea we shared last time."

She took the seat Guy offered her at the table and found Albert had jumped up in front of her, expecting more attention from his new friend. It gave her something to do while Guy poured the cordial into two glasses, checking first that at least one of them was clean.

Guy joined her at the table, having shooed Albert off first, much to the cat's disgust.

"So, tell me Amelie, how did that rogue, de Fevre persuade you to come to my apartment?" asked

Guy. "And, what plan did he come up with that enabled a betrothed young lady to be out and about without a chaperone?"

Amelie explained to Guy about the sisters of St Brigitte and the distribution of loaves to the poor. Guy roared with laughter as Amelie told him about the list of recipients, and the final address written, not by the nuns, but by Monsieur de Fevre.

"My goodness, my two good friends Leon and Luigi are like a pair of old matchmakers!" said Guy, and Amelie laughed too. She felt herself relaxing in Guy's company. It was as if they had known each other forever. She felt safe here, even though she was fully aware that her reputation would be in tatters if she was seen in another man's apartment. Perish the thought of Tobias ever finding out, although Amelie was getting to know her fiancé better these days, and knew full well that his wrath would be directed at Guy, not at her.

Finishing the last of her lemon cordial, Amelie put the glass down and went to stand. Guy followed suit. "Thank you, Guy," she said simply. "It was not my intention to see you again, but I am grateful to Monsieur de Fevre for contriving this meeting. But now I must return home."

Before she reached the door, Guy was beside her, taking her hand and planting a gentle kiss upon it. As he did so, he could see the shape of her engagement ring under the glove she wore. "It was lovely to see you, my dear," he said softly, adding in a whisper, "And I hope your charity work may bring you this way again soon."

Bending to give Albert one last tickle behind his ears, Amelie could find no answer to Guy's words, but he was in no need of it. He knew she would return. He watched from the small landing as she stepped down the metal stairs and went along the narrow passage to the street. Did she raise a hand to push back her hair, or was it a wave to bid him adieu? He rather hoped it was the latter.

Turning the corner into the square, Amelie could feel her heart beating under her blouse, and could feel the heat in her rosy cheeks. In order to gain a moment to calm herself, she walked along the street to the bakery where Monsieur de Fevre was bringing in the last of today's wares before shutting the shop. He saw Amelie approaching, and was glad to see her flushed cheeks and happy smile.

"Thank you, Monsieur," she said, as she reached the door. "Thank you."

"You are welcome, Mademoiselle," replied de

Fevre. "I am pleased to see you smile, and I am sure the gentleman is happy too."

She turned to cross the street towards home. As she did so, de Fevre called out, "Next week at the same time, perhaps?" Both the baker and Amelie knew that he meant more than just another distribution of bread to the poor.

Meanwhile, back in his apartment, Guy sat at his bare wooden table holding Amelie's empty glass in his hands as if it was a gypsy's crystal ball and would tell him what to do next. His head told him to back away, to refuse to see her again, to get out of Zurich as soon as he could. But his heart told a very different story indeed. Even though darkness fell, Guy didn't move to light a candle, nor did he get out of his chair to let Albert out, despite his urgent scratching at the door. He let his heart fight with his head, each taking its turn to present their arguments. "Get out of town," said his head. "But you love her, and she loves you," replied his heart. And so it continued, a kind of internal battle with first one taking the lead, then the other.

The clock striking the hour brought Guy out of his reverie with a start. His mind had been made up and it would take second place to his heart. He loved Amelie, and she loved him, or at least he was fairly certain of that. She had not just turned around and gone home when she realised that Leon had tricked her into coming to his apartment.

She hadn't pulled her hand away from his kiss, and he couldn't forget the comforting feeling of holding her in his arms after the avalanche.

He had another reason for letting Amelie into his life too. He was not a vindictive man, but he didn't like the way Tobias Linburg treated Amelie, as if she was a mere possession, not a real person with feelings. He vowed he would always treat her with the respect she deserved, with tenderness and love.

Since Tobias' return to Zurich, Guy had found the studio unusually quiet, almost to the point of a complete lack of custom. At first he had thought it was just a coincidence, maybe all his customers had gone on an early holiday to the mountains. But it was Luigi who told him what was really going on. Tobias Linburg and his two English friends had taken to meeting each morning at the cafe. While Edward Wingfield and Wilfred Dannay were polite young gentlemen, Tobias Linburg had no respect for those who served him. Luigi came to dread his arrival. Nothing was ever right, the coffee too cold or the pastry stale. One particular day Luigi was returning with a fresh coffee to replace the one that Tobias thought was cold. As he approached the table at which the three men sat he overheard the conversation, standing back a moment so as not to interrupt them. "I could bed that Lisbet Martinez, despite

her young age," boasted Tobias. "Or how about your sister Charlotte?" he added with a grin.
"You leave my sister out of this," replied Edward, leaping to her defence. "I won't say she is perfect, but I would prefer not to see her shamed by one of my friends."

Luigi could hardly believe what he was hearing.

"Anyway, you are betrothed to the beautiful Amelie von Truber," replied Edward.

"Bah, I have the rest of my life to take Amelie whenever I want her," said Tobias with a dismissive wave of his hand. "I may as well take my pleasures now, before I can be accused of adultery."

Luigi put the cup down on the table in front of Tobias with more force than he would normally use, splashing some of the hot liquid into the saucer. He was angry, very angry indeed. And it got worse.

"Anyway," continued Tobias, ignoring the waiter, "If my darling fiancée can eye up that Pender man, then I can do the same with Lizbet Martinez."

He took a sip of his coffee and carried on, "But I have put a stop to that gentleman's advances too.

He may find himself short of business after the tales I have put around about him. The womanising bounder!"

Luigi wasn't prepared to listen to any more of the conversation. He counted Guy Pender as a friend, and he knew that Amelie von Truber was a kind and gentle young lady. Neither of them deserved the evil attentions of Herr Tobias Linburg.

The following day Luigi found Guy at an outside table long before lunchtime. "Good morning, Luigi," said Guy. "A quiet morning for me again. It seems the good folk of Zurich have had enough of my photographic skills."

"Monsieur Pender, may I tell you something?" asked Luigi. He then went on to recount the conversation he had overheard the day before, adding that he was aware that Tobias Linburg had a reputation for vindictiveness. There were even rumours that he was implicated in the demise of a competitor in the chocolate industry, a Monsieur Auber, who had drowned in mysterious circumstances. "You would be best to avoid a battle with that man, to be sure," he added.

Guy could hardly believe what he had heard. And, once Amelie had been to see him, it was obvious that he not only needed to leave town, but that he should at least try to take Amelie with him.

Anything to get her away from Tobias Linburg's clutches. It occurred to him that his dream of seeing Amelie at Applecross could come true after all.

There was one thing that Guy had up his sleeve. Something that Tobias would not know about. In the days following his return from St Moritz Guy had been to see the lawyer who was dealing with his aunt's affairs. He had expected to have to be quite blunt with the man, scolding him for the delay. To his surprise he had found a neat pile of paperwork, tied with a red ribbon, and all that was required of him was a signature to finalise Aunt Emmeline's entire fortune passing into Guy's hands.

It was a sizeable fortune too. Without even accounting for the value of her property, there was no doubt that Guy's future was to be a secure and prosperous one. However, he would keep it very quiet for now. He certainly didn't want Tobias Linburg hearing about it. That man could do what he liked to attempt to ruin Guy's reputation, but it wouldn't break him. Now he had things to organise, things that would keep him busy over the next seven days, until Amelie's next visit.

CHAPTER NINE
Liaisons

The marriage of Amelie von Truber to Tobias Linburg was due to take place in a little over three months time. The bride and groom had much to do in the intervening weeks, but very little of it was connected to the impending ceremony. Most of the preparations had already been made.

Tobias had arranged for Edward to act as his best man, and for Wilfred to support him as usher. The two Englishmen had been somewhat surprised to be invited to take part in their friend's wedding, but had come to realise that Tobias didn't appear to have any other close friends, and being an only child, had no family members to ask either. They had intended to return to England after Easter, but neither of them had any difficulty in making arrangements to stay longer. In reality, the two young men spent much of their lives in idleness, with little to do but wait to take up their roles when their respective fathers passed on.

The two of them, and Edward's sister Charlotte, were all invited to stay as guests at the Linburgs' mansion. While the men passed their days in idle pursuits, Charlotte, Amelie and Augusta, who had very soon become friends, busied themselves with preparing the cottage, which was to become Tobias and Amelie's residence. To call it a cottage was perhaps an understatement. Although it looked from the outside every bit like an English cottage, thatched roof and roses around the door, once one stepped inside it was both spacious and comfortable. It had been Tobias' parents' home prior to the death of Herr Linburg's father and so it was to be for Tobias. Amelie thought of it as a kind of waiting room, where she would live in the shadow of her mother-in-law until they made the move into the bigger house at some point in the future. She looked forward to that with dread, which grew deeper as each day passed.

It was Charlotte who made most of the decisions about bringing the cottage up to date with the finest furnishing and the most modern conveniences. A housekeeper and cook were already employed, having been chosen, not by Amelie, but by her future mother-in-law. They would move into the servants' rooms at the back once the cottage had been renovated. No expense was spared, and Amelie had to admit that she was enjoying choosing colours and designs with her new friend, Charlotte. Augusta was pleased to be involved too. In fact, she was spending more and more time with Edward, much to her parents' delight. After all, Edward Wingfield had a title to his name and an estate to inherit in England.

Most of the time there were just the six of them; Tobias with Amelie, Edward walking with Augusta and Wilfred and Charlotte bringing up the rear. Wilfred had a soft spot for Charlotte, whom he had known all his life, but one could not call it a romantic relationship. Perhaps Wilfred would have liked it to be so at one time, but Charlotte ignored all his advances and made a point of telling everyone that she had no intention of being encumbered with a husband just yet. Not while there were so many handsome young men in the world. "Why pin yourself down to just one of them?" she had been heard to say on more than one occasion.

So the days passed. Looking at it from outside, one would see nothing more than a group of rich young people enjoying the early summer together. But it was not that simple for Tobias and Amelie.

Tobias was getting increasingly irritated with Amelie. She was just so damnably boring! She gave the impression of mild disinterest in anything he had to say, and meekly acquiesced to every suggestion made by his mother regarding the wedding ceremony and their life together afterwards. Yes, she was pretty, and he suspected, once he was given the opportunity to see more of it, her body would be a thing of great beauty to behold. But there was no chance of him knowing that for sure before the wedding night. She had made it very clear that modesty dictated a strict adherence to a mere peck on the cheek being the nearest they came to each other until they were married.

The truth of it was that he was getting frustrated. Before his engagement he had found it easy to meet girls who wanted nothing more than to be bedded by the rich and handsome Tobias Linburg. But the word was out, Tobias was betrothed to the lovely Amelie von Truber, and no self-respecting girl would want to intervene in what seemed to everyone else to be a perfect match. He missed the act of taking a woman to his bed. He missed being able to dominate them, even if only for a short time. In that act, he was physically and psychologically on top, and he missed that feeling of power. He simply couldn't understand why Amelie was not prepared to let him take her. After all, it was but a few more weeks until he could have her whenever he chose to do so.

Oblivious to the depth of Tobias' feelings, Amelie

did indeed seem to float through the days allowing others to make decisions for her. Except for Tuesday afternoons. That was her day for charity work, and for her secret visits to Guy Pender's apartment, made even more special for being the one thing in life that she felt she could control.

After her first visit to Guy, she had spent a great deal of time thinking things through. She had even feigned a mild illness of the stomach so that she had the excuse of staying in her room for a day or two, only occasionally interrupted by her sister's enthusiastic chatter. Just as Guy had been through the same battle between heart and mind, so too did Amelie. Though her battle was really between her heart and her duty to her family. She told herself that she had already made the decision to dutifully accept Tobias as her husband for the sake of her family. But decisions, she realised, could be undecided if one later became aware of other contributing factors. Would she have made the same decision now, knowing Tobias as she did, and aware of Guy's fondness for her? The answer was a very definite no.

She considered confessing all to her mother, who would likely be sympathetic, but no doubt would bow to the views of Herr von Truber. And the thought of talking to her father about such matters was far too much to bear.

The solution didn't come all at once in the end. It grew as a germ of an idea, a logical answer, or at least a justification for returning to Guy's apartment again next Tuesday. "Amelie von Truber is of age," her mind said to her. "Amelie von Truber can make her own decisions."

The little demon, who murmured those words in her ear, got more and more powerful as the days went by. "Amelie von Truber loves Guy Pender. Amelie von Truber hates Tobias Linburg." It all seemed so simple when it was put to her like that. The tipping point came on the Sunday after the group of young people walked home from church together. It was nothing but a glance exchanged between Charlotte and Tobias. A look that told Amelie all she needed to know. The demon in her head had seen it too, and that night in bed, all she could hear it saying was, "Tobias Linburg has taken Charlotte Wingfield to bed."

Well, two could play at that game, although she had no intentions of sleeping with Guy just yet. But she was almost certain she would go and see him on Tuesday afternoon. Why should she not enjoy his company for just a little while longer? But she must be careful not to show to Tobias that she knew about Charlotte, and even more careful that he didn't find out about Guy. She suspected Tobias could be vindictive if he ever found out. Or maybe he would be relieved to have an excuse to abandon her. No, on balance, she knew him well enough now to dread what he may try to do to Guy if he suspected they were meeting each other.

As it turned out, something else happened to reinforce her decision. Something which took the pressure off her. That evening, Edward Wingfield was to join them for dinner, and while the two sisters were getting dressed beforehand, Augusta confided in her sister that Edward would be asking to speak to their father after dinner.

"We have decided we will not make it public until after your marriage ceremony," said Augusta. "But we love each other so much, we just can't wait!"

Amelie immediately felt guilty. She had been so distracted by her own issues that she had barely noticed the blossoming relationship between Augusta and Edward. "Oh, congratulations, sister. I am so happy for you," she said, genuinely pleased for them both. "Oh my goodness!" she went on, "You will be Lady Augusta, and a duchess one day!"

"I know," said Augusta, dancing around the room with excitement. "Won't Papa be pleased?"

The demon in Amelie's head whispered, "Augusta has removed the pressure on you to marry Tobias now." It was as if a heavy weight had been lifted from her shoulders.

Dinner that night was a joyous occasion. Edward was good company, attentive to Augusta and, although a little nervous, polite towards her parents. Everyone knew what was to come after dinner, and conversation was light hearted and entertaining. Even Amelie seemed a little bit like her old self, laughing at Edward's stories of life in England and smiling at her sister, who looked radiant.

"Well, my boy," said Herr von Truber, once the dessert plates had been cleared away. "Shall we retire to my study for a brandy?"

The sisters stayed at the table with their mother, though nobody dared speak. It was as if they were all holding their breath. Fortunately, it was but a few minutes before the door opened and the two men came back into the dining room. Herr von Truber clapped Edward on the back, saying, "Well, you had better tell everyone what we have been discussing."

Amelie guessed that Edward had already prepared the speech he now gave. "Frau von Truber, Amelie, I am sure you both know that Augusta and I have become fond of each other," he said, looking across at Augusta with a smile. "This morning after church I asked her to be my wife, and I am thrilled to say that she accepted my proposal, subject, of course, to her father's permission."

He moved round to take Augusta's hand as she stood up from her chair and continued, "And I am further pleased to say that Herr von Truber has granted us that permission tonight."

Amelie and her mother found themselves clapping their hands together with joy before standing up and embracing the happy couple. Much discussion followed about dates and wedding venues and Edward's family, but through it all Amelie silently blessed her sister and Edward Wingfield for falling in love and making her decision to see Guy again so much easier.

Had she known about the events leading up to Tobias and Charlotte's liaison, she may not have found the decision to see Guy so difficult after all. It had all begun on the Tuesday afternoon while Amelie was helping Leon de Fevre with the delivery of bread to the poor. Ironically, at about the same time that Amelie knocked on Guy's door, Tobias lay on top of Charlotte Wingfield on the bed he would be sharing with Amelie once they were married. Tobias had not set out to seduce Charlotte that day. He was at a loose end and feeling irritated with Amelie for going off to do some ridiculous charity work. Edward and Augusta had taken themselves off to the riverbank and Wilfred had business to attend to in town. He wandered aimlessly around the garden, swiping at any poor plant that dared to get in his way. As he reached the cottage, he found the front door open and he could hear the sound of someone singing to themselves inside. Assuming it would be one of the staff, he walked inside and headed for the source of the singing. He had a desire for something to drink, and he intended to order the maid to fetch him something. As he got to the bedroom, he realised it was Charlotte, stretching up to hang the new curtains at the long windows.

All thoughts of the need for a drink were forgotten as he stood still, partially hidden behind the door and just watched for a few moments. She was a tall girl with a pert body that was accentuated by her stretching up so high. Her sweet voice continued its song and Tobias was overcome by the vision he saw in front of him. He crept up quietly behind her, waited until she reached up high again and grabbed her by the waist, causing her to drop the curtain material as she turned to face him.

"Oh my! Tobias, you frightened me!" she exclaimed.

"Then I must make you better and calm your

nerves," he replied, placing a kiss on her cheek. To his amazement, she didn't pull away from him at all. More than that, she placed her arms around his waist.

No further words were exchanged between the two of them. Tobias kissed her cheek again, but she took his chin and turned his face towards her lips, kissing him with some force. His irritation with Amelie was forgotten. In fact, Amelie was entirely forgotten as he melted under the passion of Charlotte's kiss. For a moment, he realised that Charlotte was leading the way, something he was not used to at all. But he took control and began picking desperately at the tiny buttons at the neck of her blouse. Pushing his hands away, Charlotte undid the buttons one by one, something that made Tobias' passion grow even more. It was not long before they lay on the new bedspread, their clothes in disarray around them. For the first time in his life Tobias felt as if he had been controlled by a woman, rather than being in charge. And it was rather a nice feeling. He felt as though he had been chosen by her, selected to be the object of her passion. He didn't care that Charlotte had demonstrated her obvious experience in lovemaking, and that he was not the first man to be dominated by her passion, nor he suspected the last.

In the days following they found every

opportunity to meet again. Charlotte thought the cottage was too dangerous a place to meet as Amelie could turn up at any moment. Luckily, her room in the main house was at the end of a quiet corridor, and it became the perfect tryst. Within the week Tobias found himself creeping along the corridor once his parents had gone to their bedroom, spending a night of exhausting, exhilarating passion with Charlotte and creeping back to his room before the staff were up and about in the morning. He reached a point where he didn't care a jot if the staff saw him, even though it would likely be kitchen news spreading like wildfire around the household.

He knew he needed to deal with the situation, to decide between the passionate Charlotte and the beautiful Amelie. And he knew he needed to do it soon. But something told him that Charlotte would choose to stay or go when it suited her. Maybe he would be better taking her now, whenever he felt like it, before the wedding. Then, who was to say he couldn't maintain a mistress as well as a wife after that?

Tuesday afternoon once again presented Tobias with an opportunity for lovemaking with Charlotte, and this time he was grateful for Amelie's sense of charity. Theirs was a very different liaison from the one that unfolded in Guy's apartment.

Guy had nervously prepared for Amelie's visit. He had no way of knowing if she would come, but he had a feeling she couldn't keep away. He had tidied the apartment and had even gone so far as to buy some fine new glass goblets for their cordial. That morning he had been to see Leon de Fevre who winked at him knowingly and offered to put a selection of his finest petit fours into a box. "She will come, my friend," he said, handing the box of tiny marzipan fruit-shaped delights to Guy.

With a great deal of care Guy placed the furniture where Amelie could sit comfortably in his presence, close enough that they could talk, but not so close as to be improper. As the clock approached the hour at which she had arrived last week, Guy nervously stood, then sat in one of the chairs, then moved to the other one. Briefly, he went to the door to see if he could see her coming along the passageway, but to no avail. Then he left the door ajar to save her knocking and took up residence in the chair nearest the window. Albert, sensing Guy's restlessness, sat upright on guard duty on the landing, his tail twitching as he licked a paw in the warmth of the late afternoon sun.

The truth of it was that Amelie had been late setting out, having been held up in conversation with Sister Marthe, who had wanted to know how Amelie's first visit had gone, and to tell her how pleased the sisters were to have found someone so kind and generous as to help them out in their charity work. Amelie shifted from one foot to the other, thinking of the time passing while she politely answered Sister Marthe's questions. Behind her, Leon de Fevre was quietly smiling to himself. "So, she is going to visit him again," he thought, though no further words had been spoken between them about the baker's part in their liaison since her thanks last week.

It felt to Amelie like everyone wanted to talk today. The children slowed her progress along the street by gathering in a group around her. The mothers took her hand to say thank you for the welcome gift and even Leon de Fevre seemed to be dithering over his list of addresses. Amelie rather hoped she could continue this weekly delivery on her own in future.

Eventually, only one loaf remained in the basket, and they both knew who was to be the recipient of that. Leon had not even bothered to write the address down this time. He quietly handed her the bread, took the empty basket and nodded in the direction of the passage to Guy's door. "Go on, then," he said gently.

Guy heard her footsteps on the metal staircase at the same time that Albert saw her coming. The cat stood up, stretched and yawned before sauntering down the stairs as if to say, "Well, where have you been?"

"Hello, cat," said Amelie, bending to stroke Albert's head. "Is your master at home?"

"He is indeed," laughed Guy as he reached the landing and held out a hand to indicate that she should go inside.

He followed her in and shut the door, leaving Albert mewing outside. "I am glad you came," said Guy, as Amelie took one of the seats that Guy had so carefully arranged. Amelie noticed the open box of sweet treats, and though she could not face the idea of eating anything, she appreciated the thought. She was conscious of a certain irony in this, having grown heartily sick of Tobias' regular gifts of chocolate. Somehow Guy's gift was just so much more considerate. He didn't ask if she wanted some cordial, he merely poured it into one of the new glasses and put it on the table in front of her. As he withdrew his arm, she took his hand and held it firmly. "I could not stay away," she replied in a husky voice. Guy could tell she was nervous, but he sensed a certain resolve about her today. It occurred to him that they could feel each other's emotions without the need for words, a kind of empathy that he had never experienced before.

Amelie had decided to tell Guy all about Tobias and Charlotte, as well as the latest news about her sister and Edward. It felt like there was so much secrecy in her life that she just wanted to be honest with Guy. So they just talked. Every once in a while, Guy would reach out and take her hand as she talked about her suspicions that Tobias was meeting with Charlotte. Guy kept quiet about the things Luigi told him he had overheard at the cafe table.

His heart leapt when she explained that her sister's betrothal to Edward Wingfield took the pressure off her sense of duty to her parents. He laughed out loud when she mentioned that Augusta would be a duchess one day. "Even Tobias Linburg can't compete with that," he replied.

And hearing that she felt no real loyalty to Tobias any more was wonderful news, but dreadfully sad at the same time. "I suppose I must still marry him," said Amelie, with a huge and painful sigh. Guy wanted so much to reach out and take her in his arms to offer some comfort. "It is too soon," he told himself. "Tread gently."

Instead, he just put a hand on hers. In a whisper he said, "Amelie, you can do as you wish, you know."

She looked at him in amazement, as if this was the

first time she had ever considered the idea of doing what she pleased with her life. "But I can't see a way out of it. If I don't go through with it I am worried that Tobias will find out it is because of you. He may make plans to hurt you."

Guy didn't tell Amelie that Tobias had already attempted to do so, but that it didn't matter at all. He merely answered, "Well, I suppose you had better make a decision about the marriage sooner, rather than later, my dear."

"I know I must, and I certainly have no desire to spend the rest of my life with him, especially now my sister has taken on the mantle of marrying into wealth," said Amelie.

Guy considered carefully what he was going to say next. It was important he chose the right words. He didn't want Amelie to come to him merely as a way of escaping from Tobias. What he said next had to be about their long term future together. He began, "Amelie, I don't know if this helps you to decide, but you know that I love you, don't you?"

The pair of them sat facing each other, leaning forward almost close enough to kiss. Amelie took Guy's hands before replying, "I love you too, Guy Pender. I love you very much indeed."

Guy could feel her breath on his face as she said the words he had hoped to hear from her. He stood up, still holding her hands, so that she had little choice but to follow suit. The table between them was all that was stopping Guy from taking her into his arms. Now was the moment for him to continue, "Amelie von Truber, I hope that one day soon, when the time is right, you will do me the honour of becoming my wife."

Amelie did not hesitate in her reply, "Oh Guy, it would be my great pleasure to accept. I can think of nothing I want more in life. But please, I need to work out what to say to Tobias. Let's talk no more about such things for now. I really must go home before I am missed."

"Come back next week, Amelie, please," begged Guy. "In the meantime, we should both think about a way out of your situation." Breaking away from her and heading to open the door, he added, "That is, if you really wish to be with me instead of Tobias."

Guy went to take Amelie's hands once more, but she felt brave enough to ignore it and to put her hands on his shoulders before reaching forward to place a kiss upon his cheek. "Oh, I do, Guy, I really do," was all she could whisper before taking her leave. Guy was left standing, a hand to the exact spot on his cheek where she had planted her delicate kiss.

CHAPTER TEN
Secrets

It was most unlike Luigi to deliver a fair part of Guy's coffee in the saucer rather than the cup. Guy could see that the waiter was distracted and it could only mean one thing.

"How is your wife?" asked Guy.

"Oh, Herr Pender, she is very well, thank you," replied Luigi, "and so is my new baby son, Giovanni."

"Congratulations, my friend!" exclaimed Guy, getting up from his chair and clapping the new father on the back. "Now I understand why you are distracted today."

"I am sorry," replied Luigi, reaching out to mop up the split coffee with his cloth. "But I didn't get much sleep last night."

"Babies have a habit of keeping their parents awake," laughed Guy.

"Yes, that is true," Luigi replied, "though my wife is the only one who can give the boy what he needs, of course. But I am a worried man and that is what keeps me awake."

"Can I be of assistance?" asked Guy.

"No, no, I cannot burden you with my troubles," came the reply. "Although perhaps you know of an apartment available, something not too expensive. We have an upstairs room in the house of a piano teacher, and he has already told us he will not tolerate the baby's cries interrupting his students. How can I keep the baby quiet? It is not possible. We will be homeless." Luigi threw his arms up in the air, as if accepting his fate.

Guy had a sudden thought. One he would not share with Luigi just yet though. "Hmm," he said, "leave it with me, my friend, and I will see what I can find."

Luigi took Guy's hand and thanked him before returning to fetch his customer a replacement coffee. Thankfully, it remained entirely in the cup this time.

Guy sat at the cafe's outside table deep in thought. He was doing exactly what he had told Amelie to do. To think about a way in which they could spend the rest of their lives together. In fact, he had done little else since their last meeting, and later today she would come to him again. He hoped she had made a decision about breaking off her engagement to Tobias, and then they could decide what to do next. Perhaps she had already done the deed. He couldn't wait to find out. He had lots to tell her too.

He had spent the week trying to find things to distract himself from thoughts of Amelie. He decided to untie the ribbon on the pile of papers given to him by his aunt's lawyers. He supposed he had better find out what his fortune entailed.

There were the usual bank accounts, all with a healthy balance, and some papers regarding investments held by his aunt, now transferred to Guy. At the bottom of the pile he found a folded parchment on which had been written 'Eigentumsurkunde' and the address of his apartment. His limited german language skills did not help him to understand what he held in his hand, but he did notice that, although his studio was numbered seventeen, the written address was '17-21', the seven being written in the continental style, with a line through it. He unfolded it to find a sheet of paper inside in English. At the top was written 'Translation into English'. Thank goodness his lawyer had the sense to provide such a thing. As Guy read it he came to understand that it was the deed of title for the property in which he lived, and he was the proud owner of, not only his studio and apartment, but the two adjoining properties as well. The last of these was Monsieur de Fevre's bakery. There was also a detailed breakdown of rent paid for the tiny shop next door which sold books, the owner climbing the internal spiral staircase to reach his living quarters, and the rent paid by the baker for his shop, again with a room above.

Guy had known at once what he would do with number twenty one. And now he could perhaps help his other friend out of his predicament too. Supposing, of course, that Amelie would come with him when he left Zurich. He was asking a lot of her, he knew. To give up a marriage into one of the richest families in Zurich was one thing, but to leave her family behind and travel half way around the globe was something else entirely.

Amelie had been considering what to do about Guy as well. She had at first resigned herself to a marriage to Tobias regardless, but it was Guy who had encouraged her to do what she wanted, rather than what she saw as her duty to her family. She loved Guy, of that she was certain, and she could see them spending their lives together in happiness. So the only decision she had to make was how, and when to break off her engagement to Tobias. The sooner the better in her opinion, so that all those involved could get on with their lives. To that end, she had arranged with Tobias to meet on their own at the cottage after church on Sunday morning. Being rather afraid of how he may react, she had confided in Lizzy, who promised to linger in the kitchen in case help was required. Amelie had been surprised, and somewhat amused to discover that Lizzy was fully aware of her meetings with Guy. In fact, she had been complicit in organising the initial meeting, along with Monsieur de Fevre.

On the Saturday afternoon, Amelie's mother found her oldest daughter sitting by the window in the drawing room with her embroidery on her lap. Amelie had barely added an extra stitch and had spent most of the afternoon gazing out of the window at nothing in particular. Deep in thought, she had been rehearsing the words she would say to Tobias after church tomorrow and going over and over the way she would tell her parents about the break up. While she knew her mother would be sympathetic, she dreaded the thought of what her father would say.

Amelie looked up as her mother came to join her, sitting in the chair opposite. "Amelie," said her mother gently, "There is something I want to talk to you about."

Her mother could see the sudden look of panic in her daughter's eyes. Of course, she already knew that Amelie was unhappy. It was obvious in the manner in which she had been so withdrawn of late. But her panicked expression gave away something else, and she wondered what was really going on. She hoped she could persuade Amelie to talk about it now, while it was just the two of them.

What her mother said first came as a total surprise to Amelie. "My dear, your father has had a letter from the emperor. He has been ordered back to court in Vienna as soon as possible. His next mission is a confidential one, but it is likely that we will be sent to Hungary where there are plans for our country and theirs to come together."

"Oh!" exclaimed Amelie, "that is not what I thought you would want to talk about, but Papa will be pleased. When will he go?"

"Ah, now, that is what I want to discuss with you, my dear," replied her mother. "Of course, your father is adamant he will not leave until after your marriage to Tobias. Though I am not too sure the emperor will be happy with the delay. Your father is in his study writing a reply now. But I just wanted to talk to you first to ask why you are so unhappy."

Apart from the ticking of the mantelpiece clock, there was silence in the room while Amelie gathered her thoughts together. She should have guessed that her mother would realise there was a problem, even though she had done her best to hide it from her family. Perhaps the moment was right to tell her mother everything.

"Mama, you are right," she began. "I am unhappy in some ways, and in other ways I am very happy indeed."

"Ah," replied her mother, "I rather suspected that was the case."

Slowly, hesitantly, Amelie told her mother about Tobias and Charlotte, about her feelings towards Tobias. It took a while for her to find the right words, to explain that she had felt it was her duty to marry Tobias, and that she hoped her love for him would grow over time. And then it was hard for her to explain how she had come to realise that he was selfish and uncaring, and she thought that her life with him would be a lonely one. She couldn't quite bring herself to say lonely, just like her mother's life, but Frau von Truber knew exactly what she meant.

She took her daughter's hands in hers and held

them before saying, "I too had hoped your love would blossom, even though it was a relationship born out of duty at the start. You must know that your father and I began our lives together in the same way, and yes, I did love him, perhaps I still do. But men want different things out of life. They seek power and influence, where we seek security and love. It will ever be so, and we learn to make the best of it, if we can."

Amelie thought for a moment that her mother was going to tell her to go ahead with the wedding regardless. Thankfully, her mother saw her look of panic and said gently, "But sometimes it becomes clear before a marriage that it is not the right thing to do, and it is best to break away sooner rather than later."

Relieved by what her mother said, Amelie plucked up the courage to mention Charlotte. She was not yet prepared to speak in detail about Guy, but that could come at another time, as long as she could gain her mother's support for calling off the wedding. She simply said, "Mama, I also need to tell you that I suspect Tobias is seeing someone else."

Her mother's reply surprised her once more. "Amelie, I am not as blind to these things as you might think. I know perfectly well what that brazen hussy is getting up to with Tobias Linburg!

Why else do you think I wanted to talk to you
about the wedding?"

How naive she had been to imagine that her fiancé
could keep his affair quiet? No doubt the
Linburgs' staff talked to the von Truber's kitchen
staff, or maybe Lizzy had said something to her
mother. No matter how it had happened, it helped
Amelie to make her decision.

Amelie's mother added, "I am ashamed of my
future son-in-law's sister. Her behaviour is
appalling, and I will be telling Edward what I
think of it, you can be certain."

Amelie drew on all her courage and said, "And
there's one more thing I need to tell you, mother."

In an afternoon of surprises, her mother's response
was the greatest surprise of all, "My dear
daughter, you don't need to tell me about Guy
Pender. I already know he means a lot to you. I
could tell from the first time we met him in his
studio that there was something between you."

Amelie was entirely lost for words. Her mouth
opened to reply, but nothing came out. She
decided not to mention Guy's proposal of
marriage just yet. Enough that her mother was
aware of their friendship for now. Her mother
continued, "Now my dear, let us look at the

situation in practical terms. First, we must find the right time to tell Tobias that you no longer wish to marry him."

Amelie replied, "I have already arranged to talk to him tomorrow after church."

"Good," answered her mother. "Now I have come to realise that Tobias Linburg is not averse to seeking revenge on those who get in his way. Perhaps it would be best not to mention Mr Pender."

"Thank you, Mama," said Amelie, realising that her mother had ironed out some of the complications that had been weighing her down for the last few weeks. But there was one thing still bothering her. "What about Papa?" she said, "after all, it is his desire that I marry well for the sake of the family."

"Leave your father to me," replied Amelie's mother. "You sister did you a big favour by falling in love with a man with not just riches, but a title as well. And in the end, he only wants you both to be happy, you know."

Amelie doubted that very much, but was greatly relieved that she didn't have to speak to him herself.

"Now," added her mother, getting up from her chair and heading for the door, "I must go and put a stop to your father's letter writing. There is no reason to delay our departure now. At least he will be pleased with that."

Amelie remained sitting in silence for a while longer, her sewing forgotten on her lap. Her head was full of thoughts. Her mother had known about Charlotte and about Guy. Her mother had, at one time anyway, loved her father. The family would be leaving Zurich soon. A feeling of panic came over her. Would her father expect her to go too? And where would that leave Guy? Forcing herself to get back to the issue at hand, she rehearsed her words for tomorrow morning after church. At least now she had the backing of her mother. It made everything seem a whole lot easier somehow.

It had been an anxious wait for the morning service to finish. She barely remembered what had been said in the sermon, having spent the time going through the words she would say to him one last time. However, things did not go quite as she had planned. Nervously, she had steeled herself to tell him that she had never loved him, and had come to realise that marriage would put him in an impossible position of living a life with someone he didn't love either.

But, before she could open her mouth to say

anything, Tobias spoke first, in a tone of defiance. "I suppose you have come to tell me that you know about Charlotte and me," he said. "Well, it's true, and I don't love you. I never did. I only asked you to marry me because your father begged me to."

Amelie could not believe what she was hearing. She knew that her father had encouraged the marriage, but was it true that he had been desperate enough to beg for it? She doubted it. Nevertheless, she now knew for certain that Tobias and Charlotte were involved, and she suspected it to be on a physical level too, by the way they exchanged glances with each other.

"So, I will call the wedding off," said Tobias, with about as much emotion as he would use to cancel a trip to the dentist.

Amelie couldn't believe her good fortune. There was no need for her to use the words she had rehearsed. All she had to do was agree to call things off. For a brief moment she wondered if she should say no, and make him go through with the marriage, just out of spite. But it was not what she wanted, and she really didn't care a jot if he went straight back to Charlotte's bed. After a pause, she replied, "I think that is for the best, Tobias."

The wonderful thing about it all, as far as Amelie

was concerned, was that Guy's name had not been mentioned. Tobias could not blame him for their break-up. But it was not that simple. Tobias had not quite finished.

"And you can tell that Pender chap that I'll be dealing with him too," said Tobias with real spite in his voice. "He has no right to steal you away from me."

Amelie realised that her reply was crucial to the way things were going to go for her and Guy in the next few weeks. She considered carefully before saying, "As we are no longer betrothed, it is my business alone what I choose to do with the rest of my life." As she spoke, she slipped the engagement ring from her finger and held it out for Tobias to take.

Tobias snatched it from her, saying, "We will see about that. Mark my words, that man will get his just desserts." Turning on his heel, he flung himself out of the door, slamming it closed behind him with such a crash that it caused Lizzy to come running from the kitchen.

"Miss Amelie, are you alright?" she asked, "He didn't raise his hand, did he?"

"No, no, I'm fine," replied Amelie, although the look on her face told another story.

"Is it done, Miss?" asked Lizzy, "Is the wedding off?"

Amelie recounted word for word what Tobias had said to her, including his final words. She was relieved that it had been easier than she expected to put an end to their engagement, but very worried about Tobias' threat to take it out on Guy.

"Oh, Miss Amelie," said Lizzy. "I'm sure when he thinks about it he will just be pleased to have wriggled out of a marriage he didn't want. He will forget about Guy."

Amelie was not so sure. She had a feeling Tobias would want to find someone to blame, and it was very likely to be Guy.

In years to come, Amelie would always associate the taste of lemon cordial with those precious hours in Guy's apartment. Sitting in the gloomy apartment, illuminated only by the small amount of light that made it through the narrow window, talking and talking about their future together, sometimes reaching out to hold each other's hand. One sip, and she was back there in her mind.

On their third meeting, Amelie told Guy all about her conversation with her mother, and the words that had been spoken by Tobias. Guy was pleased that it was over, especially as it had been Tobias who had broken it off in the end. And it was good news that Amelie's mother had supported her. But he shared Amelie's concerns about Tobias' vindictive streak. They would need to tread carefully for a while. But, now that the wedding was off, there was another problem. Would Amelie's family expect her to go to Vienna too? Well, Guy supposed he could go as well. Perhaps they could marry in Vienna.

Guy had news for Amelie too. He told her about the money he had inherited from his aunt and his desire to return to New Zealand now that her affairs had been put in order. He wanted her to take some time to decide if she was willing to join him. "After all," he finished, "it may be best for us to leave Zurich as soon as we can and that may need to be before your parents go to Vienna."

"I would follow you to the ends of the earth," she said, reaching out to take his hands in hers. He could see by the look in her eyes that she was telling the truth.

"New Zealand is at the end of the earth, my dear," he laughed. "But it is paradise, and you will love the country, and I am sure you will grow to love my good friends at Applecross."

Guy told Amelie all about his friends, the Mackenzies and the Lawtons. He had no difficulty in making it sound like paradise, his enthusiasm for the country shone through, and Amelie was sure she would love it just as much as Guy did. But it was a big thing he was asking her to do. What about her parents, and her sister, and Lizzy?

"We have a little time, my dear, but we do need to make a decision before your parents plan to leave Zurich," said Guy gently. He kept quiet about his idea of going to Vienna with the von Trubers. It would be adding in a further delay to his return to New Zealand. He merely added, "In the meantime, I think we should continue to keep our plans for the future secret. We don't want Tobias Linburg to know any more than he suspects already."

On the morning after Amelie's visit to Guy, he had another visitor. It was Wilfred Dannay. The day before, Wilfred had been with Tobias, Edward and Charlotte at the cafe and had seen Amelie and her mother walk across the square. Fully expecting Amelie to leave her mother to come and join them, he had been taken by surprise when she ignored them all and walked on past. He looked at Tobias who was making a point of being engrossed in conversation with Charlotte, and all of a sudden he realised what was going on.

Without a word, he got up from the table, threw a few coins down to pay for his drink and walked away. He had had more than enough of Tobias Linburg and Charlotte Wingfield's behaviour.

That afternoon, Wilfred came across Tobias leaving his father's study. It was obvious from the way Tobias slammed the door shut that he was angry. Perhaps it was not the moment to do so, but Wilfred said, "Ah, Tobias, is your father in his study? I wish to inform him that I will be leaving tomorrow. To be frank, I have had enough of your behaviour towards Amelie and do not intend to stay a moment longer than is necessary."

Wilfred, wondering if Tobias was going to raise the fist he was clenching by his side, backed past him to reach out and knock on the study door. Tobias turned to face him saying, "How dare you judge me. I'll have you know that I am the injured party here. It is Amelie who has taken up with that Pender fellow. That is what has caused her to call off the wedding." Wilfred could see the veins standing out on Tobias' temple as he continued, "You may as well pack your bags now. I have no wish to see your face ever again. Now - get out of my house!" With that Tobias stormed up the stairs leaving Wilfred standing in amazement at the depth of Tobias' anger. Ironically, his presumption that Tobias was heading for Charlotte's room was absolutely right. So there was more to this than Wilfred had at first suspected. He thought back to the morning when Amelie had been rescued from the avalanche, and yes, now he came to think of it, there was something between Guy Pender and Amelie.

In the end, Wilfred wrote Tobias' parents a note apologising for his sudden departure and found himself a bed for the night at an hotel in town. He too hoped never to set eyes on Tobias Linburg again.

Tobias' anger was, in the most part, due to his father's response to being told that the engagement had been broken off. Expecting a sympathetic father, Tobias found himself being treated like a naughty schoolboy in front of the headmaster. Herr Linburg was getting tired of his only son's selfish actions when it came to women and annoyed at his habit of blaming anyone but himself when things went wrong. Tobias told his father that Amelie had changed her mind because she had found another man. Some photographer chap with no prospects.

Herr Linburg's response was not what Tobias had expected at all. He said, "You have treated Amelie von Truber very badly indeed, my son. I presume the real reason for you wriggling out of the wedding is the woman with whom you are sharing a bed upstairs. And it is no good you using the excuse that Amelie has found someone else. Who can blame her? That Pender chap looked after her a deal better than you did after the avalanche, and from what I've heard he has more in the way of prospects than you may imagine. His aunt had amassed a sizeable fortune, though no-one knows how she did it, and I believe he is the only relative, so will have inherited the lot. Now, get out of my study and go and find your mother. You had better inform her yourself, before she hears it from the staff, that all the preparations she has made are for nothing."

Tobias was angry. Angry with his father and even more angry with Guy Pender. How dare he inherit a fortune, as well as stealing Amelie away from him! And angry with that holier-than-though, Wilfred Dannay. What did it have to do with him anyway? He would seek out his mother later. In the meantime, he would vent his rage at Charlotte. She liked a bit of a rough ride occasionally, and he would make sure she got it today.

Later that day, Wilfred chose to visit Guy Pender. If there really was something going on between him and Amelie, then he wanted to warn Guy to be wary of Tobias' revenge. It occurred to him that he may be able to help with some travel arrangements, if Guy and Amelie were planning to leave town. Something he thought they should consider doing as soon as possible. He had extensive connections through his family's shipping company and would be pleased to help the two of them to get away from Tobias Linburg.

Guy was surprised to see Wilfred at his door, but once Wilfred explained what he had said to Tobias that morning, Guy happily invited him into his apartment and poured them both a glass of wine. When Wilfred told Guy the reason for his impending departure from Zurich, it was the final confirmation in Guy's mind that he and Amelie were doing the right thing by arranging to get away from Zurich, one way or another.

"Frankly," said Wilfred, "I have been appalled at Tobias Linburg's behaviour towards Amelie, who I see as the injured party in this debacle. I have known Charlotte most of my life, and this is not the first time she has come between another man and woman. I am sad to say that she will get bored soon and move on to someone else, but not before she has caused a deal of bad feeling."

Guy hesitated before telling Wilfred what they were planning to do, but as he was returning to England the next day, he could take the secret with him. He replied, "I am rather hoping to take Amelie away from all this to New Zealand, where we will be back amongst good friends. There is a danger that Tobias will seek revenge, and I have no desire to offer him the opportunity to do so by staying in Zurich. Amelie's family are about to leave for Vienna. We could accompany them, but it would add an annoying delay into my return to New Zealand. I would prefer to get to England and find a passage to New Zealand as soon as we can."

"Then, I am happy to be of some assistance with your travel arrangements, Mr Pender," said Wilfred. "I am returning to England myself tomorrow. Perhaps I can arrange passage for you both to cross the channel to Southampton from, shall we say Antwerp? You will find it easier to take a ship from Southampton to New Zealand via Australia. Most of the shipping from Antwerp is heading for the Americas these days."

Guy was glad to accept Wilfred's offer of help and promised to let Wilfred know when they had made a decision. Wilfred finished the last of his wine and put the empty glass down on the table. He stood to take his leave, saying, "I will be in touch when I have news for you. Meanwhile, I suggest you put your affairs in order here in Zurich and take Amelie von Truber away from here as soon as you can."

CHAPTER ELEVEN
Revenge

May 1867

Just a week later, two letters arrived on the same day for Guy, both from England. The first was from Wilfred Dannay. He had indeed been able to find a way to help them on their journey, should they choose to go directly to New Zealand, though he apologised for the less than perfect timing of what he had arranged.

Firstly, he had arranged a passage across the English channel from Antwerp to Southampton on a coaster, including cartage for Guy's mobile studio, leaving Antwerp whenever it suited them. The ship ran a regular service to and fro, with departures from Antwerp on a Monday, Wednesday or Friday, so they only needed to contact the harbourside offices of the Dannay Line when they arrived. However, Wilfred had been unable to find suitable berths on a ship bound for New Zealand until the middle of August. He explained that most ships were heading for New York these days, there being a huge demand to travel to the Americas, but that, if Guy was prepared to wait that long, Wilfred would be more than happy to accommodate them both in comfort on a ship of the Dannay Shipping Company.

Wilfred also invited them to stay at the family home in Hampshire in the meantime, finally asking a question that Guy could not immediately answer. Would Amelie be bringing a maid with her? Guy had not considered the implications of the two of them travelling alone before they married, but Wilfred's question led him to wonder if he should seek a suitable chaperone to accompany them. It was a risky thing to do to bring someone else into their plan, but he would consider doing so in order to preserve Amelie's good name.

His second letter of the day was one he had been half expecting, but dreading at the same time. It came from Reverend Bestwick, the vicar of Upton Barwood, the small village in which Nanny Bee had her home. It read,

Dear Mr Pender,

I am so sorry to have to inform you that only yesterday we laid your old nanny, Beatrice Webster to rest in the churchyard. She had grown frail of late but did not suffer at the end. I was with her in her final hours and she was at pains to beg me to let you know how proud she was of you. I do so with sadness, but also with gladness for the love she gave you, and that you returned in providing her with a comfortable home for her final years.

I must tell you also that the whole village turned out for her funeral. She was much loved by her neighbours and will be sorely missed.

Perhaps you will, at your earliest convenience, find yourself in a position to call at the vicarage. In the meantime, I believe you will be hearing from your solicitor regarding arrangements with the property.

Yours in Christian spirit,
Reverend Charles Bestwick.

Guy remained seated at his table for quite some time, the letter from Reverend Bestwick in his hand. He was remembering the happy times of his childhood, almost all of which involved Nanny Bee. To all intents and purposes, she had been his mother, the one person who had made him what he was today. He sent a silent message of gratitude heavenwards, while wondering what on earth Nanny Bee would make of recent events. He rather hoped she would approve. She would most certainly have liked Amelie, if they had been given the opportunity to meet.

The sound of footsteps on the stairs outside brought Guy back to the present with a start. The door was already open to catch the morning's sunshine, so Amelie had no need to knock.

"Good morning, Albert," she said to the cat as he sidled up to his favourite visitor. "And good morning, Guy," she continued, "I have Lizzy with me today, and we have something to tell you."

Lizzy couldn't help herself from offering a tiny curtsy towards Guy, although, after the conversation she had just had with Amelie, it meant that she would need to get used to being his equal rather than his servant.

With a passing thought that it was wonderful that Amelie could just visit whenever she liked now, he offered them both a chair, standing between them while they told him their news. The von Trubers would be heading for Vienna as soon as possible. Amelie's father was to leave at once, leaving her mother to oversee the packing up of their few possessions. The staff had all been given notice, except for Lizzy, who was supposed to accompany Augusta to England. Amelie's sister was to be the guest of her future parents-in-law until the wedding had been arranged. There was a question to be answered about the timing of the wedding in England, but Augusta hoped that her parents would be able to travel from wherever they were posted in time for the ceremony.

These arrangements left Amelie with something of a dilemma. Should she go to Vienna with her mother, and would Guy come too? Or should the two of them begin their journey to New Zealand? And how could they fit a wedding into things now? She had no desire to go to Vienna and had spent a sleepless night worrying about the implications of travelling unaccompanied with a man who was yet to be her husband. However, at breakfast time, her mother had informed them that she had decided to go directly to England with Augusta and Edward until the wedding had taken place. Herr von Truber had much to do in Vienna, or wherever he was to be sent, and had made it clear his mission was a secret one, which would be easier for him to manage without a family to consider. This, of course, meant that Lizzy was no longer required as a chaperone for Augusta, and it had occurred to her mother that Amelie may be in need of Lizzy as both a chaperone and a companion. After all, Lizzy had acted as a chaperone on the day of the avalanche, so she could do so again.

Lizzy and Amelie had discussed it and agreed it was the perfect solution. Lizzy had no desire to live in England again and doubted whether she would be a popular addition to the staff of such a wealthy family anyway. And, from what Amelie told her, she had an idea she rather liked the sound of New Zealand. She wasn't too sure about Amelie's request that she travel as a companion, rather than as a maid, but she supposed she would get used to it in time.

The two young ladies told Guy all this news in a rush, excited by the plans they had made. It seemed to Guy it had all been decided for him. But he didn't mind a bit. It all sounded absolutely perfect. So they would decide on a suitable date to leave, head for Antwerp and take up Wilfred Dannay's offer of a crossing to England.

The rest of his plans had still to be put straight in his head, but he decided to share his ideas with Amelie and Lizzy. But Lizzy put her hand out to stop Guy. "No," she said, "I will leave you two to talk alone. I am only your chaperone in public places. I am still a servant for now, and I have jobs to do."

Guy accompanied her to the door, taking her hand and kissing it gently as she went to leave. "Thank you, Lizzy," he said. "Thank you for coming with us. I am sure you will love New Zealand, and perhaps we can find a young man for you too, once we get there."

"Ooh, sir," replied Lizzy, with a giggle. "Now, that would be something, wouldn't it?"

Once Lizzy had gone, Guy sat down in the empty chair and said, "Amelie, I have news myself, and, now you have worked out how we manage the first part of our journey, I have an idea of what we do next, which I want to share with you."

Guy told Amelie about Wilfred Dannay's visit and his subsequent offer of help. Amelie hadn't realised that Wilfred had confronted Tobias on her behalf. She had always thought he was a real gentleman, and she wondered if she would get an opportunity to thank him in person. Guy also explained how he planned to give his apartment to Luigi and his new family, and to give Monsieur de Fevre the freehold of the bakery. He would, he said, need a little time to put all this in place, so perhaps they needed to consider whether a fortnight's time would fit into the von Truber's plans too. He then went on to show Amelie the letter from Reverend Bestwick. Amelie knew all about Nanny Bee, and she was sad for Guy, realising it was almost like losing a mother to him.

"The Reverend Bestwick has suggested that I visit," said Guy, "and, to begin with I thought it would be an impossible thing to do. But I wondered, in the light of the time we are likely to have in England before we sail, if perhaps we could go to the house, and I can pay my respects at Nanny Bee's grave."

Amelie replied, "I think that would be a lovely thing to do. I wonder how far it is from Wilfred's home. Maybe it is close enough to travel there in just a day."

"While we are at the church, perhaps we can persuade Reverend Bestwick to marry us too," joked Guy, although it was, now he came to think of it, not a silly idea at all.

"I like that idea," Amelie replied, adding, "My mother and sister may be in England by then."

Guy said, "In that case, there is something I need to do as a matter of urgency before your father leaves Zurich. I must ask his permission."

"Oh Guy, of course you should, but we haven't got much time before he leaves," said Amelie. "I know, why don't you join us for dinner tonight? It is to be a special evening to see my father off, and I would like you to have more time to speak to Mama and my sister too. Now I had better go home and let everyone know that you will be joining us this evening."

Guy watched Amelie go down the stairs. She paused to wave to him at the end of the path and was gone. He didn't particularly relish the idea of dinner with the von Trubers tonight, but it sounded like his only opportunity to speak to Amelie's father. There was a lot to do in the next two weeks, so he decided he may as well start by packing his photographic equipment away. He had already been through it all and decided on just what was necessary to take with him. The rest was becoming obsolete due to the huge developments in the photographic process in recent years. He wondered if he would have time to find a buyer for what was left, or perhaps it merely needed to be thrown out.

By the end of the afternoon he had everything stored neatly in the apartment. It would have been a great deal easier to pack it away in the cart, rather than carry it up the stairs, but Guy was somewhat concerned about everything getting damp over the next week or so under the canvas cover. There was also a box containing some books and other small items from his aunt's apartment, just a few keepsakes as he was leaving the furniture and all the household items for Luigi and his wife. There would still be plenty of room for Amelie's travelling trunks and anything Lizzy wanted to bring along. He would pack it all into the cart just before they left. All he had to do now was to arrange for a horse to be hired and that was an easy task. He would just repeat what he had done for the journey to St Moritz, although he wondered what the arrangements would be for a one way journey.

He just had time to write a reply to each of his letters. First a brief note of thanks to Wilfred Dannay, accepting with gratitude the offer of passage across the channel, hospitality at Wilfred's home and his help with the voyage to New Zealand. He explained about the need to visit the grave of his childhood nanny and wondered if Wilfred could make arrangements for them both to visit Upton Barwood, either overnight, or in a day, depending on the distance. At the last minute, he remembered to tell Wilfred about Lizzy being an extra passenger. His letter to Reverend Bestwick included the news that he would be travelling to Upton Barwood in the not too distant future, accompanied by his fiancée and her companion.

Conveniently, he was able to drop the letters into

the postbox on his way across the square. There were still people about, even at this hour. The weather was warm and sunny and dusk grew later by the day at this time of year. A young couple, arm in arm passed Guy just as he waved an arm in greeting to Leon de Fevre. A group of young ladies looked up as he walked by. They watched in silence as the handsome Guy Pender walked towards them. He could hear their giggles as soon as he had passed by. Luigi saw Guy striding past the cafe and called out his name, but Guy merely waved back and kept going. He didn't want to be late to dinner with his future father-in-law. What he failed to see, because they were hiding in the dark doorway to one side of the cafe, was a group of three swarthy men. When they heard Guy's name called out, they nodded to each other before pulling their hats down to cover their faces.

Somewhat to his surprise, Guy was made very welcome indeed to the von Truber household. Amelie's mother took his hand and greeted him warmly, saying, "Herr Pender, may I call you Guy? Come, come and meet my husband once more. It is good to see you again, and we are so very pleased to welcome you to our family."

Guy felt as though they had already accepted his proposal to Amelie, but he still needed to take Herr von Truber on one side before dinner. Amelie's father spoke little English, but had already been brought up-to-date by his wife. So it didn't take long for the two men to appear again with smiles on their faces. Herr von Truber made a formal announcement of his agreement to the marriage, and while Amelie and Guy embraced, Herr von Truber said in German, "I cannot stand in the way of love, and it is clear that these two young people love each other very much. Not only that, but Herr Pender assures me that he has the means to support my daughter. She will want for nothing."

Knowing how important it was to Amelie's father to see his daughters marrying into money, Guy had been pleased to be able to tell his future father-in-law about his aunt's legacy. Guy had come prepared and now felt in his pocket for the tiny leather box containing his mother's engagement ring, a gold band with a single bright diamond. Or, at least, that is what he assumed he had found in Aunt Emmeline's jewellery box. The jeweller's name inscribed in the lid was from his home town in England, and the box had been wrapped in paper with a silver locket containing a curl of hair. Aunt Emmeline had written a note on a little scrap of paper which fell out as Guy carefully unwrapped the paper. In his aunt's flowery handwriting, it said, 'My dear sister's jewellery'. The silver locket had been packed with the other items to be taken to New Zealand, and he now pulled the box from his pocket, opened the lid and, taking Amelie's left hand, he slipped the ring onto her finger. With the merest pressure, it fell into place perfectly, as if it had been made for her.

With congratulations from Augusta and Edward and Amelie's mother, the family made their way into the dining room. Dinner was a lively affair with so much to talk about. Herr von Truber would be leaving very early in the morning, a carriage having been arranged to pick him up. Edward would be moving into the guest rooms upstairs until he and Augusta left for England with Augusta's mother, and Amelie and Lizzy could stay in the house until Guy was ready to leave too. Everything seemed to be falling into place very nicely indeed.

There was one bit of news from Edward, something he hadn't been sure about telling Amelie, but Augusta insisted upon it. Apparently, Charlotte had already left for England, somewhat unexpectedly. Edward chose not to relate the details of the incident that caused her to leave, but it had involved a deal of shouting from his sister, and from Tobias, which could be heard all over the house. Tobias had a gash across his forehead caused by an expensive porcelain vase being thrown at him, and since Charlotte's sudden departure, Tobias had refused to speak to anyone in the household. Edward was only too thankful that he had already arranged to move his things to the von Truber's home, and rather hoped he would have no further dealings with the Linburg family.

At this news, Guy exchanged a worried glance across the table with Amelie. They were both still concerned about the possibility of Tobias seeking revenge against Guy for stealing Amelie from him. With the end of his relationship with Charlotte, the likelihood of such vengeance was, Guy thought, even greater.

The three men remained at the table after the plates had been cleared away, while the ladies retired to the drawing room. Sipping a glass of port, Herr von Truber said, "Have you decided when the wedding will take place, Herr Pender?" Guy told him about the idea of marrying in the small English village where his childhood nanny was buried. He also mentioned that it would need to be before they sailed for New Zealand in mid-August.

"I will try to be there," said Herr von Truber. "I will try my very best."

"And I will be there too, my friend," said Edward. "We are not so far away from the village you mention, and I am sure Amelie will want her mother and sister to be at her wedding."

So that was another piece of the plan neatly put in

place. As Guy made his farewell, in particular wishing Herr von Truber a safe journey to Vienna, he set off for home across the square feeling more optimistic than he had been in a very long while. Everything seemed to be coming together very well indeed.

As he approached the pavement on his side of the square, he looked up at the frontages of the three houses he had inherited from Aunt Emmeline. It reminded him that he needed to speak to the current tenant of the bookshop and to Leon de Fevre in the morning, and he had better see Luigi too. So much to do! Deep in thought, he almost didn't notice that the front door of his studio was slightly ajar.

Wondering if he had simply forgotten to shut it that afternoon when he had been carrying boxes around to the back, he pushed the door open in order to get the key which, when it was not in his pocket, always hung from a hook above the counter. The light from the street cast enough of a glow to show him that the key was not there, and feeling in his pocket he felt the cold of metal safely there. As he gathered his thoughts to wonder who else could have opened the door, he found himself being spun round to face his attackers. There were three of them. Two men held him firmly by the shoulders, while the third, a broad-shouldered man with a stubbly face, which he held far too close for Guy's liking, spat out in English, "Get out of town, Herr Pender, or you will find yourself as broken as your shop."

"Now, look here," replied Guy, wriggling as much as he could to release himself from the firm grip of the two heavies.

"No, you look here," replied the man, as he reached out to take hold of Guy's collar, pulling Guy's face towards his own. Guy could feel the wet of his spittle on his cheeks as the man went on, "Be gone by this time tomorrow, or the lovely Fraulien von Truber may lose her good looks too. Herr Linburg told us not to finish you off like we did that other chap, else you would be getting more than this from me." With that, he let go of Guy's collar, pulled his arm back and planted a vicious punch to the side of Guy's head.

With his head swimming from the impact, and feeling blood coursing down his cheek, Guy fell to the floor as soon as the two men let go of him. He was vaguely aware of the man who had done all the talking turning away to go out through the door, but began to lose consciousness as the remaining two men planted their heavy boots in a series of cruel blows to his body. He managed to curl himself into a ball to avoid too much damage, but not before he felt the sharp crack of several ribs breaking in his chest. Once the men had gone, he lay still, his breathing laboured with the pain, not daring to move a muscle lest they return.

All three men, checking that they hadn't been seen or heard, sidled along the pavement, keeping to the shadows as much as possible. Once out of the square, they were stopped by a fourth man who had been waiting for them. "Is it done?" he said in German.

"Yes, sir," replied the man who seemed to be in charge of the group. He spoke in English, knowing that he would be understood. The other two men had not spoken at all. "He will be hurting for a while. Just enough to warn him off, as you asked. We told him you had said not to finish him off."

"Good grief, man," came the swift reply, "did you mention my name? Please tell me you did not mention Auber's name too."

The leader of the gang hung his head in shame, suddenly realised his stupid error. "No, sir, I did not mention Monsieur Auber's name," he said. He had no need to say that he had indeed used Tobias' name. It was written all over his face. His boss was a dangerous man, and he knew immediately that his own life was now in serious danger.

"So, now you have not only implicated me, but you have told Pender of a previous occasion where murder was a necessary revenge. Now I need to change my plans because of you, you stupid man," Tobias said, reaching for the knife in his pocket, before thinking better of it. He would deal with the idiot later. "Be gone, there will be no pay for you tonight, and keep an eye behind you lest I choose to deal with you in a similar manner to Herr Auber."

The man needed no second bidding to leave. He turned away, pulled his collar up to protect his neck and slunk away into the shadows. Throughout the whole conversation the other two thugs had stayed silent and motionless.

This changed everything for Tobias Linburg. If Pender was aware of the words the stupid henchman had spoken, then he needed to be rid of the man entirely. He had murdered once, though others had done his dirty work, and he could do so again. After all, a man can only lose his head once in execution however many acts of murder he commits. Now he had to find out where Guy was going and mobilise his contacts across Europe, as well as dealing out some form of punishment to the man who had spilled the beans to Pender.

"Now go." With that he handed each of the two remaining men a coin, glistening gold in the moonlight. Although they had been hanging back, they didn't hesitate in accepting their blood money, each of them touching a finger to their hat before disappearing swiftly into the darkness.

With a swirl of his cape, Tobias Linburg turned for home. The meagre light from a half-moon lit up his face to show an expression of sheer hatred. Tobias wanted nothing more than to be a winner, and he had thought tonight would end in victory. Now, however, he was left with a dangerous confidence being shared, which could lead him to the executioner's block, a man he hated who now needed to be disposed of entirely and a vacancy as leader of his pack of thugs to fill.

CHAPTER TWELVE
Escape

Leon de Fevre was surprised to see light at the windows of number forty two at such an early hour. It was only when he saw the carriage draw up outside that he realised it must be the day for Herr von Truber to leave for Vienna. Today's batch of bread was in the oven already, so Leon had time to busy himself at the front of the shop where he could see Frau von Truber, Amelie and Augusta standing on the step to wave a tearful goodbye to the master of the house.

It was a time of change in the square. What with the von Trubers on the move and his friend Guy Pender packing up to return to New Zealand, Leon wondered who would take their place as his neighbours. "Ah well," he said to himself with a deep sigh, "I daresay they will all need their daily bread."

The coachman was climbing up onto his seat, and with a crack of his whip, the covered carriage began to move forward. It had been raining all night by the look of the wet cobbles, and Leon could hear the horses' hooves scrabbling to get a grip as they built up momentum. The three ladies remained on the step until the carriage had disappeared from view, turning to go back inside just as Leon saw Luigi walking towards the cafe. As he did every morning, the waiter lifted his hat in the direction of the bakery, and Leon waved back to say good morning to his friend.

However, this morning Luigi seemed to have stopped walking. He had seen something along the street and was turning back to investigate. Leon, sensing Luigi's concern, also turned in that direction and began to hurry past the bookshop next door and towards Guy's studio. There was what looked like a pile of clothes outside Guy's door. Luigi got there first and bent down as if to pick it up. As Leon reached the door too, he could see it was a person laying on the ground, half in, half out of the open door. With a shock he realised it was Guy, and it looked like he had been there all night.

As Luigi turned the body of their friend over, Guy groaned with the pain, and although neither of them wanted him to be hurt, they were both glad to hear a sound from him. At least he was alive.

But barely, by the look of things. Luigi gently hooked his arms under Guy's shoulders and pulled him into the studio, leaning him up against the counter. The heels of his shoes made two damp tracks across the floor showing how wet he had got overnight, and they could see his whole body shivering with cold and shock.

With a great deal of effort, Guy whispered, "Thank you my friends," before closing his eyes in relief. He had drifted in and out of consciousness all night, occasionally wondering if he would ever see the dawn. He felt so cold and every bone in his body ached. Taking a breath was difficult, and his two friends were greatly concerned by his rasping breathing and his grey face, drained of all colour.

"Leon, fetch some blankets," ordered Luigi, "and then go and wake up the physician."

As Leon went to do as he had been bidden, he met Amelie and Edward at the door. Just as they had all gone inside after seeing Herr von Truber off, Amelie had seen Luigi stop and look back across the square. All she could see was that he was looking towards Guy's studio and something made her quickly wrap a shawl around her shoulders and run down the steps. Edward, who was waiting in the hall behind her, followed her just as quickly, in case he could be of assistance.

Amelie knelt beside Guy but could do no more than hold his hand. Little did she realise how much comfort that simple act was for the patient. He tried to speak, saying, "It was Tobias….."

"Don't try to talk now," said Amelie gently. "You can tell us all about it once we've got you comfortable."

Leon came back with a blanket and a pillow before hurrying across the square to the home of Doctor Kuscher. Luigi gently lifted Guy by the shoulders so that Amelie could tuck the pillow behind his head, and they were just laying the blanket over him when the doctor arrived with his leather bag.

Amelie stayed with Guy while the doctor took stock of his injuries. It gave the other three a chance to look round at the state of the room. The curtain separating the front room from the studio had been torn down and a knife had been used to slash deep cuts into the mountain scenery backdrop. There was broken glass everywhere, photographic plates in pieces and bottles of chemicals smashed, their contents spread in pools across the floor.

The doctor pronounced that Guy was fit to be moved, but he would need to be carried gently to bed where his wounds could be cleaned and the extent of his broken ribs assessed properly. The blanket was already warming him up, and the doctor prescribed a change out of the wet clothes and a warm bed as being all that was necessary to stop the shivering.

"He's a lucky man in some ways," said the doctor to Amelie. "The cut on his head is shallow, despite the copious amount of blood to be seen. And I rather think he will have the services of a good nurse to help him heal," he added with a smile.

Guy remembered nothing of being rolled onto the blanket and carried on a slow journey across the square by the four men. Amelie went on ahead to warn her mother and to arrange for their patient to be put to bed in the guest bedroom. Thanks to the good doctor's application of a strong sedative draft before he was lifted up, Guy was asleep almost immediately. Between them Amelie and Lizzy gently pulled his wet clothes off his lifeless body and tucked him under the covers. There was no reason for the doctor to stay while Guy slept, so with a promise to return around noon, he left Guy in the care of his nurse.

In the meantime, it was Edward who went back to the scene of the crime to see if he could find any clues as to the reason for the attack. Leon and Luigi both had work to do, although neither of them were able to concentrate on their customers while their thoughts were on the health of their good friend. Edward had his suspicions about the attack, although he doubted it was actually Tobias Linburg who had performed the act. There was no doubt he had access to hired men and would have paid them well to carry out his dirty work. The studio was in a fair mess, and Edward could see no evidence of Guy's cameras and other equipment apart from the broken glass plates and bottles.

Leon was concerned about the cart and the upstairs apartment, so Edward went around the back of the building. If he was honest with himself, he was expecting to find both in ruins. His heart sank when he found the cart sitting at an odd angle where the wooden cartwheels had been broken to pieces with a heavy hammer. Just as in the studio, someone had taken a sharp blade to the canvas covers and the leather trappings for attaching a horse were all cut to shreds as well.

Fully expecting the apartment to be in a similar state of disarray, Edward drew a sigh of relief when he reached the top of the stairs to find the door still locked. He had removed all the keys he could find in Guy's discarded clothing and now found one that would fit the door. Thankfully, the apartment remained untouched, although Edward could see that Guy did not have the regular services of a maid. It was an untidy room and full of boxes and crates. On inspection, Edward was again relieved to find Guy's camera equipment, a pile of photographs and several albums of portraits and landscapes, as well as some assorted books and bits and pieces. He realised that these items had been saved from destruction because Guy had already started to prepare for his journey. Thank goodness he had not started to pack everything into the cart.

Over the road at number forty two, Guy had woken up. He felt himself lying in a soft and comfortable bed, he was warm and dry, and he could hear an angel humming softly to herself. Surely this was heaven? He tried to move to see where the angel's music was coming from, but it hurt so much that he groaned out loud.

The angel stopped humming that glorious tune, but if he opened his eyes he could see her face. Well, at least he could open one eye. For some reason the other one felt as if it was stuck together with glue.

"Guy, my darling, you are awake," said the angel. "Now, don't try to move."

With a growing consciousness, Guy realised it was Amelie bending over him, a look of great concern on her face. The events of the night before came rushing back to him, with snippets of being found by his two friends, just at the time when he thought he was going to die.

"We have to go," he said, with panic in his voice. "We have to go today." Again he tried to move, this time pushing his elbows into the soft mattress to sit himself up. Every movement hurt, but he had to tell Amelie about the three men. He had to tell Amelie about the threat they had made to hurt her too, if he didn't take her away today.

"Now, Guy, I want you to lie still and close your eyes again," ordered Amelie. "I am going to talk to the doctor now, but Lizzy will be sitting here with you, if you need anything."

Once Amelie had left the room, Guy called Lizzy over to the bed. With much hesitation, and an occasional gap while he took a sharp intake of breath, Guy told Lizzy all about the attack, and his suspicions that it was Tobias at the root of it. He also related the threat that had been made to hurt Amelie too, unless they left town by tonight. As he mentioned what the thug had said about Amelie, it reminded him of the rest of the conversation. His memory was a bit muddled, but if he had heard it correctly, it confirmed Tobias Linburg's involvement in the death of a man, just as Luigi had suggested.

"Please don't say anything to Amelie about all

this, though," said Guy. "I don't want to worry her unduly."

"No sir, of course I won't. But, sir," said Lizzy, "you can't go travelling anywhere for a while. And you certainly can't be driving a horse and cart."

"We must do something, Lizzy," Guy replied, before sinking back onto the bed, exhausted by the sheer effort of talking. Even so, he continued, "Lizzy, could you pack some clothes for Amelie into her travel chest and put your things together too? We need to be ready to go."

"Yes sir, I will," replied Lizzy. "But now you must sleep."

Guy did indeed close his eyes, but his mind was far too active for sleep now. He had such a lot to organise, even if he had to do it all while lying flat on his back.

The doctor was of the opinion that sleep is always the very best healer. Guy Pender proved this theory. On his return to check on the patient, Doctor Kuscher found him in a much better condition than he had been when first discovered. Amelie had cleaned his head wound. It transpired to be a shallow cut which, other than likely leaving a scar, would not cause any long term damage. His body was bruised and battered and the blue, green and red marks would be with him for a while, but as far as could be told there were only two cracked ribs, neither of which had punctured the skin, nor his lungs. After some heavy strapping was applied around his torso, Guy felt considerably better and was able to be propped up in bed.

"Well, young man," pronounced the doctor. "I cannot say that you were lucky to be set upon in the first place, but luck was on your side with the extent of your injuries. Unless you feel the need to call for me, I think we can just let nature take her course. Your bruises will fade, your bones will mend, and you will have barely a scar to remind you of the occasion. Just take life gently for a few days."

"Thank you doctor, I will try," replied Guy, knowing full well that the next twenty four hours would be nowhere near as gentle as the good doctor expected.

If Guy had wanted a quiet afternoon, he was destined not to get it as a series of visitors arrived. The first of these was a policeman, informed of the crime by Edward Wingfield. The officer made copious notes as Guy told him what had occurred, including the words spoken by the leader of the gang concerning Tobias Linburg and a possible previous murder. The officer added to his notes at this point, but gave nothing away to the men in the room. He had been waiting for a chance to deal with Herr Linburg, and Mr Pender's words may be just the break he needed.

When Guy told him of the threat to Amelie, he agreed to make his presence felt in the square while Guy put together his plans for leaving town. Edward was listening to this conversation and, although disconcerted that Guy was even considering making a move so soon, he agreed to help out.

However, he drew the line at Guy leaving with Amelie and Lizzy by horse and cart. Edward told Guy all about the damage to his studio and to the cart. For the first time today, Guy tried a laugh, despite the pain. "I should be grateful to the rain," he joked. "Had the weather been kinder, I would have placed all my worldly goods into the cart by now."

"Why don't you travel by train?" asked Edward. "There is no better way to get from one place to another nowadays. How else do you think Wilfred and I could get here so easily each season?"

It had not occurred to Guy to consider the railway as a means of transport. He had never been on a train, there being none that he was aware of in

New Zealand and there had always been the constraint of being able to afford a ticket. That was not an issue now, and he had to admit that he wasn't relishing the idea of handling a horse in his current condition. Edward was more than happy to make arrangements on his behalf for the first available train to take them north towards either Antwerp, or to Paris and on to Le Havre. This was the route that Edward normally used, and he assured Guy that the Dannay Shipping Line had offices in both ports, and he would happily send a telegraph to Wilfred to expect them at one port or the other.

While Guy was explaining all this to Amelie, there was a commotion downstairs as Luigi and Leon arrived to see their friend. Guy assured Amelie that, not only did he feel well enough to see them both, but he really did need to talk to them about some important issues as a matter of some urgency. He suggested that she should leave them to it and find her mother to explain that they would be leaving as soon as was practical. Then she may want to see how Lizzy was getting on with packing.

"I'll leave you gentlemen to talk then," said Amelie, once she had ushered Luigi and Leon into the bedroom.

Of course, the first thing they wanted to know was

how Guy was feeling, and Guy needed to thank them both for coming to his rescue. Then, he waved a hand to stop them talking and said, "Now, I have news for you both and some urgent business to discuss. I must tell you both now because we are leaving tonight on the first available train."

Both Luigi and Leon realised the significance of the word 'we', so it came as no real surprise when Guy told them that he and Amelie would be marrying as soon as they reached England where they would be waiting for a passage to New Zealand. They were, of course, thrilled for him, and for Amelie, although sad that they would not be able to attend the ceremony.

Guy went on to tell them about his ownership of the three houses across the square. Leon was astonished to find out that he had been paying his rent to Guy ever since his aunt had died, but always through a lawyer, so he never needed to know who owned the building. But this was nothing to his amazement when Guy told him that he could stop paying rent to anyone from this day forward. Edward had brought the pile of papers from Guy's apartment before going to arrange transport, so now Guy asked Leon to undo the ribbon and take out the first document. It was already signed by Guy in the presence of his lawyer, so all Leon needed to do was to take it and sign himself. The freehold was then his, to do with as he pleased. Leon could not believe his good fortune, and he vowed to keep in touch with Guy and let him know how the business thrived.

"Now, Luigi," said Guy. "I have not forgotten my other friend."

Guy went on to explain that the studio and apartment were to be gifted to Luigi and his wife and child with the same conditions as the bakery. There was a similar document for Luigi to sign. However, as Guy pointed out, the studio would need some work before it was straightened out, and he had already spoken to a builder who was willing to create an internal staircase. There was an amount set aside to pay for this work. It was up to Luigi how he wanted to proceed, perhaps he may even consider opening his own premises one day. Whilst Guy still owned the bookshop in between his friends' houses, with its sitting tenant, he was aware that Herr Schmit was considering retiring soon, in which case Guy would be more than happy to come to some arrangement about expansion. Laughingly, he suggested they may combine their skills into a fine patisserie where Leon's wonderful baking could be served by Luigi, le patron.

Guy could see tears in his friend Luigi's eyes and was glad that he had the means to help him and his young family out.

"But, there is one more thing," said Guy, once the two men had gently taken his hand in thanks for their good fortune.

Wondering what conditions Guy was to put on them, Leon and Luigi, both at once said, "Anything you ask of us."

"I ask you both to look after Albert," said Guy with a serious face. He had a feeling that Luigi's young son would grow up to love having a pet cat. "That cat needs a good home and will reward you both with his hunting skills to keep the mice down."

The three men laughed together, somewhat painfully in Guy's case. It may be a small thing to be discussing the cat, but it was another thing sorted out for Guy. "Goodness," he thought to himself with some trepidation, "we are nearly ready to go."

Despite Amelie's protestations, Guy was determined to get out of bed. He needed to make sure he had all his belongings packed as well. Amelie and Lizzy had everything they needed in two large travel chests, and a smaller bag to carry things closer to hand during the journey. Feeling proud, but very uncomfortable in borrowed clothes, Lizzy had been transformed from a maid in her black dress and pinafore to a lady's companion. Both ladies had their warm coats with short capes and their sensible hats and best boots ready to put on when the journey started. Cook had been given instructions to prepare a hamper of food to be taken onto the train. She had already put cakes and biscuits in tins, but was awaiting news of the time of their departure before adding more.

That news came with Edward's return from the railway station. Guy was thankful that Edward was a seasoned traveller and had no problem in organising a first class carriage for the journey right through to Le Havre. Yes, it was to be France, rather than Antwerp, but Edward had sent a telegraph message to Wilfred explaining the reason for the change. Unfortunately, the next train to leave Zurich was not until early the following day, a matter which concerned Guy greatly, but could not be helped. However, Edward had thought about that too, and had managed to put things in place to avoid any more visits from Tobias Linburg's thugs just because they would be missing the midnight deadline. A burly policeman in uniform would be stationed outside the von Truber's house tonight, and Luigi and Leon would sit in Guy's apartment to ensure there were no unwanted callers. Edward would be keeping an eye on the studio too.

Guy was in far more discomfort than he cared to show as he made his way slowly and painfully across the square, with Edward beside him putting out a hand to steady Guy when necessary. The hardest part was climbing the stairs to the apartment, a feat he could only manage one slow step at a time. His left side, where the broken ribs throbbed painfully, could not bear the weight of a step up, but by leaning heavily on the rail, he could push himself up one step with his right foot, and then drag the other foot up to join it. Edward hovered behind him, hands out ready to catch him if he stumbled.

It didn't take long for Guy to finish his packing. Most of it had been made ready the day before, but so much had happened in that short time that Guy felt as though he had been tidying things away a very long time ago. Just as he closed the lid on the travel trunk, Albert sidled into the room and wound himself around Guy's legs purring softly.

"You'll be fine, Albert," said Guy, bending carefully to tickle the cat behind his ear. Albert jumped up onto the table and watched as Edward began the slow job of helping Guy down the stairs again. Guy took one last glance around the room that had been his home for so long, one last nod to Albert, and was gone. It felt to him like the turning of a page. He wasn't sad at all, except perhaps for leaving Albert behind, more excited by the beginning of his new life with Amelie and his return to New Zealand. It was just that the journey was to begin a little sooner than expected.

Later that day, Luigi and Leon carried Guy's belongings across to join the growing pile of luggage in the hallway of the von Truber's home, before setting off to spend the evening over a bottle of wine and a supper of fresh baked bread and cheeses in the apartment that now belonged to Luigi.

There were just five of them at the supper table, Amelie and her mother and sister, Edward and Guy. Lizzy had insisted that, despite her new clothes, she wanted to spend her last evening in the kitchen with her friends. The talk was all about the journey, of course. Edward had all the necessary papers for the train, including those needed to cross the border into France. He assured Guy that the journey was a straightforward one, and that they should call upon a porter at each station to help them in and out of the carriage and to point them in the direction of the facilities. He told them that there was adequate time at most of the stopping places to disembark to use the lavatories. With a smile, he suggested that, once they changed at Strasbourg they would have their own small closet, making life a little easier, especially for the ladies.

Amelie's mother had tried to discourage Guy from leaving so soon, despite the threat from Tobias' thugs. But she had come to realise that Guy was a determined young man who, once he set his mind to something, would ensure that it came about. A quality that would stand him and Amelie in good stead over the next few months. She was sad that their departure marked the first stage of Amelie's move across the world, but glad for them too. Having lived for many years in a loveless marriage, one could hardly be sad to see two people so much in love. And, at least the current plans gave her the opportunity to see both her daughters married to men they obviously adored. After all, it would only be a matter of days before she set out for England herself.

An early night was in order for everyone, though nobody actually got much sleep. It was Amelie and Augusta's last night sharing their bedroom, and it was very late indeed before they stopped whispering to each other. Even then, Amelie lay wide awake, a whole range of thoughts running through her head. Her love for Guy, her hatred of Tobias and all that he had done, her fear of the journey into the unknown, all mixed up with the excitement of the whole adventure. She must have dozed off eventually, because it didn't seem very long before Lizzy was gently shaking her to wake her up.

"Time to go, Miss," said Lizzy.

For the second time in two days a coach rolled to a halt outside the von Truber's just as the dawn was breaking. The same coachman jumped down to take the baggage. He was helped by the constable who had been on duty on the step all night. The two men tied everything down before turning to help the passengers onto their seats.

The policeman chose not to make mention to anyone of the two men he had seen approaching the house at dead of night. He did not doubt they meant mischief, but had beaten a hasty retreat when they spotted someone guarding the door. Luigi and Leon had just arrived with Edward, all three reporting no signs of intruders in the apartment or studio. It would be obvious, even to Tobias, that they were leaving town now, so the policeman doubted there would be any further issues. Despite that, he knew that one of his colleagues was to be on duty at the railway station, just in case. He rather hoped his superior officer would be able to bring Tobias Linburg to justice. It was well known by the officers that the young gentleman had an evil streak and the finances to allow others to do his dirty work. It was time he paid for his crimes, in the officer's opinion. It was also time for him to go home and get some breakfast, so he wished everyone a good morning and took his leave.

Meanwhile, Amelie was saying her farewells to her mother and sister. In the end, Edward had to push things along so that they would reach the railway station in plenty of time. Having loaded cook's hamper on top of the other bags, he turned to Guy.

"Good luck, my friend," he said, "and travel safely. I look forward to seeing you in England soon, where we will not just be friends, but brothers-in-law." He refrained from clapping Guy on the back, but took his hands in a firm handshake.

"Thank you, Edward," was Guy's reply. "Thank you for everything you have done for us. I look forward to meeting again soon."

The coachman had already helped Amelie and Lizzy into the carriage, and he now did the same for Guy. It was a painful experience indeed, and Guy fell into his seat with a groan. Amelie reached across to take his hand before pulling the curtain to one side to wave to her mother and sister as the coach began to move away. The three of them were silent, the sound of the horses' hooves and the rattle of the carriage the only noises to be heard, each thinking their own thoughts as they set off on their grand adventure together.

As the coach left the square, the coachman saw a man standing in the shadows. He tipped his horsewhip in salute, and the man lifted the brim of his hat in reply, briefly revealing his face. It was Tobias Linburg.

"So they are on their way," he thought to himself. "And I have won the battle to rid myself of Amelie von Truber. But the battle goes on to rid the world of Mr Guy Pender."

CHAPTER THIRTEEN
Journeys

The rhythmical sound of the carriage rattling along the tracks was sending them all to sleep. Guy lay along the upholstered bench seat on one side of the carriage while Amelie and Lizzy sat opposite, their heads tipping sideways towards each other. At last, they were on their way, the early morning light showing through the window, as the houses began to spread out more thinly on the edge of the town and green fields started to appear, dotted with brown and white cows.

None of them were used to railway travelling. In fact, Amelie was the only person who had been on a train when the family went from Vienna to Venice. She had been but a babe in arms then, so had no memory of it at all, but her mother had found it uncomfortable and frightening, the carriages lurching from side to side as if they were just about to topple over. She had passed something of this fear onto her daughter. Lizzy was terrified of the fire-breathing monster of an engine and firmly believed that no man could survive travelling at such speeds. If truth be told, Guy was just as scared, but was working hard at looking unconcerned for the sake of the ladies.

Arriving at the railway station and getting onto the train had been easier than he expected. A porter had appeared out of nowhere to magic their luggage away to their allotted carriage, returning quickly to accompany them to the steps. In normal circumstances, he would help the gentleman into the carriage first, who would then reach down to help the ladies aboard, but he could tell by the way this gentleman winced in pain as he got out of the coach that he would need to help the ladies aboard first. Then, gently, he helped Guy to pull himself up. His final duty was to slide cook's hamper into the carriage and to shut the door. Before he did this, he stood expectantly looking in Guy's direction. It took a moment for Guy to realise he should tip the man a coin. Once he did so, the porter grinned from ear to ear, wished them a comfortable journey and slammed the door shut.

Once more there was silence while the three travellers took in their new surroundings. Apart from the occasional hiss of steam from the engine, which was only just in front of them, there was little noise. Passengers were disinclined to take this train at such an early departure time, so most of the rest of the carriages contained freight, made up mainly of letters and parcels addressed to all corners of Europe.

Guy consulted his pocket watch and said, "We will be off soon." And with the shrill whistle of the guard and a screech of metal on metal from beneath their feet, the carriage lurched forward. Amelie couldn't stop herself from jumping up to look out of the window as they began to slide forward.

"Hold on to your hat," shouted Lizzy, as she joined Amelie at the small window. In only a few moments they were going so fast that the ladies needed to hold onto the window frame to save themselves from falling over. They took up the seats nearest to the window and continued to watch the world flying by while Guy made himself as comfortable as possible on the well upholstered seats. Fear turned to excitement as this stage of their journey got under way.

The porter had told them that they would reach the final stopping point of this train in Strasbourg early the next morning, but stops would be made at various points along the line. Someone would tell them if there was time to disembark or not at each stop. He had also pointed them to the mechanism for dropping the seats into position to form a bed of sorts and curtains that could be drawn across to provide some privacy. Once they had left the town behind them, Guy could start to relax. His chest still ached with every breath and his head throbbed with a dull pain, but there were signs of a definite improvement. There was also an enormous relief at getting away from the clutches of Tobias Linburg. It did not cross his mind that Tobias had contacts outside of Zurich on whom he could call. He would perhaps have felt less comfortable had he known that Tobias was already aware of their travel plans.

The ladies were now asleep, with Amelie's head in Lizzy's lap, and Lizzy's head dropping forward, her nose being tickled by Amelie's hair. Guy worried that they would wake with stiff necks, but they needed their rest after all the trauma of the last few days so he left them to snooze. It gave him time to think too. Despite the speed with which they had made their escape, things were actually turning out positively. He was on his way to New Zealand, although just at the moment they were pointing in exactly the opposite direction. He was travelling with the woman he was to marry soon, and he even had that partially arranged. Lizzy was turning out to be a resourceful young lady with a sharp wit. She made the ideal companion for Amelie, while being good company for them both. The danger of Tobias carrying out his threat to harm Amelie had passed, and there was always the hope that the constables would follow up their enquiries and bring Tobias to justice for inflicting injury, albeit not in person. Tobias was a bully, and it was about time he received some punishment for it. Guy had no real desire to see Tobias charged with further crimes, but if it turned out that he had some involvement in a man's death, then he deserved what he got for it.

Amelie would always look back on their dash across Europe as a series of snapshots of passing scenes interrupted by the occasional break from the monotony of the journey. Leaning on Lizzy with her eyes closed, glancing across to see Guy stretched out on his makeshift bed, or taking an occasional glance out of the window as the world whistled past. The odd small town, a church tower, animals running away from the noisy monster of an engine, and then the train slowing to a crawl until it pulled up at a platform in one or other town with names she didn't recognise painted neatly on signs next to the platform. It surprised her that these platforms were all so neat and tidy. Many had displays of flowers growing in wooden boxes or pots. She lost count of the number of times they stopped at such places during the day. As the sun began to throw long shadows across the carriage they drew into a much bigger place. Amelie put her head out of the window and was greeted by a porter speaking German, but in an accent she could barely understand. As far as she could tell, they were to be here for an hour and could disembark while the porter prepared their carriage for sleep.

Lizzy had been woken up by the sudden lack of movement, and Guy was beginning to stir too. The three of them were relieved to get onto solid ground for a while, to stretch their legs and to seek out somewhere to eat. The porter pointed them in the direction of a small room set out with tables where they were served a meal which, though bland and over-cooked, did at least fill their bellies with warm food. By the time they got back to the carriage it had been laid out for the night with a heavy curtain separating the two couches for the ladies from Guy's single bed.

They chose to wait for the train to get under way again before getting under the blankets provided to keep them warm. Guy lay down as he was, not seeing the point of struggling out of his clothes, but he smiled to himself as the ladies giggled to each other as they attempted to disrobe, despite the lurching of the carriage. Eventually, everything was quiet, but just as Guy was on the point of dropping off Amelie whispered, "Guy, when do we need to wake up?"

"Well, I suppose we just wait for the train to stop,"

replied Guy before tiredness overcame him. He fell asleep with a picture in his mind of them sleeping all the way to the train's final destination to be woken by a porter. He had no idea where that would be, but he imagined it would be a long way from their desired route, maybe as far away as Russia. He hoped they would all wake up in time to make a change of trains in Strasbourg.

In truth, they were all awake before that and perhaps it was just as well. Dawn came early at this time of year and the three passengers had already pushed back the curtain and were sitting on the edge of their makeshift beds when the train came to a halt. Guy, who was feeling much better after a good sleep, pushed the window open expecting to see another railway station, but they seemed to be in the middle of nowhere. Edward had warned Guy that they would need to show their travel documents when they crossed the Rhine from Germany into France, so he guessed the wide river running alongside the track was that river. No papers had been needed to leave Switzerland, but Edward had told him there were tensions between France and Germany at the moment, which meant that the border officials were taking their job seriously.

It wasn't long before Guy could see a man in a blue uniform with a strange military style hat making his way down the length of the train stopping wherever there were passengers. Fortunately, apart from a crowded third class carriage made up of travellers who had embarked at the smaller stations along the line, Guy's party were the only other passengers. The man placed a short wooden ladder at the carriage door, Guy opened the door and the officer climbed up the steps and into the carriage to join them. "Papiers, s'il vous plait," he ordered.

Guy had everything ready for him and, apart from questioning the reason for an Austrian woman to be travelling from Switzerland to England, all was in order. Amelie was fluent in French and could answer his questions with ease, though Guy couldn't understand all her words. He got the feeling that Amelie's disarming smile did the trick, rather than what she said. Without any further delay, the man pulled a small metal stamp out of his pocket and used it to emboss a mark onto their papers, then lifted his hat and retreated down the steps saying, "Bon voyage."

Not long after that the train started up again with a jolt sending the last of cook's shortbread biscuits flying from Amelie's plate to the dusty floor. They all looked out of the window as they rolled and rattled over the bridge crossing the mighty river Rhine, and a short while later the train came to a halt in the city of Strasbourg.

Once on the platform, the three travellers stared in awe at the glass roofed railway station building. It was by far and away the biggest building they had ever seen. The noise of screeching brakes, steaming engines, whistling guards and the rattling of hand-held carts echoed down from the high ceiling all around them.

All of a sudden, a porter appeared to escort them to the train that would take them to Paris. He explained to Guy that breakfast was already waiting for them at their buffet table and that, if they all cared to follow him, a boy would deal with transferring their luggage. The train for Paris would leave in a little over an hour's time.

The French railway carriage was a much grander affair than the small German train. They had a carriage to themselves and a man would be travelling with them to serve food and attend to their every need. There was, as Edward had said, a small room containing a water closet in the corner which Amelie would have liked to use straight away, but their porter warned her that it was only to be used while the train was in motion, not in a station. The dining table was set for breakfast and there were several comfortable chairs placed to give the best view out of the window. Their porter explained that, although beds could be made available in the adjoining rooms, there no need for such things on this journey as they would be travelling during daylight hours only. They would be reaching the hotel in time for a late supper tonight.

Their journey through the French countryside was uneventful. The land was flat and verdant. It reminded Guy of the plains between Applecross and the sea. Sheep and cows could be seen, always running away from the noisy engine, but coming to rest again as the railway carriages passed by. Amelie and Lizzy sat facing each other, chatting of this and that, while Guy took the chance to exercise his aching body, pacing backwards and forwards, pausing to stretch occasionally. His broken ribs were still very sore, but he felt better for the enforced rest whilst travelling. He realised now that he could not have managed the horse and cart in his current state. The railway certainly made a big difference to travel over long distances. Perhaps he would find that tracks had been laid in New Zealand by the time he got back there. He remembered Samuel talking about a train running from the coast to Marytown and back, something that would make life a lot easier for those like James Mackenzie, who transported great quantities of wool to be sent overseas. He looked forward to seeing if any progress had been made.

His mind wandered back to thoughts of introducing his new wife to his friends over there on the other side of the world. He knew for certain that Sophia and Nancy would welcome Amelie with open arms, and when children came along, he could think of no better place for them to grow up.

Amelie woke him from his daydreams saying, "You are quiet, my dear. Are you feeling better?"

Lizzy had drifted off to sleep again, so Amelie now took Guy by the arm and guided him to sit next to her on the bench seat. It was the first moment they had shared in each other's company for several days.

"Yes, my aches and pains are easing as we travel along," replied Guy, almost truthfully. "I hope you are finding this method of transport a little more luxurious than a horse and cart," he added, with a smile.

"Isn't is incredible that we can go so fast?" said Amelie in reply. "This part of the journey is like travelling in a luxurious house. I thought I would be frightened by the speed of the engine, but I find it strangely calming, despite the rattling noises and the occasional lurch of the carriage."

"I have not had time to ask you this before, but are you happy my dear? Have we done the right thing?" asked Guy.

"Oh yes," Amelie replied without hesitation. "Oh yes, of course we have. We just left Zurich a little sooner than we intended and with a little more haste."

"And, Lizzy?" asked Guy, suddenly overcome by the magnitude of their sudden departure and the effect it was to have on all of their lives. "Do you think Lizzy is happy?"

"I believe she is," replied Amelie, although Guy could see a small cloud of doubt pass across her face. "I think perhaps she is yet to realise quite what she has agreed to do. But she is more of a friend than a servant and has been so since she first came to us in Venice, and we must do our best to make sure she is happy too. Perhaps you spoke the truth when you told her there may be a suitable husband for her in New Zealand."

The subject of their conversation was just beginning to stir from her sleep and could hear her travelling companions talking to each other. She purposely kept her eyes closed for a little longer than was necessary to give them a chance to spend a little bit of time together. Eventually, her eyes opened, she yawned as discreetly as she could and said, "Ooh, Miss, I ain't never slept in the daytime in my whole life!" Guy and Amelie couldn't help themselves from laughing out loud.

The journey continued with little to interrupt them. It was as if they were travelling in a vacuum, but a pleasant one, where someone else was taking responsibility for the direction in which they travelled and there was no threat of being followed by a murderous Tobias Linburg, or constricted by their parents' expectations. They were just three young people on an adventure, travelling in style and comfort on their way to a new life. The sense of freedom caused them all to relax in each other's company, and in many ways, they got to know each other better in that day's journey than they had been able to do in the weeks beforehand.

By the time they reached Paris, pulling into the Gare d'Est, they were feeling relaxed and ready for the next stage of the journey. Yet again, staff appeared, as if by magic, to whisk them and their luggage away to a nearby hotel, where they were looking forward to spending a night in proper beds without the constant movement of the carriage.

As they approached the reception desk at the hotel and gave their names, the gentleman behind the desk said, "Ah, Monsieur Pender, il y a un message pour vous." Guy didn't really need to understand what was said, so he merely took the folded paper that was being held out to him. It was from Edward and had been written in a flowery hand by the telegraph operator at the hotel. The message told them that Edward had been in touch with Wilfred and that it had been arranged for a representative of the Dannay shipping company to be waiting for them at the railway station in Le Havre. This part of the message he shared with Amelie and Lizzy, but he chose to keep to himself that Edward had also warned him to keep an eye out for 'Linburg's spies', as he called them, in Le Havre.

There were several other passengers staying at the same hotel. Some were joining Guy and the ladies on the journey north in the morning, others travelling elsewhere. A buffet supper had been set out for them all, but nobody lingered long in the dining room. Early nights were taken by all, the ladies in particular enjoying a warm bath before retiring to their beds. There was plenty of time in the morning with no reason to rise early. A real treat after a series of early starts.

A line of carriages awaited the passengers outside the hotel, each one already loaded with their trunks and bags. Those at the front of the queue were heading only a short ride away to Gare du Nord, which Amelie had told Guy and Lizzy translated as the northern station. Trains left for Calais from that station, which was all very well for the majority of passengers who wanted to end their journey in London, but those who hoped to cross the English Channel to Southampton needed to leave for Le Havre from Gare St Lazare.

Guy was looking forward to a glimpse of the basilica of the Sacre Coeur, or the cathedral on an island, Notre Dame. Indeed, he thought he caught sight of the domed roof of the basilica as they sped along a tree-lined boulevard. But their station was not far away either, so there was little time to take in the sights of the famous city before they pulled up outside a building with a most impressive facade. Guy wondered why the three railway stations had not been combined into one through route, rather than all three being a terminus, but presumed correctly that there was rivalry between the separate railway companies. It occurred to him that a system of linking railways together without such gaps would need to be created if the train was to become the answer to easier travel over long distances. For now, however, they had no choice but to revert to horse and carriage between the rival stations.

Once they were inside the building they were glad they had a porter to lead the way. There were so many more people here and so many platforms to choose from, engines steaming gently at most of them, but their guide led them deftly through the crowds to a gate over which was a painted sign saying 'Le Havre'.

This time there were no individual carriages, although, as they walked the length of the platform they could see how uncomfortable it would be to travel without the luxury of first class. Third class consisted of bare wooden benches, crowded with people and packages. Some even contained chickens and various farmyard animals appeared to be tethered to the wooden benches too. The second class carriages offered a little more comfort with upholstered seats. Here it seemed the majority of passengers were professional gentlemen travelling on business, or young couples returning from a treasured trip to the city of romance.

As they approached the engine, the final carriage was reserved for first class passengers. They climbed aboard and took their seats, the ladies facing forward while Guy sat opposite them and would see the journey in reverse. Not all the seats were occupied by any means, but Guy tipped his hat to the three young gentlemen sitting in the adjoining group and to the well-dressed elderly couple who were on the other side. A piercing whistle from the guard standing just outside the carriage door was the signal for the engine to move forward. Once again they were on their way. The journey was to take most of the day, including a stop in Rouen where there was time to alight for some much needed exercise. Throughout the day, the railway line meandered along the banks of the river Seine, crossing and recrossing at several points. It was something of a relief to them all when the train slowed to a crawl, finally coming to a halt at the end of the line in Le Havre. Alighting from the carriage, they caught a glimpse of the harbour, the seawater glistening in the late afternoon sun. The air smelt of the sea too, a welcome aroma, which made them all feel as though they were getting closer to their destination at last.

Guy cast a glance around to see if there was someone waiting for them on the platform, although he had to wait for the clouds of steam from the engine to clear first. A young man had obviously recognised the elderly couple, perhaps he was their son, and he reached up the take his mother's hand to help her down from the carriage. The three other gentlemen, who had travelled with them, were already striding towards the exit carrying their bags with them. That left just the three of them standing alone, not quite sure where to go next. A porter was placing their baggage onto a hand cart and would need to know where to take it, but Guy had no idea what to tell him. To add to his concern there were two men leaning nonchalantly against a pillar, their hats pulled down over their faces. Were these Tobias' henchmen? Guy hesitated before guiding the two ladies right past these shifty characters, but just as he was wondering what to do, two gentlemen appeared at a run, holding on to their hats to stop them flying off their heads, their coat tails flapping as they ran. "Monsieur Pender?" one of them questioned. "Je suit desole nous sommes en retard."

Guy had to rely on Amelie to translate what the man said as they both came to a halt in front of the group of travellers. It turned out that the gentleman who had called his name was Dannay's man in Le Havre, a Monsieur Pierre Bergier. He apologised for not being there to meet them, blaming the early arrival of the Paris train today. He introduced his companion as Inspector Pascal of the local constabulary. Amelie raised her eyebrows at Guy as she translated this introduction, but said no more. Guy also noticed that the two mystery men were no longer there, having sidled away as soon as they set eyes upon the inspector.

Monsieur Bergier told Amelie that their cabins were ready for them on board the channel steamer that would take them to Southampton overnight, and that, if they were ready to do so, he would take them straight to the harbour. A carriage was waiting for them outside the station. The inspector had, at the same time, spoken to the porter who had been patiently waiting for instructions. He immediately pulled his handcart along the platform towards the exit in search of the carriage belonging to the Dannay Shipping Company.

The whole group travelled the short distance to the waterfront, the inspector and Monsieur Bergier sitting alongside the coachman while Guy, Amelie and Lizzy sat on more comfortable seats inside. Their baggage had been strapped behind them. As soon as they reached the pier and came to a halt, two men dressed in sailors' uniforms began to unload the chests and bags and carried them on their shoulders up the gangplank. As the coachman helped the travellers to step down from the carriage, the inspector stood to one side casting his eyes to left and right as if he was looking for someone. Guy let the ladies go on ahead with Monsieur Bergier, up the gangplank and on board the ship, while Guy waited for the inspector at the bottom of the gangplank.

"Thank you, inspector," said Guy.

"My pleasure, sir," was the inspector's reply in heavily accented English. "Bien sur, you will be safe once you leave our shores."

These words did nothing to ease Guy's concerns, having not been aware of any signs of danger over the last couple of days. As he followed the ladies on board, he wondered what may have befallen them if Inspector Pascal had not been available to meet them on the platform. He certainly breathed a sigh of relief when he heard the two sailors pulling on the ropes holding the gangplank to leave a sizeable gap between the deck and the coast of France that even Tobias Linburg's henchmen would find too wide to cross.

CHAPTER FOURTEEN
England

The captain of the steamship 'Maida' showed Guy to his cabin. A small room with a single bunk and just about enough room to stand beside it. His travel chest had been stored elsewhere but the small valise Guy had carried with him throughout the journey was already on the bed. It contained everything he needed overnight. All of a sudden, Guy felt utterly exhausted and could do nothing but sink onto the bed. Captain Bickerton looked at him anxiously.

He asked, "I hear from Mr Dannay that you have been injured in some way. Is there anything I can do to help?"

"No, thank you, Captain, but perhaps I can rest a while," replied Guy, thankful for hearing an English speaking voice at last. His ribs were now throbbing with pain. It was as if he had forgotten about his injuries for the journey, and now he could relax, the intense pain could no longer be ignored.

"I am at your service for the journey across the channel," said the captain. "Mr Dannay has sent instructions to treat you as his personal guests. We leave in about an hour, once the full tide turns. This gives us plenty of time to reach Southampton on the next incoming tide. Now, rest a while. I will send a man to let you know when dinner is served in the galley."

Guy was already placing his head on the pillow as the captain left the tiny cabin. "Thank you," was all he had time to say before he fell into a deep sleep.

By the time he awoke, he could hear the throb of the engine room in the depths of the ship, meaning they must be underway already. Guy found a water jug set into a hole on top of a small corner table. As Guy was splashing his face with cold water, there was a light tap on the door. It was one of the sailors who had loaded their luggage aboard, coming to tell him that supper was ready, communicated by a series of hand signals and a few words in french that Guy did not entirely understand.

He followed the sailor up a steep wooden staircase and into a large open galley with a heavy wooden table running down the middle of the room. Captain Bickerton sat at the head of the table at the far end of the room, while Amelie sat next to Pierre Bergier on one side with Lizzy on her own on the other side. Guy took the seat next to her as the food was served. The crew may have been french, but the cook was a broad-shouldered Yorkshireman with a fearsome voice that could be heard by the diners as he barked orders to his staff. It came as something of a relief to Guy to be served good, solid English fare. First came a steaming meat pudding, the suet crust encasing tender beef and kidneys in a succulent gravy. Dessert was a sweet and delicious apple charlotte. Guy, who had grown up eating such staples at school and at Nanny Bee's nursery table, found himself very much at home. He wondered, however, how Amelie would find such stodgy food, as she was used to a more delicate menu. Lizzy was tucking into her portion with gusto, perhaps it reminded her of home too.

Amelie and Monsieur Bergier were chatting in French while Lizzy felt the same sense of relief as Guy at being able to use her mother tongue in conversation with the captain. Guy told Captain Bickerton about their intention to head for New Zealand and Lizzy listened with fascination to the two men discussing the route the ship would take.

Captain Bickerton had sailed to Australia and New Zealand on several occasions, but in his latter years he claimed to have left the long voyages to younger men. It suited him to ply the short crossing between Le Havre and Southampton these days.

"Guy," said Lizzy, "can I ask you a question?"

"Of course you can," replied Guy. "I will do my best to answer it."

"Well, can you tell me what language they speak in New Zealand, please?" she asked, a worried expression on her face. "I need to learn it as soon as I can. I find it difficult to know what to reply and how to behave when I don't understand what is being said."

"Why, they speak English there, my dear," said Guy with a laugh. "Though the natives have their own language with words it is hard for us to say. But when you meet Atewhai you will find she somehow understands you without you even needing to speak at all."

Of course, then Guy had to tell Lizzy all about the elderly Maori woman who had been such a help to Sophia and James, and how Atewhai's niece had even been a surrogate mother for baby Lily when her mother died. The more Guy spoke about this place Applecross, the more Lizzy liked the sound of it. She couldn't wait to meet everyone.

"Not long to wait now, Lizzy," said Guy. "It is May, and if everything goes to plan we will reach New Zealand in November. Perhaps we will get to spend Christmas with the Mackenzies."

"Will there be snow?" asked Lizzy with a look of excitement on her face.

Again Guy laughed as he explained that summer and winter were back to front on the other side of the world. So they would leave England in the summer and arrive in New Zealand as summer started again. There would, of course, be snow, but not until June or July.

Lizzy was finding it hard to take all that in, but she had travelled before and was not in the least bit scared of making another journey. Once more, Guy realised how fortunate he was to have Lizzy accompanying them on their journey. She had that stoic character that meant she could take anything in her stride, and he had no doubt that they would all need that kind of spirit over the next few months.

Perhaps it was the sense of relief at leaving french shores, or the effects of a good supper, but nobody was keen to leave the table. The group relaxed in each other's company and talked of this and that until the candles started to sputter as they reached the end of the wick. Captain Bickerton assured them that they need not hurry in the morning. Breakfast would be served in the same room regardless of the fact that they would be docked in Southampton by then, and he expected Wilfred Dannay to arrive in the morning to greet them.

They all slept well in their tiny wooden beds, the gentle rocking of the ship and the rhythmic beat of the engine sending them all off to sleep in no time. Thankfully, it was a calm crossing and, as the captain had predicted, the ship was in port before breakfast. Guy woke to the sound of the anchor chains being dropped and met the two ladies coming out of their cabins at the same time on their way up to the dining galley.

They were all thrilled to find Wilfred Dannay waiting for them at the table and Amelie took his hands in hers and said, "Thank you for your help in making this journey possible."

"It is the least I could do to make amends for the way you have been treated," replied Wilfred. "And it is a pleasure to be able to assist in bringing you two lovers together."

"Now, have some breakfast while the men load your bags into my carriage," he continued. "My townhouse is but a short distance from the quayside, so I have arranged for you to stay there tonight. I wondered if the ladies would like a chance to do some shopping. My mother has suggested a trip to the dressmaker may be in order, as I believe there may be a need for a special outfit."

The ladies were very happy indeed to make a visit to Mrs Dannay's dressmaker. It turned out that Wilfred's mother was a charming, elegant woman with firm ideas about suitable attire for a bride, and with Guy's permission to spend whatever was necessary, the three ladies enjoyed a wonderful day choosing materials, accessories and all manner of necessities to be delivered to the Dannays' country house in time for the wedding. This time Amelie was able to enjoy all the preparations. Indeed, her spirits soared with the realisation that she was to marry the man she loved. Choosing designs and materials and being measured for her wedding dress made it feel very real indeed.

Meanwhile, Guy and Wilfred had the day to themselves. Wilfred's father remained at their country house, which, to Guy's delight, turned out to be only a mile or two away from Upton Barwood. For a short time they would almost be neighbours. The two men sat over a long and lazy luncheon talking of plans for the wedding and for the voyage to New Zealand. Wilfred once more apologised for there being some time before the next available ship. Guy pointed out that it gave them the opportunity of allowing Amelie's family to be at the wedding too, so in many ways it was the best possible outcome.

Then Wilfred said, "Guy, there are things I must tell you that I did not want to share with the ladies."

The pleasant journey across the channel and the excitement of the ladies going shopping had given Guy time to forget about Tobias Linburg and his devilish intentions, but Wilfred's words brought it all back.

Wilfred had received news from Edward in the form of a letter which had only been delivered on the day before Guy's arrival in Southampton on the 'Maida'. Wilfred took the letter from his pocket and handed it to Guy to read himself. It came as no surprise to Guy that Tobias was not content with merely dishing out a beating. Fortunately, the policeman who had stood guard outside Amelie's house that night had made some enquiries which led to the arrest of one of the three thugs who had injured Guy so badly. He had apparently been found leaving the city after some kind of fall-out with his master. In exchange for a lenient sentence, this man had been more than willing to tell the policeman everything he knew. And it was damning evidence of Tobias' ill-doing. First of all, this criminal had spilled the beans about a whole network of men who earned a few coins doing the nefarious deeds of Herr Linburg. A man who issued tickets at the railway station had been paid to pass Guy's travel details to Tobias, who had then arranged for more attacks to take place along the route. It was lucky that none of this had come into effect, mainly due to Edward's well-organised arrangements where they changed trains. It was in Le Havre that the local police had solid evidence of a possible attack and, at the time of Edward writing the letter, he hoped there would be some protection in place, as indeed had been the case.

Furthermore, the person who had been arrested in Zurich confessed to there being an attack planned on Leon de Fevre's bakery, a plan which had been thwarted by the police and resulted in two further arrests being made. It was however, harder to build a case against Tobias Linburg himself. Although, Edward said that the local constabulary were of the opinion that they had opened a can of worms. They were indeed considering a serious charge involving the mysterious death of the chocolate manufacturer, Monsieur Auber. Rumour had it that Linburg had some involvement in this man's untimely drowning in the river.

Wilfred assured Guy that Tobias' influence did not reach beyond the continent, and that they would be safe in England and on the journey to New Zealand. Nevertheless, Edward had suggested that Guy write down as much as he could remember about the night of his attack and the reasons behind it, to be sent to the police in Zurich to add to their case. Otherwise, there was a possibility that he may be called back to the city to give evidence in court. It was unlikely to happen before they left for New Zealand, and even less likely that the authorities would expect him to return then, but a written statement may avoid such demands.

"The reason I am telling you this," said Wilfred, "is that you need to decide whether you wish to talk to Amelie about it. If a connection is made between that man's body and Tobias Linburg, there is a chance he may be found guilty of murder and be sentenced to death. In England he would hang, but in Switzerland the method of execution remains a barbaric decapitation by sword or guillotine."

Guy shivered at the thought of Tobias' severed head rolling off the executioner's block. No, he had kept quiet about the things his attacker had said on the night he was injured, and he had sworn Lizzy to secrecy too, so he would not tell Amelie about it now. Unless he found himself summoned back to Switzerland, that is, and he hoped to avoid that. Despite her current feelings for the man, she had at one time considered marrying him, and she did not deserve to share the dreadful mental picture that he carried now. Guy certainly would not put it past Tobias to commit murder as a result of revenge, and he strongly believed that, had he not made a hasty escape from the city, he would have come in for even more punishment. Though, whether the man deserved to lose his head was another thing entirely.

"I will do as you say in writing down what I remember, but I think it is best we say nothing to Amelie at the moment," replied Guy.

"Say nothing to Amelie about what?" said Amelie as she entered the room with Wilfred's mother and Lizzy, having returned from their shopping expedition.

"Nothing you need to worry about, my darling," replied Guy, cursing under his breath and hoping she hadn't overheard the rest of their conversation. In order to divert her, he added, "Now, show me all your purchases."

"I will not do any such thing," said an indignant Amelie. "It is bad luck indeed for the groom to see anything the bride will be wearing."

Guy was pleased to see a smile on her face, and equally pleased that he had managed to draw her away from any discussions about Tobias Linburg's disjointed head.

The rest of the day was spent relaxing. All three travellers were glad to have found solid ground, with neither the rattle of railway tracks nor the throb of a ship's engine to disturb them. Amelie and Mrs Dannay found themselves immediate soulmates. Wilfred's mother had borne only sons and craved the special kind of relationship one had with a daughter. Amelie found herself able to share her thoughts about the wedding, her desires for her future life with Guy and her concerns about leaving her family behind.

Lizzy, on the other hand, found herself drifting towards the kitchen where, once the staff had got over the shock of a visitor to their side of the green baize door, they made her welcome with tea and cakes. She was getting used to her newfound status, but she still found herself relaxing in the company of fellow housemaids and kitchen skivvies.

Over dinner it was agreed that Amelie should be a guest at Dannay Court, even spending the night before the wedding ceremony there. Her family would also be invited to stay there prior to the wedding. On the day, providing Herr von Truber was able to leave Hungary, a carriage would bring Amelie and her father to the church, and the guests would all return there afterwards for a wedding breakfast. Amelie and Guy would then retire to the cottage Guy owned in the village, where Nanny Bee had lived, leaving everyone else as guests of the Dannays for as long as they liked. It was to be quite a summer party, though the actual date had yet to be agreed with Reverend Bestwick. In the meantime, Guy would live in Nanny Bee's cottage and spend his time sorting out her meagre belongings and the few affairs she had that needed to be wound up.

It was a happy and relaxed group of travellers who left the next day. The carriage would stop first at Dannay Court where Lizzy would alight with Wilfred and his mother, before taking Guy and Amelie on to Upton Barwood to see Reverend Bestwick, visit Nanny Bee's grave and see the cottage that would be Guy's temporary home.

Lizzy felt very much alone as the carriage made its way down the long drive with Amelie and Guy sitting next to each other. But she need not have worried. Wilfred's mother took her under her wing, aware of the awkward position she was in, as neither fish nor fowl in the household. Mrs Dannay had taken a liking to Lizzy's honest opinions and her loyalty to Amelie, and the two of them had a most pleasant afternoon exploring the extensive gardens of Dannay Court. When rain began to fall all of a sudden, they retired upstairs where Lizzy found herself the new owner of a beautiful ball gown and several day dresses, which Mrs Dannay assured her would be better put to use on board ship than hanging unloved in her wardrobe.

Meanwhile, Amelie was enjoying her first taste of the English countryside in May. As the carriage bobbed along the narrow lanes they passed trees in full blossom, hedges springing into bud and the odd well-ordered garden with vegetables growing in neat rows. Swallows scooped along the road, just in front of the horses, as tiny insects took flight, only to be caught mid-air by the swift flying birds. A skylark could be heard singing as they drew to a slow pace on the edge of the village, but neither of them could spot the tiny creature against the billowing white clouds. Guy was reminded of Lucy's birds singing their tunes in the sky above Applecross station.

Upton Barwood was laid out like so many villages in the south of England, centred around a village green where ducks waddled across the grass to slide with a plop into a kidney-shaped pond. Around the green were higgledy-piggledy cottages of all sorts, some with thatch, some with grey slates or orange tiles. At one corner of the green a lane led slightly uphill towards the church. St

Margaret's church tower stood taller than any other building in the parish and was topped by a huge brass weather vane in the form of a proud cockerel, swinging currently to show a westerly breeze.

Guy indicated to the driver of the carriage to pull up outside the Royal Oak public house, a long, low building washed white with lime, under a thatched roof. He suggested that the coachman may like to take some refreshment in the inn while Amelie and Guy walked first to the churchyard and then to the vicarage, which could be approached by use of a gate in the churchyard wall.

Not a soul was about in the village at this time of the day, though Amelie wondered if the inhabitants of the tiny cottages they walked past were peeking out from behind their patterned curtains to see who Guy Pender was going to marry. They took it in turns to go through the church gate. It was what Guy called a kissing gate, swinging only wide enough for one person at a time to wriggle through the gap. Amelie went first and then held the gate open for Guy to follow, but he would not do so until he had paid the toll of a kiss on her cheek. For some reason she found that small thing to be one of the most romantic things she had ever experienced. She took Guy's hand as they walked together up the path. It was easy to see the new earth piled high where Nanny Bee's grave had been dug, and they only needed to take one step off the path for Amelie to lay down the flowers she had bought that morning from a market stall. It was one of the things Guy loved about Amelie. Her thoughtfulness for others. She knew how much Nanny Bee meant to him and had the forethought to bring flowers. As they stood together looking down at the brown earth, Amelie squeezed Guy's hand gently. He was lost in thought for a time, remembering his childhood where all the happiest memories included Nanny Bee.

As sometimes happens on a summer's afternoon in England, there was a sudden change in the weather. Huge spots of rain started to hit the ground around Guy and Amelie, just an odd one or two to begin with, but Guy could tell by the looming clouds that they were in for a soaking. He pulled on Amelie's arm and said, "Come. Let's seek shelter in the church."

They dashed as fast as they could towards the church porch, reaching it just before the rain set in properly and just as Reverend Bestwick turned the latch and opened the ancient wooden church door. Taken aback to see two people heading straight for him, it was a moment before he recognised Guy Pender.

"Come in, come in children," he said, turning back into the silent church. Guy laughed to himself at being referred to as a child. Perhaps Amelie could still be mistaken for a girl not yet of age, but he was nearing thirty these days. He supposed the good vicar was referring in a generic way to the children of God.

"My goodness, is it raining?" asked the vicar who watched as Guy took off his hat and shook the spots of rain from it. "I am so pleased you have been able to visit us, Mr Pender, and to bring Miss von Truber to meet us too. Mrs Bestwick is very excited by the prospect of offering you tea, my dear."

Amelie wondered how the vicar knew her name, but all became clear when Guy said, "Ah, so I presume you received my letter, Reverend, and can I also presume you have put things in motion as I asked?"

"Indeed I have, indeed I have," Reverend Bestwick replied, walking towards the vestry at the back of the church. "On my desk somewhere are the papers for you to sign. Now, where did I put them?" Guy and Amelie joined him in the tiny office, not really a separate room, just a corner curtained off from the main church with a heavy and dusty curtain of maroon material, thick enough to be a blanket, suspended on brass rings from a rickety metal rail. They found Reverend Bestwick searching his desk upon which were piled all sorts of papers, open books, a box of beeswax candles and, bizarrely, a half eaten pie on a china plate. It was obvious to them both that the vicar was not a tidy man, and Amelie guessed correctly that he depended on his wife to ensure he had an appropriate sermon written on time, turned up at the bedside of a sick parishioner and otherwise performed all the duties expected of a village priest. Guy was reminded of Job Nicol, the much loved vicar at Applecross. It was his wife, Clara who steered the ship in that household too.

Reverend Bestwick uncovered the paper he was looking for and waving it in the air in triumph he said, "Here we are. The notice of marriage needs your signature. We have already announced the banns once last Sunday."

Amelie realised that Guy had already started organising the marriage ceremony, but was struggling to understand everything that was said in English. She heard one word that concerned her and said, "Banns? Am I to be banned from something?"

"No, no, my dear," said Reverend Bestwick with a smile. "The banns are just a proclamation to the parish that Guy intends to take a wife. It is the law of the land and all that is required because Guy owns a property in the village. I have all your details too, as Guy was good enough to include them in his letter, but perhaps you could check that I have everything correct before we read them out for a second time on Sunday morning."

Amelie read the names Reverend Bestwick had written in a neat hand on a long thin piece of paper. The same details had already been written in a ledger which lay open on the vicar's desk. Guy Andrew Pender, of full age, bachelor of this parish, photographer and Amelie Louisa von Truber, 22, spinster, overseas (Austria and Switzerland). How quaint these English customs seemed to her, and how lovely it would be to kneel with Guy before the altar, above which was a glorious stained glass window depicting a shepherd and his flock. How appropriate an image that was too. She almost felt that Guy's friends James and Sophia would be looking down upon them. She was suddenly overtaken by a feeling of absolute contentment, as if she knew that everything they were doing was right. It was a very pleasant feeling indeed.

Bringing herself back from her thoughts, she realised that the vicar was asking a question. Fortunately, Guy was answering for her. The vicar had asked if they would like to meet Mrs Bestwick straight away, or go to the cottage today, and visit the vicarage another day.

"If you don't mind, and your wife will not take offence, we will make a quick visit to the cottage now," said Guy. "Our coachman is waiting for us at the Royal Oak to take us back to Dannay Court. But we will return tomorrow with a whole day to organise everything and would very much enjoy taking tea with you and your wife."

"Of course," replied the vicar. "Now I had better get home or my wife will be sending out a search party to find me. She worries that I may get lost between here and the vicarage."

They all laughed as Guy swung the heavy oak door open, and they could see that the rain had all but stopped. Reverend Bestwick waved a goodbye to them both as he turned left out of the porch, heading across the wet grass to a gate in the ancient wall that surrounded the church. Amelie presumed it led to the vicarage, but she and Guy turned right to walk around the base of the tower and along a short path to another kissing gate. Guy insisted on paying another toll by planting a kiss on Amelie's cheek before leading her across the narrow lane to the sweetest little cottage she had ever set eyes upon.

"Let's just take a peek inside now," said Guy. "We haven't much time if we want to get back to Dannay Court before dark."

Amelie just had time to marvel at the riot of flowers growing in the tiny front garden before they reached a door so low that Guy had to stoop down to go inside. In contrast to the vicar's office, Nanny Bee must have been a very tidy person. Everything was neatly organised, even the books on the shelf were lined up perfectly with each other. Guy stopped in his tracks, overcome by the presence of his old nanny in the room. There was a smell of lavender that reminded him of sitting on her knee as a child, and a sewing basket that he recognised was still open on the tiny table next to her favourite chair. It was as if she had just stepped outside for a moment.

Once more, Amelie sensed Guy's feelings and she took his hand again, giving it a gentle squeeze to show that she understood.

"Come now," she said gently. "All looks well here, and we can see what needs to be done tomorrow. Let us go and find that coachman to take us home before he drinks the keg dry of your warm English ale."

It lightened the moment, for which Guy was grateful. There was plenty of time for him to sort things out here, and he would return tomorrow with his belongings, while Amelie enjoyed some company at Dannay Court.

Fortunately, the coachman had kept his drinking to a single jug of ale, knowing very well that he would need to keep his wits about him on a slippery wet road in twilight. The journey back to Dannay Court was uneventful, but they all had lots to talk about over dinner that evening. Once again, Guy was feeling positive about things. His aches and pains were improving by the hour, the danger of Tobias Linburg following them had diminished and, though he hadn't put these thoughts to Amelie, he would not have been surprised to find that she shared a deep contentment for the way things were turning out. Guy was reminded of something Nanny Bee had said to him when he set out for New Zealand all those years ago. "If it is the right thing to do," she had said, "Why then, it will all work out right along the way."

CHAPTER FIFTEEN
Marriage

England - July 1867

The joining of Guy Andrew Pender with Amelie
Louisa von Truber in holy wedlock took place in
the tiny church of St Margaret, Upton Barwood on
a glorious day at the beginning of July. The sun
shone through the stained glass window above the
altar, casting glorious patches of primary red, blue
and green light over the bride's magnificent pale
pink wedding gown and reflecting shadows of the
tiny embroidered flower motifs on the cream veil
across Amelie's face.

It would have been the best day of her life if she
was marrying Guy with no more than a priest and
witnesses in attendance, but to add to her delight,
all her family were able to be there too. Her father

had been given permission by the emperor himself to travel to England for his daughter's marriage. Herr von Truber made it by the skin of his teeth, arriving at Dannay Court the evening before the wedding. Wilfred Dannay was more than happy to relinquish his role in giving the bride away, although it took Guy by surprise to see Amelie walking down the aisle on her father's arm. Augusta and Lizzy followed Amelie, acting as bridesmaids, while Edward stood next to Guy as his best man. Amelie's mother, Wilfred Dannay and Charlotte Wingfield formed the front row on the bride's side of the church while on Guy's side the pews were filled with people from the village who had known and loved Nanny Bee. It followed naturally that the boy she had cared for, as if he was her son, would be loved by the village folk too.

The tiny church was packed to overflowing. It being a hot day it was necessary to leave the door ajar to circulate some fresh air, the added advantage of this being that those who could not find a seat inside could hear every word in the churchyard and were waiting to greet the happy couple when they made their way outside again as husband and wife.

The organist playing the opening notes of the processional hymn was the signal for the village bellringers to announce that there was something to celebrate. As they walked together to the door, Amelie and Guy caught a glimpse of the bellringers at the back of the church, coloured ropes of red, white and blue flying up and down as the six local men rung each bell in turn. It was a glorious sound which spread across the open countryside, stopping distant workers in their fields and causing a flock of noisy crows to rise from the churchyard trees in protestation. Those who crowded around the bride and groom had to shout their congratulations in order to be heard above the peal of bells, but nobody minded at all. Although, the man holding the horse harnessed to the decorated wedding carriage was having difficulty in keeping it from bolting at the sudden sound.

In no time at all, peace returned to the church. The bellringers, hot after their exertions, wiped their brows on their shirt sleeves before making their way back to work. One to the mill, another to the smithy and the rest to their fields. They would down their payment in ale at the Royal Oak the following evening, once they had finished their practice for Sunday service ringing.

The organist put her sheet music away in the space under the seat where she sat, her short legs barely able to reach the pedals. Then she headed back to her tiny village shop, turning the sign on the door to 'open' again.

Meanwhile, Amelie and Guy led the procession back to Dannay Court for the wedding breakfast, their carriage decorated with an arch of white flowers, trailing ivy wound amongst them to symbolise eternity and fidelity. Behind them came a carriage containing Amelie's parents with Augusta and Lizzy, then, somewhat squashed into their carriage came Wilfred, Edward, Charlotte and the vicar and his wife. Bringing up the rear was a motley collection of carts, riders and walkers from the village, straggling along in twos and threes to join the party at Dannay Court.

And it was quite a party! One cannot always depend on the good weather in an English summer to allow dining outdoors, but the day was warm, with not a breath of a breeze, so tables had been set in the rose garden. Amelie and Guy welcomed each guest in person before directing them to enjoy a glass of sparkling wine in the sunshine until the meal was served. There was an awkward moment when Charlotte Wingfield came forward.

"Amelie, I am so sorry for the way I behaved towards you," she said, gratefully accepting Amelie's outstretched hand, with a sense that such a gesture offered forgiveness in itself.

"Charlotte, you do not need to apologise at all. Look what it has brought me," Amelie replied, indicating her new husband with a wave of her free hand.

"Then we must be friends again, dear Amelie," continued Charlotte. "After all, we both know now that we are better off without a certain gentleman."

Guy was pleased to see his wife laughing with Charlotte Wingfield. This was not a day for ill feeling, and in many ways he had a lot to thank Charlotte for. Not only that, but when Augusta and Edward married they would be related by marriage, and the last thing he wanted was some kind of longstanding family feud.

"His wife!" Guy thought to himself. How easily he had found himself referring to Amelie as his wife. He had never been happier at any moment in his life, standing next to the woman he loved, surrounded by friends and family. What more could he want? Except perhaps his other friends on the other side of the globe, the friends who would be going about their everyday lives unaware that Guy Pender had a wife. He must write to them soon and tell them all about it. But for now, he would concentrate on celebrating with the new Mrs Pender. As the last of the guests was welcomed, he took Amelie's arm and led her proudly to a seat at the head of the table to begin the wedding breakfast.

As the sun set, the village folk began to drift away from the celebrations. Reverend Bestwick and his wife left first, offering a seat to a few of the more elderly villagers who would find the walk too much at this time of the evening. Before they took their leave Mrs Bestwick drew Amelie to one side and said, "Amelie, my dear, I am here for you. I know that there are things which may scare you about married life, but you may come to the vicarage for advice if ever you need it."

Amelie thanked Mrs Bestwick, who she had grown close to over the past few weeks while preparing for the wedding. She was a practical woman, a no-nonsense sort of a person, and Amelie was sure she could indeed seek advice from her without embarrassment. But the truth of it was that she was not scared of anything with Guy beside her. Her mother had given her some idea of what she should expect on her wedding night, and she wasn't frightened by it one tiny bit. Rather more excited by the prospect and intrigued by her feelings and desires. She would hardly be likely to share it with the wife of a vicar, but she couldn't wait to see more of her husband's body. Thinking back to that night after the avalanche, she wondered what might have happened had she not kept her body primly covered despite their closeness. Tonight she could change all that, and she couldn't wait.

Soon it was just the Dannays, Amelie's family, Lizzy, Edward and Charlotte who remained, and they were all to stay at Dannay Court that night. Once they had changed out of their wedding attire and Amelie was wearing her 'going away' outfit, it was time for the bride and groom to take their leave. The coachman waited patiently for them on the driveway outside the house.

"We will send the coach to bring you back for luncheon tomorrow," said Wilfred's mother as she fondly kissed Amelie goodbye.

"Thank you for everything," said Amelie, though it didn't seem an adequate thank you for all that the Dannay family had done for them both.

"It is my pleasure, my dear," replied Mrs Dannay. "I have enjoyed having a daughter for a while."

Next, Amelie hugged her mother, who whispered, "Good luck, my darling daughter. I am so very happy for you."

Even her father gave her a hug, something he had not done for a very long time. "I am sorry, Amelie, that I very nearly forced you into an unhappy marriage," he said. "But I am glad that you have found someone you love. I am very proud of you, my dear."

Then, of course, she had to hug her sister and Lizzy and say thank you to Edward, Wilfred and Charlotte. So it took some time before she could take Guy's hand to step up into the carriage. He followed to sit beside her, reaching for a rug to spread across their knees. Her beautiful bouquet of flowers lay on the seat opposite, still tied with pink ribbons to match her dress. "How thoughtful," she thought to herself. "One of the staff has put these here for me, and I know just what I have to do."

She could see her sister near the back of the group as they stepped away to let the coach move forward. She picked up her flowers, and turning away from everyone, tossed them over her head in Augusta's direction. She was next to be married, surely, and would catch the bouquet. However, as Amelie turned back to face everyone she saw Augusta reach up, but only the tips of her fingers could touch the flowers as they flew over her head and landed in Lizzy's open arms.

"Well, there's a surprise," whispered Guy, as the coach pulled off and made its way down the drive, Amelie waving to her family until they lost sight of each other.

Arriving outside the tiny cottage, the coachman only paused long enough to help the bride and groom down to the ground. He then jumped up quickly, took the reins and was gone. For a moment, Guy and Amelie stood together in the near darkness, absorbing the quietness after all the excitement of the day. With a screech of an owl breaking the silence, Guy took Amelie's hand to lead her to the door. She paused to breathe in the night time scent of the rambling rose that surrounded the door and then cried out with surprise as Guy scooped her up in his arms to carry her over the threshold.

"It will bring us good luck," said Guy, as he deposited his new bride in the hallway. It hadn't been an easy thing to do, to carry Amelie through the low doorway. They both had to duck to avoid cracking their heads on the lintel and Guy came very close to overbalancing before they made it through the door.

"I have all the luck I need," replied Amelie, leading Guy straight to the bedroom. Over the last few weeks Nanny Bee's cottage had been transformed into a haven for the pair of them to live comfortably until the time came to embark on their journey to New Zealand. A new and bigger bed almost filled the main bedroom and it was not long before the two of them lay together.

"Are you sure, my darling?" asked Guy. "We can wait if you are too tired."

"No we can't," was Amelie's reply. "I have wanted you since we first met in your studio, and since we spent the night in the shepherd's hut. I cannot wait any longer."

With that she lay back and let her new husband take her, consummating their marriage with tenderness and love.

Amelie woke first, the sun streaming over their bodies through a crack in the curtains. As Guy slept, she lay awake, thinking how different it would have been if she had married Tobias. She suspected he would have been a more dominant and demanding lover, disregarding her needs entirely. How lucky she was to have found a man who loved her, who treated her with respect and who had a gentle touch which drove her crazy with passion. She put both hands on her belly, wondering if a new life was already stirring there as a result of their activities last night. But she must be patient. Her mind wandered into the future, wondering what kind of life a child would have in New Zealand, imagining a small version of Guy running through the green pastures with a black and white dog cavorting alongside, just as Guy had described it to her.

A dog, that's what she needed. She laughed out loud at the thought, causing Guy to open his eyes, though he didn't move a muscle. He lay watching his bride, silently counting his blessings. As so often happened, his thoughts matched Amelie's and his attention was drawn to her beautiful smooth belly and what may now lay inside.

"What are you smiling at?" he asked, propping himself up on his elbow. Her answer was not what he was expecting at all.

"Can we have a dog when we get to New Zealand?" she asked.

"My darling, you can have anything you like," replied Guy, reaching out to pull her body close to his own. "But, of course you can have a dog. In fact, I insist upon it. Then you can learn to round up sheep, and I can send you out as a shepherdess while I stay at home and do nothing at all."

"We will see about that," she replied, pulling herself away and jumping to her feet. Guy found himself incapable of removing his eyes from her beautiful body. "Now come on husband, get out of bed. We have things to do."

"I suppose I had better obey your orders, darling wife," said Guy, leaping out of bed too.

It was fortunate that they had risen by the time they heard a sharp tap on the front door. It was the coachman, who had arrived to take them back to

Dannay Court for luncheon. He explained that he had arrived early because Amelie's father was to leave soon, and he wanted to have time to see his daughter and son-in-law before he returned to his diplomatic duties.

Guy was glad to get there in time, not only for Amelie to say a final goodbye to her father, but because he had made arrangements to take a photograph of the whole wedding party. Once they reached Dannay Court, they all donned their wedding clothes one last time and, under Guy's direction, arranged themselves on the front steps. Guy had been training one of the footmen to open the shutter of his camera at the right moment, which meant that the groom himself could be in the portrait.

What a treasured possession that small portrait was to become for Amelie! The last time she was to see her father and only a few short weeks until she left her mother and sister behind too. Once she had given her father one last fond farewell, she found Guy holding the newly developed precious photograph in the air to dry it. It was a wonderful picture of a group of very happy people.

"We will frame it," said Guy, "and it will take pride of place in our new home in New Zealand."

CHAPTER SIXTEEN
High Seas

August 1867

The thin dark line of the distant English coast was merging into the horizon. All that Lizzy could see was sea, grey sea, apart from the white scars made by the ship's wake, criss-crossed by low-flying seagulls. She stood on tip-toe, leaning over the stern rail, trying to decide if she could still see England, or not.

Was she sad to be leaving England behind for good? In truth, she wasn't really sure, but it wasn't the first time Eliza Berry had packed one life away and started afresh. In her mind, the excitement of the new door opening dominated any thoughts of what lay behind the door just closed. In a symbolic gesture, Lizzy turned away from the stern of the ship and made her way forward, purposefully dodging other passengers as they dawdled along in ones and twos, going as far as she could get along the promenade deck towards the bow of the ship. All she could see in that direction was sea as well, but it was where they were heading, rather than where they had been. It was as if she had turned the page with anticipation to see where the story took her.

The sea mesmerised her. She loved the feeling of sitting on top of it, unknown depths beneath the ship. She loved the constant movement and the power of the water, moving side to side, breaking into white caps before rolling on and on until it hit a distant shore somewhere. She wondered if it was possible to spend the whole journey watching it, feeling the salty air in her face, pushing her damp hair back from her eyes. It made her feel alive.

She knew she should go down the steep stairs to join Guy and Amelie in the suite of rooms which was to be their home for the next three months, but, using the excuse that they needed time together as a married couple now, she had no reason to hurry down into the depths of the ship. A seagull landed on the rail beside her, leaving its white deposit to be sluiced away by a poor deckhand with his bucket and mop. With a shake of his black and white feathers, he regarded this human with a studious expression which made

Lizzy laugh out loud.

"What am I doing here?" she asked the seagull. Its reply was an indignant squawk before taking off across the waves.

Lizzy continued the conversation in her own head. Well, she knew what she was doing here, but what had brought her to this point, and what was to come? Her, an urchin from the filthy squalor of London's East End, the eldest child of a drunken dockworker and a country girl who, like so many others, had left the rural life behind because she thought the city streets were paved with gold. Lizzy had no idea how her father and mother had come together, neither did she care much. All she knew was that her father spent most of his time looking for work, grumbling about work, or downing copious quantities of ale while avoiding work. On his rare waking moments at home it was obvious how he spent his time, because her mother seemed to be in a permanent state of being with child, various brothers and sisters appearing with alarming regularity.

Once Lizzy reached an age where she could be of use to her mother, she became the main carer in the squalid single room where they all ate and slept together. By the time Lizzy was ten, not only was she caring for her siblings, she was cooking, cleaning and shopping with what little money she could eke out from the tin on the mantelpiece, while her mother took to a worn out armchair in the corner of the room. More often than not she tried in vain to hide the bruises on her face and arms, inflicted as a result of her husband's drunken rages.

Looking back on it now, Lizzy could see that her father's interest in her mother had waned, and that was no surprise when you looked at the woman who cared not a jot for her family or herself. But that lack of interest coincided with Lizzy blossoming into a young woman. Inevitably, his attentions turned to Lizzy as the only attractive female available to him. She shivered as she thought back to the occasions when he had pushed himself upon her. At her young age, she knew no better than to allow him to do so. It had taken several years before she realised that what he was doing was most improper and that life could not go on like that. But she also knew that, if she left home, her younger sister would be next in line for her father's attentions.

Her only friend was Mary, who lived in the room across the staircase. Lizzy thought Mary was the lucky one because her father had gone to work one day and simply never returned. Mary's mother was left with three children and no income, but they managed to get by on the charity of neighbours and occasional gifts from the local church. It was at this church that Mary and Lizzy learned to read and write, sitting at their double desk, scratching on their little slate boards with a sharp stylus pen.

The girls remained good friends even after they were too old for school. Both had sharp brains and a good eye for picking skills up by watching others. By the time they were sixteen years old they knew how to run a household, how to sew and mend all manner of things and how to make meals out of nothing. Mary was keen to leave home and find a place in service as soon as she could, partly to get away from the slums and partly to be able to send money back to her mother. The only thing holding Lizzy back was the worry of her father's attentions being transferred to her younger sister, especially as little Lucy was a weak child with a wheezing chest, often leading to a wracking cough in winter.

Lizzy shivered once more when she looked back on that dreadful day when Mary told her she would be leaving for a kitchen maid's position in Rickmansworth, a place to the north west of the city. It was also the day that Lizzy knew for certain that she was with child. She knew by then that a child born to a girl and sired by her father was against God's rules, but Mary scared her even more by suggesting that the child could well be deformed in some way too. Mary also said that she knew a woman who could 'dispose of the problem', as she put it, but Lizzy had heard all the dreadful stories of infections and injuries caused by these back street abortionists and was not prepared to consider that option.

In the end, she tried what many women have attempted over the years. She filled a copper bath with water almost too hot to bear, stepped gingerly into the scalding water and swallowed the best part of a bottle of her mother's gin while watching her bare legs go red and blotchy with the heat. She would never know if it was this old wives' tale that did the trick, or a case of mind over matter forcing her brain to hate the disfigured and gruesome thing that grew inside her. Whatever the cause, that night she was hit by a pain in her belly like no pain she had felt before, and by morning she found blood staining her undergarments. For several days she wondered if she might die from the loss of blood, or the pain inside her, and at times she rather wished that to be the result.

But she was generally fit and strong despite her poor diet and dreadful living conditions, and within a week the bleeding had ceased and she felt able to get out of her bed. At first, she could only assume the child had left her body, but when her normal course returned and her belly failed to swell she was confident of it being gone. She had expected to feel nothing at all except relief, but there was a period of regret, particularly as she wondered if she would be able bear more children in the future, when the time was right.

Throughout the whole episode, her mother remained oblivious to her daughter's condition, addled as she was by alcohol for breakfast, lunch and supper. It was Mary who looked after Lizzy, and when she reluctantly left to take up her new position, it was Lucy who continued to care for her big sister. And it was Lucy who persuaded Lizzy to leave. Lucy knew all about her father's drunken behaviour and assured Lizzy that she could fend him off by feigning illness. Even their father was unwilling to lay hands on a child who was regularly wracked by chest-heaving bouts of coughing.

The local children had all grown up around the port of London. The dockside was their playground, the comings and goings of ships from exotic places around the globe was familiar to them all. It was no surprise that Lizzy chose to escape on board the first vessel she found where the gangplank was unattended. She slipped aboard with nothing more than an old pillowcase to hold her meagre possessions and found a place to hide inside one of the small lifeboats attached to the side of the ship.

Although she had no idea of the ship's final destination, it was a surprise to her when the journey was over in less than a night and a day. She heard the sound of the engine ceasing and anchor chains being lowered, followed by lots of shouting from the quayside in a language she didn't recognise. Waiting until darkness, she sneaked onto dry land and set about discovering where she was. It turned out to be Hamburg, and it was German she had heard being spoken.

"Lizzy," she heard Amelie calling her name. "There you are. We've been looking for you. We thought you had fallen overboard!"

Lizzy's thoughts came back to the present day in a rush. "I'm sorry, Amelie," she said. "I just love watching the sea."

"You have three months to do that, my dear," replied Amelie. "Now come and join us for luncheon." She linked arms with Lizzy and led her back along the deck and down the steep stairs to the state rooms.

Later that afternoon, Guy went in search of the captain of the 'Dannay Felicity' to ask about their intended route, and Amelie pulled out her sewing and took a seat near the porthole window, in order to see her stitches better. Amelie suggested that Lizzy may like a lie down, and indeed she tried to lay on her bed and shut her eyes, but she felt so idle doing so. A rest after luncheon was not for people like her, but then again, what sort of person was she now? She was still finding it hard to be Amelie's equal, and to behave as she should in the company of people of a class many steps above her humble beginnings. Though she may dress like Amelie and sit at the same dinner table, she rather felt the illusion fell apart when she opened her mouth to speak. At dinner the previous evening, before they had left Southampton, she had found herself seated next to a tall and handsome gentleman in naval uniform. She was pleased when he struck up a conversation, but could instantly see a change in his manner when she replied in the accent of the east end of London. Perhaps she should ask Amelie to give her some lessons in speaking correctly? It was all so confusing, and she missed doing Amelie's hair and helping her to dress for dinner and all the little things that maids do for their ladies. Heavens above, she even had the services of a maid of her own on this voyage!

Leaving Amelie to her embroidery, Lizzy made her way on deck to get some fresh air. The sea had changed and huge dark clouds were billowing on the horizon to the south. It looked very much like a storm was heading their way. There were a few fellow passengers taking a promenade after lunch, and Lizzy had to stop herself from making a curtsy to them as they passed by. Instead, she adopted the nod of the head that she had seen Amelie use in greeting and was rewarded with a similar gesture from the women she met, and a gentleman's hand tipping the brim of his hat. Most people were hurrying back to their berths before the storm hit, but Lizzy stopped to watch the sea grow in strength as the clouds approached. She could feel the ship moving up and down and had to hold the rail to keep herself from being tossed along the deck.

Guy was standing on the bridge with the captain, who was now issuing orders to the crew around him to bring in the sails and sending messages down to the engine room with the movement of a brass handle. Each time he moved the handle, a bell would sound and a muffled voice from the depths of the ship would come out of a speaking tube beside the captain. Guy felt as though he was in the way, so when he saw Lizzy standing alone on deck he went to join her.

"There's a storm coming," he said, as he approached her. He needed to shout above the sound of the wind. "We had best go below."

With his words, the rain hit. Coming down like a volley of tiny missiles, they both covered their heads with their arms and headed as fast as they could to the nearest doorway for shelter. Guy found himself leaning on the doorpost and holding on to Lizzy's arm as the ship lurched into the huge waves. They were dry under the shelter and both exhilarated by the weather.

"Are you happy, Lizzy?" asked Guy, out of the blue.

"Why yes, sir," replied Lizzy. "Of course I am happy."

"I worry that we have forced you into this journey against your will," said Guy.

"Oh sir, I am more than happy to be going to New Zealand, but perhaps I will be happier when we get there," she replied.

"Why?" said Guy, surprised by her answer. "Do you not like the movement of the ship? Does it make you feel ill?"

"No," Lizzy shook her head in reply. "It's not that at all, I love the sea, and I don't mind the ship being tossed about. It is just that I feel awkward amongst people of class, and sometimes I wish I was just a simple maid again." Guy watched as she tried to hide the fact that she was wiping away a tear from the corner of her eye.

"You manage better than you think you do, my

dear," said Guy. "I saw that young officer in conversation at the table last night. He could barely remove his eyes from you."

"Sometimes I feel like a swan on the water," was Lizzy's reply. "I may do my best to look beautiful on the outside and sail along smoothly, but underneath I am paddling frantically to say and do the right thing."

"I daresay we all feel like that at times," said Guy, knowing that he too sometimes felt out of his depth in conversation. "But the best we can do is to learn the rules and carry on trying to be a swan rather than an ugly goose!"

Guy was pleased to see Lizzy laugh out loud. The rain was now coming at them in sheets, blown into their faces by the strong wind. Guy pushed the doors open and guided Lizzy inside where the sudden lack of noise made them both stop in their tracks. "Come," said Guy, "Shall we see if we can find someone to make us tea?"

"So now I am a swan, I have to ask others to make my tea," laughed Lizzy. "When I was a goose I could make my own."

"Let's go and find a goose then," replied Guy, heading down the long corridor towards their suite of rooms.

They were still laughing when their tray of tea was delivered by the steward, who had been disturbed from the small cabin where he was polishing silver for the dinner table.

"Tell me, Lizzy," said Guy, as she poured their tea into fine bone china cups. "However did you end up in Venice, working for the von Trubers?"

Not wishing to tell Guy every detail, Lizzy explained her need to escape from her drunken parents. She then went on to tell him about jumping on a boat, not knowing where it would end up, and finding herself seeking shelter inside a church in Hamburg. Luck had been on her side because the priest was in need of a housemaid and had employed her on the spot. But, not long after that, his time in Hamburg was up, and he was sent to Venice to work alongside the senior priest of the church of San Simeone Piccolo. It was a promotion for the priest and it came with a comfortable, furnished house already staffed with a cook and a housemaid. However, the priest insisted that Lizzy should accompany him, especially as his elderly sister was to join him. Lizzy, to all intents and purpose, and despite no formal training, became her personal maid. It was only after the old lady died that Lizzy found herself out of work, but her reputation as a good worker and her experience as a ladies' maid meant it was not long before she came to the attention of the von Truber family.

Their conversation was interrupted by the arrival of the steward who had served their tea. "Excuse me, sir," he said, "I believe your wife is feeling the effects of the sea. She is asking for you both."

Guy and Lizzy were on their feet in no time. They found Amelie sitting on the edge of her bed clutching a porcelain chamber pot. Guy had never seen anyone look quite so green in the face and was not at all surprised when his poor wife was hit by another bout of sickness. The ship's doctor arrived, having been called by the steward, and though he could do little to stem the nausea, he administered a sleeping draught so that Amelie could sleep through the storm. It was a task he would repeat many times throughout the ship as the storm raged, and he knew very well that the only real cure was a calmer sea. He knew, as well, that they would need to get beyond the Bay of Biscay first, with its fearsome reputation for stormy waters.

For the next few days, Guy and Lizzy remained healthy. They, along with a small band of passengers who were equally not afflicted by sea sickness, became regular visitors to the main deck. The smell of the salty air and the freshness of the wind in their faces was in stark contrast to the stench of sickness below deck. They both felt guilty that Amelie remained in bed, unable to keep down anything but a weak broth to keep her strength up. Guy knew from his previous trips that he could withstand rough seas, and Lizzy was thrilled that it did not seem to worry her at all either.

As they ploughed on through high seas towards the equator, the rolling of the ship became a more gentle sway and the warmer climes made everyone feel better. After five days below deck, Amelie made her first visit aloft, with Guy's arm around her to help her up the steps. Weak as a kitten, she fell into the wooden chair that Lizzy had prepared for her, a blanket around her knees, even though the sun shone warmly on them all.

For the first time in days the sails were used to speed their journey. People who had hardly seen daylight since their departure started to make their way up on deck. For some, there was the occasional need to rush to the rail to bring up their last meal for the seagulls, but on the whole pale, sallow complexions began to be replaced with rosy cheeks. Amelie decided that she quite liked this form of transport after all, and the three of them could be found out and about as much as possible, taking a walk from stem to stern, or leaning on the rail looking out for something to relieve the plainness of the vista. Indeed, they spotted the odd ship on the horizon and even the occasional island passing them by.

Guy had been fascinated to hear from the captain that their route would not be the same as the one which first took him to New Zealand some nine or ten years ago now. At that time, they hugged the coast of Africa until they reached Cape Town, where there was a welcome break to replenish stocks on board. This time, the captain explained to Guy that, once they passed the Canary Isles, it would seem that the ship was heading in entirely the wrong direction, heading south-west towards the Americas before catching the winds which would speed them on their way around the 'Great Circle', as he called it. This arc of travel took advantage of the prevailing winds in the southern oceans and though it brought with it some danger of icebergs, should they venture too far south, it was a risk worth taking to make good use of the wind. Thus, they would sweep under the horn of Africa by many hundreds of miles, using the power of sail, in the main, to reach Fremantle on the western coast of Australia.

But this would not be their first port of call. Even though the ship carried a good supply of coal to feed the boilers in her engine room, it was not enough to get them to their final destination. It was therefore necessary to make a brief stop at the Cape Verde Islands, dropping anchor at the port of Mindelo to take coal on board. Though the passengers found the ship's lack of movement a welcome relief, there was no time to disembark, although they were grateful for the chance to enjoy fresh fruit and vegetables for the next few days, their first for some time.

Some days later, the passengers could all tell that the ship was turning to port. At the same time, crew were busy ensuring that the fresh winds could be used to best effect to move the ship along at speed. It was quite a sight to see the sails being unfurled by sailors climbing precariously up the masts and across the spars. The huge sheets flapped loosely at first, before catching the wind and billowing out to do their job of carrying the ship forward at great speed. And speed they did, heading straight towards the setting sun. There was a shift in mood for passengers and crew. According to the captain's log, they picked up the Great Arc on the first day of October. Only three weeks to go before reaching Australia and just three more to New Zealand.

Nearly half the passengers left the ship at Fremantle. The majority of these were single men travelling in steerage, off to the interior of the vast Australian continent to seek their fortune in mining gold and precious gemstones. Ironically, they were replaced on board by those who had failed to make their fortune, or thought there was a better chance of doing so in New Zealand.

Amelie and Lizzy took the opportunity to disembark as soon as they were able, although the captain warned them not to wander into the parts of town he called, 'lawless and godless areas, full of pickpockets and prostitutes'.

The ship would take two full days to be restocked, so they had ample opportunity to explore the port of 'Freo', as everyone called it. There was plenty to see, ships coming and going all the time and throngs of passengers moving around the wharves amongst the crates and packages, sacks and barrels of goods to be imported into Australia or shipped overseas. At one point, a policeman held them back while a long line of miserable looking convicts made their way slowly down the gangplank, their leg chains clanking on the cobbled quay as they were marched towards the prison. They also came across a group of bedraggled children being herded towards the church door by a well-dressed lady who seemed to be in charge. Other people had come to a halt as this sorry group were led away, and Amelie asked the person next to her if they knew what had brought such young children to this side of the world.

"Why, my dear," replied the lady. "They are the young convicts, sent here for some misdemeanour at home. Perhaps for stealing a loaf, or picking a pocket."

"What becomes of them? Do they go to prison too?" asked Lizzy.

"No, no, we do not lock them up," was the reply. "They become wards of the church and are found homes locally where they can be of use as servants or workers in the field."

Lizzy felt a shiver run down her spine. How close she and her brothers and sisters had come to being in the self-same situation! Although, she wondered if their lives would be better here than back in the slums of London. Perhaps, at least for some of these poor creatures, there was hope of a better way of life here.

Once Amelie and Lizzy had their land legs back and the cobbled streets stopped feeling like jelly, they didn't need to cling to each other for support. But they still linked arms to avoid being separated in the crowds of people. For the first time since their departure, they had the pleasure of peeking through shop windows or examining the wares on a market stall. Amelie managed to replenish her stock of thread for her embroidery and Lizzy bought a length of lace from an old leather-skinned lady who sat on her doorstep with her bobbins laid out on a cushion, her fingers flying to turn the bobbins and twist the threads into intricate patterns. Lizzy liked the look of the process of making lace and wondered if it was something she could try for herself. The bobbins

Amanda Giorgis

appeared to be made of wood or bone, intricately carved and weighted down with beads. She thought she would try to find someone to make her some when she reached New Zealand. What fun it would be to pass the threads backwards and forwards to create long lengths of lace. It reminded her of the maypole dance they had been taught at school where the girls went one way and the boys the other, passing ribbons over and under to form a woven pattern.

While the ladies went shopping, Guy found a seat in a dockside bar where, as he sipped his mug of ale, he had a chance to watch the crowds. A group of people gathered to watch a man who had trained a monkey to tap on a drum at his command. The man's hat lay on the ground next to the monkey, and once he had finished his drumming, the animal had been trained to take the hat around the crowd collecting coins. Guy felt rather sorry for the monkey. Had Lucy been travelling with them, she would probably have put all the coins she owned in the hat and walked away with the monkey, although goodness knows what havoc would be caused by a monkey in Lucy's beloved orchard.

His thoughts remained in New Zealand as he sat in the sunshine, people from all corners of the world passing him by. So near, and yet so far. He knew the rest of the journey could be rough and unpleasant, with the Roaring Forties to come. Strong and gusty winds often caused the ship to roll into the waves in a corkscrew movement, and many passengers who had prided themselves on staying hale and hearty for the journey so far would succumb to sea-sickness as the ship sailed south of the Australian coast and across the Tasman Sea.

He worried about Amelie, who had recovered from her early sickness, as far as he could tell. But, in the last few days, she had been quiet and withdrawn, even excusing herself from breakfast this morning. He had suggested that she stay on board the ship for the day, but she was having none of it, and said she was looking forward to wandering around the town on ground that wasn't constantly moving from side to side. Nevertheless, she looked pale and drawn as she linked arms with Lizzy and gave a final wave to her husband before turning away from the quayside.

He had to admit to himself that the colour had returned to her cheeks by the time they met up at the bottom of the gangplank. They were to sleep on board tonight, but before that there was a dinner planned at the captain's table with the Dannay Shipping Company's representative in Fremantle and his wife and daughter.

The conversation was convivial over the dinner

table. Dannay's man in Fremantle, Mr Israel Eaton, turned out to be a portly gentleman with many a story to tell about the comings and goings of the busy port. Guy was pleased to see Amelie and Lizzy laughing at these stories and enjoying conversation with Mrs Eaton and her daughter, Louisa. Lizzy was thrilled to discover that Louisa had a skill for lace-making too and even more excited when she promised to send a spare bobbin on board the next day, so that Lizzy could use it as a pattern to have more made.

"Of course, you will need a pin cushion for your knee and some tiny pins and thread too," explained Louisa's mother.

The following morning, armed with a shopping list, Lizzy set off for the haberdasher's shop again. She was concerned that Amelie had declined to join her today, declaring that she had found the warm sunshine a little too much the previous day and would be spending the morning in her cabin.

To her delight, Lizzy found Mrs Eaton and Louisa inside the tiny shop buying a supply of wool for stockings. Mrs Eaton explained to Lizzy that they both knitted socks for the young convicts, who often arrived in bare feet with nothing but the tattered clothes they were wearing. Louisa helped Lizzy to select some fine thread for making lace, a tin of short end pins and a sheet of pricking card to mark out the patterns. She suggested that Lizzy wait until she reached her destination before getting a board and cushion made to fit her knees. As they left the shop, Louisa handed Lizzy an envelope containing a spare bobbin made of a soft, dark wood and weighted down with a string of cloudy blue beads. Lizzy held the bobbin in her hand for a moment. It felt soft and tactile, a thing of great beauty, even though it was a mere tool in the process of making lace. She thanked Louisa for the gift and promised to keep in touch by letter once they reached New Zealand.

As they made their farewells, Mrs Eaton asked, "Is Mrs Pender not with you today?"

"No," answered Lizzy, "she was not feeling well this morning. I think the sun is a little strong for her."

"Hmm," replied Mrs Eaton, after a moment's thought. "I rather think the sun is her excuse to stay inside. One comes to recognise the signs, and I think perhaps she is with child."

"Oh, goodness me," was Lizzy's flustered reply. "Perhaps you are right."

"I do hope so," said Mrs Eaton, "and I look forward to hearing news of a safe arrival. Now let me see, if my calculations are right, I daresay it may be an Easter baby."

CHAPTER SEVENTEEN
Christchurch

New Zealand - November 1867

During the three week voyage from Fremantle to Lyttelton, Amelie managed to hide her pregnancy behind a facade of sea sickness. She was almost certain that she carried Guy's child in her belly, but was determined to keep it from him until she was sure. When she retired to her cabin again, as soon as the Roaring Forties took hold of the ship and tossed it around, Guy thought no more of it than to assume her sea sickness had returned. Lizzy, however, could not be fooled so easily and had recounted her conversation with Mrs Eaton.

"I wonder how she can tell?" Amelie pondered.

"I suppose there is a glow about you that wasn't there before," said Lizzy. "However she can tell, I am so pleased for you and excited to welcome a child into our new lives."

"But we must keep it quiet for now," said Amelie. "I would prefer to wait until we are sure before I tell Guy."

"Of course," replied Lizzy. "Though I will find it hard to keep silent."

Amelie had gone on to say that she would stay in her cabin for the last part of the journey, something that would not be a surprise to Guy as he was expecting rough seas. Not for the first time, Amelie blessed her mother for the conversations they had shared before the wedding. At least she now knew a little of what to expect, and she could face the next few months with a little less trepidation than would have been the case had she not learned so much from her mother. If the child had come about on her wedding night, then Mrs Eaton may well be right that it would be born around Easter time. Given that, she hoped she would begin to see a thickening of her waist by the time they came in sight of the New Zealand coast, and if that was the case, she would break the news to her husband before they docked. To some extent, she was nervous of telling him at all. Beginning a new life half a world away from home was hard enough, but she would be adding to the disruption by her confinement.

She need not have been concerned. After a rough journey in the latitudes below Australia and across the Tasman Sea, it was a relief to everyone when land was sighted. Even those who had been confined to their berths with sea sickness made it up on deck, gathering by the rail to see the grey line of the land they would soon call home, as it grew clearer on the horizon.

That morning, for the first time, Lizzy had struggled to tie Amelie's corsets and to button up her dress.

"These will need letting out soon," she said.

"I know," replied Amelie, "and I think we can be sure we know the reason for my growing belly. Perhaps today it is time to tell Guy."

As the three of them stood together watching the land come closer, a huge black and white seabird flew gracefully by, its long wingtips almost touching the water.

"An albatross!" shouted Guy, pointing as the bird sailed close to the ship's hull. "A sign of good luck. What a graceful creature he is!"

They watched entranced as the majestic bird sailed over the waves, not a single beat of its wings required to keep it in the air.

"They spend almost all their lives on the wing," Guy continued, "Landing only to breed, and they have but one partner throughout their long lives."

Sensing that this was the perfect moment to give Guy her news, Amelie glanced sideways at Lizzy, who knew it was time for her to leave the couple alone to talk. She walked along the deck as the bird flew almost beside her, so close that she could see his enormous beak and piercing eyes before he broke away, skimming across the waves. Lizzy kept her eyes on the bird until it was nothing more than a tiny dot against the ocean.

Meanwhile, Amelie had taken Guy's hands in hers. Hesitatingly, she said, "Guy, my darling, we are just like the albatross, aren't we?"

Guy laughed and replied, "Yes, I hope we will be together for all our lives as well."

"Yes, of course," said Amelie. "But we are also landing for the same reason."

It took a moment for Guy to understand what Amelie was saying in her convoluted way. What did she mean about landing for the same reason?

His puzzled look made Amelie smile to herself, but then she could see his expression change as it all fell into place in his mind. Her recent sickness, the pallor of her face, and now he came to look at it, her thickening waist.

"What?" he said, "Do you mean....?"

"Yes, that is exactly what I mean, Guy," replied Amelie with a smile, as she placed Guy's hands on her growing belly. "I am with child."

"Oh my goodness!" said Guy, breaking away from her and taking a few steps along the deck. He needed time to take in this news. Then he turned back towards her, took her in his arms and whirled her round and round. The other passengers watched on in amazement at this show of affection. When Guy announced to everyone that he was to be a father, there was a spontaneous round of applause, which caused Amelie's cheeks to blush, a sharp contrast to her usually pale features.

"Oh my goodness," he said again. "Oh, Amelie, I love you so much, and I am so excited that we will start our new life with a family. Our son will grow up in paradise."

"She may be our daughter," laughed Amelie.

"I don't care, as long as he or she is ours and is happy and healthy," replied Guy, continuing to hold onto his wife as if she may fall overboard if he let go. Suddenly, he stopped twirling her around in circles and said, "But, Amelie, I must look after you. You should rest, for the baby's sake."

"Now Guy," said Amelie, with a stern expression on her face. "Before our marriage my mother told me what to expect when I carried your child. And the thing she told me to remember most of all is that it is not an illness. It is a blessing that a young, fit woman should suffer without the need to be shut away for the duration. Sunshine, good food and exercise are all of benefit to our child, and I hope to take advantage of all those things once we get off this wretched ship."

Guy laughed out loud. "Patience, my dear, it will not be long now. Look how you can already see trees and waterfalls along the coast. We sail in sight of the coast in calmer waters now and will be in Lyttelton before you know it. Now, whatever your mother says, you must come below so that you can sit down and rest for a while." With that, he proudly led his wife past the gathering of other passengers and down to their cabins.

In no time at all they were approaching Lyttelton harbour. Perhaps, because they had the ever-changing landscape to show the passage of time, the last few days of the journey passed very quickly. Travelling chests had been packed, last minute items gathered together into their valise cases and decisions made about their travelling outfits. Amelie and Lizzy had, at first, laid out their warm woollen dresses and a cape, as they would have done in November in Europe. But, of course, the summer was approaching here, and so cooler cotton clothing had to be found instead, with a shawl for the evenings and a wide brimmed hat to keep the sun off their faces.

The 'Felicity' drew gracefully into her regular berth at the port of Lyttelton on fourteenth day of November 1867. The passengers who travelled in cabins were able to disembark as soon as the anchor was dropped and the gangplank put in place. Those in steerage, of which there were a good deal more than on the higher decks, were forced to wait below in semi-darkness before reaching dry land, their eyes streaming in the unexpected sunlight as they made their way on deck. By that time, Guy, Amelie and Lizzy were being made welcome in the Dannay Shipping Company offices. So far, New Zealand seemed very similar to England as far as the ladies were concerned, but Guy assured them that they would soon see more of the countryside and possibly the native people, once they got away from the busy port.

Before they left Lyttelton, there were some things that needed to be done. Amelie had written letters to her family to tell them about her condition and these could now go into the mailbag to be sent via the 'Felicity' back to England. There was mail for them to collect too, including a short note from Dorcas Paget. Guy had written to the Pagets not long before the wedding, to let them know about his new bride and to give them the glad tidings of his return to New Zealand. His plan had been to spend a night or two in an hotel in Christchurch, a town which had grown bigger since his last visit, before heading south to stay with the Pagets in Rhodestown. From there it was a mere day's travel inland to Marytown, where he felt sure they would be made welcome overnight at Betsy Franks' shop before beginning the climb into the basin the next day. They should easily reach Applecross before Christmas.

However, he had not accounted for the short but difficult journey to Christchurch. Had they arrived but a week or two later they would have had the luxury of a short train journey through the newly built tunnel. Instead, they had to brave the arduous journey over steep terrain on a narrow path hewn out of the solid rock and clinging to the edge of the cliffs. As they made their slow and painstaking way along this treacherous route, Guy told them the story of James Mackenzie's part in the building of the road while he was imprisoned for a crime he did not commit.

It was well into the evening before they reached level ground and Guy was thankful that Dorcas Paget's note had instructed him to join them at their Christchurch home, rather than an hotel. Noah Paget had a business interest in the new railway and in the building of the tunnel, and they had come up to the city to be amongst the first passengers to make the rail journey back to Lyttelton in a few weeks time.

Just as Guy expected, Dorcas and Noah made wonderful hosts, pleased to see Guy again and thrilled to meet Amelie and Lizzy. Dorcas flapped and fussed around the ladies like a mother hen, and even more so when she heard Amelie's news. In Guy's opinion, Lizzy and Amelie were in need of being mothered and it was the perfect solution for their first few days in New Zealand, while they recovered from the journey and got to know their surroundings.

After an early night, Guy rose swiftly to take advantage of the long, light days. He found Noah already at the breakfast table, and after they had eaten, the two men took a walk from the house, which lay to the side of the huge Hagley Park, into the centre of the town. Passing down the street, Guy was surprised to see most of the houses boarded up, their gardens overgrown with new spring growth, obviously untended for some time.

"It is as a result of the storm," explained Noah Paget. "In July the country suffered the worst snow in memory, bringing everything to a halt for several weeks. There were dreadful losses of stock, leading to equally dreadful losses of income and investment. Many of our neighbours have gone in search of riches elsewhere."

"Were they badly affected at Applecross?" asked Guy. He had a sudden image of the place being abandoned to the weather, not at all as he had described it to Amelie.

"They lost animals," said Noah, "to be sure, but James is a wise man and had made time to bring the majority of his flock near the homestead. I will leave them to tell the full story when you reach Applecross, but you may find them in disarray. They lost a fine tree to the weight of snow, it causing some damage to the house. Sophia has insisted on some renovations!"

"I'll bet she has!" replied Guy with a smile. "James may not approve of spending money on it, but he will do as he is told, no doubt." The two men laughed.

"As you will find out now you are a married man, that is the way of a woman," said Noah, clapping his friend on the back.

They continued their walk through the park, taking the bridge over the meandering river and into the centre of town. Guy could not help thinking he had travelled all around the world, only to end up in England again. The layout of the place was as familiar as any English town, and the people they met wore just the same styles as those he had seen in Southampton, despite the distinctly un-English climate. He saw more than one gentleman reaching for a handkerchief to mop their brow. Even at this early hour there was the promise of a hot day to come.

Reaching what Noah said was the centre of town, they found a statue of a man overlooking an almost empty square. To one side a building had been started, something quite big by the look of the foundations. Noah explained that the statue had been recently erected and was in honour of John Godley, who had founded the Canterbury Association, bringing new migrants to the area. A grand unveiling had happened only a few days ago, and Guy could see that the bronze, cast in the foundries of Shropshire according to Noah, had not had time to tarnish. It glistened magnificently in the sun. Noah went on to say that the building Guy had seen was to be the cathedral, though money had run out with nothing more than the foundation stones to show for it. He said that he was hopeful of progress in the town. It was a small place now, but, with the support of some forward thinking men, he thought the town would become a great city in the future, and that the cathedral would be completed soon and would be a great symbol of its wealth.

Guy could appreciate what Noah was saying, but wondered why in God's name someone had chosen a flat and seemingly swamp-like place to build a town, especially as the journey from port to town was fraught with so many problems in getting over the steep, volcanic hills between the two. But, as Noah pointed out, the new tunnel would solve that problem, bringing the port closer to the town with a mere six minutes of train travel.

"I am hoping to persuade you to stay for the first journey for passengers on that train in three weeks, on the ninth of December," said Noah. "It will give the ladies some time to acclimatise, and you may still reach Applecross for Christmas."

"Well," replied Guy, "it is not what I intended, but I see no reason why we should not stay longer here. Though I would like Amelie to reach Applecross before travel becomes a problem in her condition."

"Mrs Paget will be delighted to look after your wife, I am sure," said Noah. "She enjoys having someone to care for. And we can all travel back to Rhodestown together. Though I must tell you that, more often than not, we call it Timaru these days. Samuel Morling should be with us by then. You remember Samuel? Sophia Mackenzie's brother? He has become something of an asset to me lately and is due to arrive here today, having been dealing with some railway business on my behalf in a place called Rangiora, to the north."

"It will be most pleasant to meet him again," said Guy. "I am glad to hear he is doing well after the loss of his wife and the injury to his arm."

"We see a lot of him these days," said Noah. "He has come a long way since he turned up on my doorstep with the money he had made from finding gold. I knew then that he had the makings of a businessman, and in many ways he has taken the place of the son we lost to that dreadful war. It pleases my wife too that he brings young Caroline and Samuel with him, and sometimes little Lily, when he stays with us at Hither House. Perhaps you will bring your family to stay with us soon too? Once you have made a decision about where you will live, that is."

"I look forward to that very much indeed, sir," replied Guy. "I have spent much of the voyage trying to decide what to do with the rest of my life, and I have reached no definite decision yet. It is, of course, made harder by having a wife and child to consider too. We will live at Applecross, if Sophia and Nancy will allow us to do so. How I spend my days? Well, I am not sure. I just know I wish to be of some use as a settler, to contribute something to the future of this land."

"Well said, young man," replied Noah, clapping Guy on the back. "I don't blame you for wanting to let your child grow up in that paradise, but don't forget to come and see us occasionally. My study door is always open if you have a notion to get involved in opening up this young country. Not only will the railways enable better transport links for goods leaving our shores, they will provide the opportunity for people to reach places like Applecross more easily. I see a boom in travelling for leisure, for those with the money to do so, at least."

Guy was not sure that he wanted to share his piece of paradise with anyone else, although there was little hope of halting progress with men like Noah Paget involved. He chose to give a non-committal reply, "We will see, but I will certainly consider your idea, thank you."

As the two gentlemen talked, they had been making their way back home. Reaching the front door, it occurred to Guy that things had changed in the six years he had been away. Everyone was six years older, and Samuel's business had, by all accounts, thrived. He wondered what other changes he would find at Applecross. He could hardly wait to see everyone again, but these days he had to think of his wife too, and she would appreciate the company of the Pagets for a while before he took her off into the wilds of the high country basin. He was certainly excited about seeing Samuel again. The two of them had become good friends all those years ago.

The ladies had the same idea as Guy and Noah. The men found Amelie and Lizzy putting their sunhats on in the hall before taking a stroll around the park. Dorcas Paget was keen to show them around, but had warned them to use the relative coolness of the morning for their walk. By midday they would find it best to stay indoors at this time of the year.

Guy had time to thank Dorcas for making his wife and Lizzy so welcome already. She replied, patting his hands, "It is a pleasure to have some female conversation again. You men have nothing to talk about but money and engines. Though I make an exception for you, dear Guy. I have missed your company these last few years."

With that, the three ladies turned towards the town in search of a tea shop. Guy watched them proudly, a feeling of contentment pouring over his soul. It was good to be back.

Samuel arrived in time for luncheon and just before the ladies returned from their walk. It was a most pleasant reunion. Samuel congratulated Guy on his marriage and then felt in his jacket for a letter he had carried from Applecross. Guy was just about to read it when the ladies appeared, so he put it in his pocket, promising himself the chance to read it after lunch. A cold buffet had been laid out in the dining room with the doors opened onto the garden to keep the room cool. As there were just the six of them, they piled their plates with food and took their seats under the verandah at two round tables. It was yet another reminder to Guy that things tended to be more relaxed in New Zealand. Eating luncheon with guests in England or Switzerland would generally be a much more formal affair. He glanced across at Amelie, who had taken a seat with Dorcas and Noah. She appeared to be dealing with the situation very well indeed. That left Guy to sit down with Samuel and Lizzy. Guy knew that Lizzy would cope with whatever was thrown at her and the less formal the better, he suspected.

In six years, Samuel had become used to meeting new people and making polite conversation at the regular events organised by the Pagets for their business acquaintances. Usually, he found himself able to talk easily, often finding himself being listened to, his opinions valued by his fellow diners. Today, however, he found himself tongue tied and ignorant, the heat of the day making him red in the face and having a need to loosen his stiff collar every few minutes. It was all Lizzy Berry's fault. There had been a formal introduction, of course. He had admired Guy's choice of a wife at once. Amelie was just beautiful. And then Amelie had introduced her companion, Lizzy Berry.

"I am pleased to meet you, Samuel Morling," she had said in an accent he recognised as coming from London, and then disarmingly, "I hear you have three lovely children. I can't wait to meet them all."

It had quite taken the wind out of his sails, and the final blow came when their eyes met. Was this what they called love at first sight? Whatever it was, he now seemed incapable of forming a sentence, aware of his fluttering heartbeat under his shirt and even more aware that Guy was laughing at him from across the table.

Guy was indeed smiling to himself. Only a fool would fail to notice the instant attraction between these two, and although it was somewhat unexpected, he was thrilled to see it. It was early days, but maybe, just maybe, his prediction that Lizzy would find herself a man in New Zealand was coming true. She deserved it, and he knew that Samuel would be a most suitable match.

After they had eaten, Guy left Samuel and Lizzy to talk while he strolled into the garden, leaning against a tree for shade while he read Sophia's letter. As he read, he could hear her voice saying the words she had written :-

Dearest Guy

We cannot wait for your visit. To see you again, of course, but more importantly to meet your new wife. We know already that she is lovely, or you would not have married her, but we are so looking forward to welcoming her to Applecross. Nancy is very excited too, and Lucy sends her love.

There is a room set aside for you whenever you arrive, though you will find us in the midst of a muddle with the changes being made here. No matter, we will manage, even if I have to send James to sleep in the stables.

Now, you mention Lizzy in your letter. She is, of course, welcome too. But tell me, how should we greet her? Is she your wife Amelie's maid? I love the name

Amelie, by the way, with such a nice name she must be a nice person.

Samuel will deliver this letter to you, and tells me you may stay in Christchurch to see a tunnel being opened. I am sure it will be interesting and that you may take a photograph of it with your equipment. Perhaps you have time to answer my question regarding Lizzy. The postal service will get a reply to me before you arrive, I daresay. If you send it on a postcard Betsy Franks will read it as it passes through Marytown, which will save me letting her know. You know how she likes to be aware of our comings and goings.

Oh, Guy, you do not know how much we have missed you all this time. Come soon, and bring your lovely new wife with you.

*Yours with love,
Sophia Mackenzie*

Guy wiped a most ungentlemanly tear from the corner of his eye. Sophia wrote just as if she was standing in front of him and speaking, her words bringing all his feelings for Applecross back. Now he knew why he had been so homesick. How could you not be so, when it was obvious you had been missed? He would write back straight away, on a postcard so that Betsy Franks could read it too. After all, they may need a bed for the night there too. He rather thought he would wait to tell them news of the baby. He knew they would all be excited about another birth in the basin, especially Nancy. He wondered how many more babies Nancy had added to her family since he left. He would soon find out.

Over the next few days they all fell into something of a routine. The day began with a walk, sometimes the gentlemen and ladies went their separate ways, sometimes they all walked together. It was not uncommon for the six of them to walk in pairs, Mr and Mrs Paget, Guy and Amelie, followed by the two new lovebirds, Samuel and Lizzy. By the time the sun reached its zenith it was too hot to be outside, so a long lunchtime was taken. In the afternoons the ladies took to their sewing or reading. Samuel and Noah would, more often than not, have business to see to, and Guy could be found in Noah's study catching up on the correspondence he had received once they docked.

There had been quite a pile of letters to attend to, apart from Sophia's note. He had passed on another long letter from Amelie's mother and had been amused to find it, dog-eared from being read over and over, open on the dressing table in their bedroom. Frau von Truber was looking forward to hearing news of becoming a grandmother soon, but was sad that she would not be able to be there to see such a child born. Guy laughed to think that the letter had crossed with Amelie's message to say that, indeed, Frau von Truber would be a grandmother very soon indeed. He was saddened to read that there had been no news of Amelie's father in recent weeks, and they were all concerned for his welfare.

Wilfred Dannay had written to Guy, who had chosen not to tell Amelie that the letter contained news of Herr Linburg. A case of murder had indeed been put together against the man, along with the attempted murder of Guy Pender, even though it was others who had done the deed on his behalf. However, when the time came to make an arrest, Herr Linburg had been found to have left the country. Wilfred was of the opinion that his parents had got wind of the details of the crime, and not wishing to have their name dishonoured, they had sent Tobias across the Atlantic to their cocoa plantations in the Americas. The police in Switzerland would be taking no further action against him, whereas those who had actually perpetrated the crimes, albeit under Linburg's instructions, would be punished accordingly and were expected to face execution. Guy could not shake off the image of that awful thug's head rolling around in the dirt, severed from its body with a sword.

Edward Wingfield's letter contained news of a much happier tone, as it gave details of the date of his marriage to Amelie's sister, which would take place just after the following Easter. Edward said that Augusta was missing her sister more than he expected, but that arrangements for the ceremony and for her to take over her role in running the estate had kept her busy so far. Much to Guy's delight, he also mentioned that they were considering a visit to New Zealand, having heard that the route may be shortened soon by the opening of a canal into the Arabian Sea at Suez.

There was a letter from Reverend Bestwick too, informing him that a young couple had taken up residence in the cottage belonging to Guy and would, as per Guy's instructions, pay a peppercorn rent directly to the church. Guy was pleased that the cottage could provide someone in need with a home and pleased that the small income would benefit the church where he had married Amelie.

The final letter was in a hand he did not recognise, but was marked with the stamp of Zurich. It turned out to be from Luigi, although it had taken Amelie's language skills to help him decipher it. She had written an English translation which Guy read with great delight. Luigi and his wife had moved into the apartment almost immediately, apparently. All together in one room to begin with. However, the staircase had been installed, meaning that the entrance to the studio now formed their front door, and a wall had been built across the downstairs room. In this way, they had a downstairs living room and only needed to go upstairs to sleep. The very front of the studio was reserved for Luigi to set up a few tables to serve coffee alongside cakes made by his friend, Monsieur Le Fevre. It was a start, but Luigi added that he and Leon were already talking to the bookseller who rented the shop between their two homes, with a view to opening a much grander cafe, rivalling the one across the square. Luigi ended by passing on Leon's regards and sending his love and eternal gratitude to Guy and Amelie. There was a postscript that made Guy laugh out loud. It said simply that 'Albert puts up with my son's grabbing hands and is getting fat on Le Fevre's baking.'

Lovely as it was to hear news from his past, Guy couldn't wait to finish his journey to Applecross now. He was resigned to kicking his heels until the tunnel opening ceremony, but would be glad to get started as soon as possible after that.

CHAPTER EIGHTEEN
The Last Leg

December 1867

Amelie declared herself well and truly tired of travelling by train so she had decided to stay at home on the morning of the grand opening. Lizzy had, somewhat reluctantly, offered to stay with her, but Amelie insisted that she accompany the Pagets, Guy and Samuel. Amelie knew how much Lizzy was looking forward to spending some more time with Samuel.

The five of them joined a crowd of people on the platform at Heathcote. Samuel and Noah, who were business acquaintances of the people involved in its construction, had already travelled through the tunnel and back, but today was the first day that tickets could be purchased by the general public. Lizzy was, of course, quite used to trains after their journey across Europe, but she let out a startled cry when the carriage entered the total darkness of the tunnel. Guy smiled to himself as they came out into the daylight at the Lyttelton end and Samuel hastily let go of Lizzy's hand.

The journey was all over in just a few minutes, but there were speeches and celebrations on the Lyttelton platform before their return journey. A band played as the train drew to a halt and there were crowds of interested onlookers cheering and waving flags. Noah and Samuel were thrilled with the journey, and even Guy, who saw transport merely as a means to go from one place to another, had to admit it was an achievement. The construction had gone on longer than expected because the first company to work on it had hit hard rock, declared it impenetrable, packed up their tools and gone back to England. However, an Australian company had subsequently agreed to give it a try, and found they were able to drill through the volcanic rock. Guy was most impressed to hear that the workers from both ends of the tunnel had met exactly in the middle and within a day of breaking through had made a hole big enough to step through.

They all boarded the train for the return journey and were home again in time for lunch. Noah and Samuel talked excitedly about the connection of the tunnel to the railway line being built in Christchurch and of their plans to be involved in a line to run the length of the island. They had high hopes for it becoming a fast and reliable way for goods to be transported into the country and exports, particularly wool, to be sent to the port before being shipped out to the rest of the world.

Guy kicked his heels for the last afternoon, restless to get moving now. He had considered taking some photographs of the morning's events, but in the end had decided not to unpack all his equipment, only to have to pack it all away immediately. Sophia would have to make do with a copy of the following day's newspaper. He must remember to buy a copy in the morning.

It took him no time at all to have his bags packed. This was not the case for the ladies of the household who fussed and flapped all afternoon in order to have everything put away. In the end, Guy left them to it and took a final walk around the growing town. It was not a place he felt drawn to, preferring the hills to the flat plains of Canterbury. But there were positive signs of growth everywhere, despite the temporary setback caused by the snow in July. You couldn't help but feel the town was set to blossom into a major centre very soon. Give it ten years, Guy felt, and it could very well outstrip Dunedin as the South Island's major town, especially as there was now a practical route to and from the nearby port of Lyttelton.

They were all set to travel back to Timaru together, though Samuel would be on horseback. It would be quite a squash in the Paget's carriage for five people, but one of the gentlemen could always join their footman, who was to drive a cart with all the baggage on board, if things got a bit uncomfortable. They set off as early as they could to avoid the heat, and by a lunchtime they had reached the Rakaia river. For the most part the road now ran alongside the beginning of a railway line, not yet in use, but all part of the route to Timaru, and beyond. The wide river beds running at right angles to the route, formed by numerous fast flowing streams and banks of gravel, were a major barrier to construction, and Noah told Guy that financing the building of bridges was one of their biggest concerns for the completion of the project.

How things had changed in only six years. Guy noted that the road was flatter and wider, and the carriage in which they travelled faster and more comfortable than anything he had used in his previous journeys around New Zealand. They made good progress on their first day, crossing the river without incident and reaching Ashburton as dusk fell.

Amelie and Lizzy had found the river crossing to be quite alarming. Dorcas assured them that, despite the carriage lurching from side to side, the horses knew how to pick their way between the deep pools of water, and the coachman was experienced in navigating through the safest route. Despite this, the ladies were alarmed to hear that they had another river to cross at Rangitata the following day. Guy kept quiet about the occasions when horses were swept away by the floods and carriages tipped into the racing waters in the major rivers along this route. In the early days, the settlers saw so many drownings at such crossings that they christened it 'The New Zealand death'. It was no comfort for Amelie to hear that bridges would soon be constructed across all these rivers, as she had no intention of returning this way, if it could be avoided.

A pleasant night was spent in a tavern at Ashburton, followed by as early a start as possible. The Rangitata crossing went smoothly, despite the ladies' concerns, and they made it to Hither House without incident, Guy travelling the last leg on the board seat next to the footman, partly to give the passengers a bit more room in the carriage, and partly to afford him a better view of the mountains inland. Tomorrow's journey would take them in that direction.

Hither House was just as Guy remembered it, and

he felt very much at home there. This time, however, he slept in the main guest room overlooking the sea, with Amelie by his side. Visiting the lavatory across the corridor he was suddenly accosted by a memory of Frewin staying here too. "Goodness," he thought to himself, "I haven't thought about Frewin for a very long time." He would try to remember to ask Noah if they had heard from him at all, assuming of course that he was still in New Zealand. He wished him no ill these days and blamed himself entirely for his poor reaction to Frewin's advances. No doubt, with some more experience in life generally, he could well have treated him quite differently. He hoped he had found happiness now.

Getting back into bed, he asked Amelie, "Are you happy, my darling? Are you beginning to love this country as much as I do?"

"My darling, you know I would be happy wherever we go, as long as we are together," replied Amelie. "Yes, I am beginning to see why you love it so much. It is the people who make it, in my opinion. Perhaps because they all come from overseas, they appear not to make any judgments about background or class. I find it refreshing that they are so friendly, relaxed and happy to welcome strangers in their midst."

"Yes, that's true," said Guy, considering the matter before he lay his head on the pillow next to his wife. "Though you have to wait another day or two before we meet the best of them."

Amelie had read Sophia's letter and could tell at once from her words that they were going to be great friends. It was all so new and different, and she had the added burden of a growing belly, but she was truly beginning to see why this place was so special to Guy. In truth, she couldn't wait to stay still in one place for a while. They had been travelling in one way or another for many months, and she was tired of sleeping in different beds, getting used to new ways of doing things and generally being on the move all the time.

As she lay her head down, she said, "I can't wait to get to Applecross, if only so that we don't need to go anywhere else for a while."

Guy laughed, "Oh, I agree. It will be very pleasant to stay in one place at last, but we have just a little further to go yet, and I have saved the best until last." He planted a gentle kiss on his beloved wife's cheek before settling down next to her.

Amelie had to agree that the road to Marytown was indeed a most pleasant route, although it was not the most comfortable seat next to Guy as he drove the open cart gently uphill towards the mountains. The weather was warm and the two ladies held parasols over their heads to keep the bright sun from their fair skin. Lizzy had been very quiet since they set off, and Amelie guessed correctly that she was already missing Samuel.

The two of them had said a fond farewell on the steps of Hither House, although it was not for long because Samuel would be at Applecross for Christmas.

"I wouldn't dare miss an Applecross Christmas," he said, "Sophia would never speak to me again!"

"I still don't know how you can have Christmas in the summer," replied Lizzy. "It all seems very strange."

"Ah, you will get used to our upside down ways," said Samuel, with a laugh. "And we sometimes have another Christmas in June, just so that we can remember our roots."

Guy and Amelie looked on as the two laughed together about something Samuel had said. They were both delighted at the relationship and were hoping it would flourish into a proposal of marriage one day soon.

Samuel stood with Noah and Dorcas on the steps, waving a final goodbye as the cart disappeared down the drive. In his pocket was the wooden bobbin that Lizzy had been given in Fremantle. He knew exactly what he would give her as a gift at Christmas, but it would mean a fair bit of work with his tools. He had some things to do in Timaru, gifts to buy for his family, and he must find some coloured beads to add to the bobbins he would make. Then he would follow Lizzy, Guy and Amelie up the valley to Marytown. In the workshop attached to his tiny cottage there, he had all the necessary tools, and he had just about enough time to get it all done before Christmas morning.

Guy could hardly contain his excitement as they approached the small settlement of Marytown. Not much had changed while he had been away, perhaps the odd new house here and there, but he took the cart straight into the centre of the village and came to a halt in front of Betsy Franks' shop. He hardly had time to get down from the cart before Betsy came rushing out of the shop, wiping her hands on her apron.

"Oh Mr Pender," she said, "How wonderful to see you again!"

Guy helped Lizzy and Amelie down before replying, "Mrs Franks, why you have not changed a bit in six years, still as lovely as ever."

It was what Betsy liked about Guy Pender. He was so polite and always managed to make you feel special in some way.

Guy was glad he had written a separate letter to Betsy, rather than just assume she would read Sophia's postcard. So she knew already that Amelie was with child, and that Lizzy and Samuel had taken something of a fancy to each other.

Betsy Franks chivvied her visitors out of the sun and into the cool atmosphere inside the shop. Her husband Edgar was introduced, and standing tall behind the counter was young Joshua, no longer a lanky boy, but now a handsome young man with an air of confidence about him. Guy shook hands warmly with them both before introducing his wife and Lizzy. Guy had warned the ladies about Betsy's baking, but even he was taken aback by the huge pile of cakes and biscuits on the table in the parlour. Betsy had been busy all morning baking all of Guy's favourites.

There were many memories for Guy in the shop. He had been there for celebrations and for sad occasions too. He felt very comfortable at Betsy's table, and he could see Amelie and Lizzy relaxing as they got used to the pleasant atmosphere that Betsy offered all her guests. Nothing was too much trouble and there were no airs and graces. It didn't matter that Lizzy automatically rose to help serve the tea, neither did it matter that Amelie could hardly manage a bite of anything.

The rest of the afternoon flew by while Guy caught up with all the gossip and Amelie and Lizzy listened in. They were beginning to realise that Marytown, although isolated by geography, was by no means a backwater. There was lots going on, and it was a prosperous settlement, due mainly to the success of the wool industry.

Amelie took to her bed straight after supper, but it was Betsy who followed her to her room to make sure she was comfortable.

"Now, my dear," said Betsy, sitting on Amelie and Guy's bed and patting the cover to encourage Amelie to sit down beside her. "You must be exhausted, and I wouldn't wonder if your mind and body are confused by all this travelling and meeting new people. But please remember that we all love your husband, and we are very happy to know he has found such a wonderful wife. You are welcome here, and we know you will be very happy."

It was a long speech for Betsy, but one which Amelie appreciated very much indeed.

"Thank you, Mrs Franks," she replied, "I am tired, both from the journey, and from carrying this child around with me." She put both hands on her growing belly before continuing, "Despite my weariness, I feel as though I have reached home. I left my family behind to come here, but I find I have a new one who are making me welcome. Thank you."

It was the kindest thing that Amelie could have said to Betsy Franks. Feeling like the old fool that she was, Betsy wiped away a tear with her handkerchief. If she had ever had a daughter, she would want her to be like this young lady, that was for sure. Pulling herself together, she stood, straightened her apron and said, "Now, sleep my dear. Sleep as long as you need. Tomorrow you get to meet the rest of your family."

Amelie needed no further instructions. By the time Guy joined her, some hours later having spent a pleasant evening in Edgar's company, Amelie was sleeping peacefully. Guy thought she looked more relaxed than he had seen for a long time.

Meanwhile, Lizzy had her bed made up on the red couch that had been the overnight haven of many a visitor over the years. It felt to Lizzy like the softest and most comfortable bed she had ever slept in, and she lay awake savouring the absolute silence of the night. It was so unlike her childhood home where it was never quiet, with ships coming and going and people always passing by in the street below their one room apartment. She could hardly believe she was here, half way across the globe, in a comfortable bed, amongst friends, and in love with a man she had known for such a short time. Her dreams were full of that man and her hopes for their future together.

The day dawned early at this time of the year and Guy was not going to waste a single moment of it. Leaving Amelie to sleep peacefully, he joined Betsy and Edgar at the breakfast table while Joshua prepared the shop for opening. The first customer was Jane Hartley with her son, Percy who had taken over Joshua's job as post boy. Neither Jane nor Percy had made themselves popular in Marytown when they first arrived, but that was a long time ago now, and Percy had grown into a strong boy with a willingness to work hard and to turn his hand to any task. Jane was pleased to hear about Guy's return with a wife, but her attitude changed when Betsy mentioned Lizzy had accompanied Amelie, and that they had all met up with Samuel in Christchurch. Guy wondered if Jane had put two and two together. Perhaps she had designs on Samuel for herself. He hoped there would not be any ill feeling between the women. Fortunately, Jane had left the shop before Lizzy appeared, apologising for sleeping in so late in her comfortable bed.

There were letters for Applecross and Combe stations, so Guy agreed to take them with him, to save Percy the long walk. Although these days, he rode a horse up and back saving a good few hours on the journey. Edgar told Guy that the journey into the basin would be a lot easier than the last time he had been that way. The track was well-trodden now and wide enough for carts to meet and pass each other. Which perhaps, was just as well because it was quite late in the morning before Amelie was out of her bed. She blamed the mountain air for her good sleep, but Guy was inclined to think it was more a matter of her feeling relaxed at last.

So began the final leg of their long journey, splashing over the main river before turning up the valley. They passed the place where Guy said Sophia and her first husband had built their home, and where George was drowned in the swollen river. Then a little further up was Nancy and Edmund Lawton's abandoned home, now little more than a ruin. There was still plenty of melt water in the stream and the trees were fully in leaf, their branches full of birds of all kinds. Many were familiar to Amelie and Lizzy, a welcome reminder of home. The ground dwelling birds were not of a type they recognised, particularly the weka, who Lizzy said resembled a duck's head on a pheasant's body. Guy laughed at her description and added that they made a very tasty bird for the table too.

With every passing mile Guy was feeling more and more excited about seeing his Applecross friends. He was driving the horse on as much as he could on the steep incline until Amelie put her hand on his and said, "Give the horse a rest, my dear. We could stop here for a moment." She pointed at a flat and grassy area next to the stream, a perfect place for a picnic lunch.

It was a good place to stop for a rest. The horse took a long drink while standing up to its fetlocks in the river, and Amelie and Lizzy laid out the fresh bread and cheese that Betsy had provided for them. It reminded them all of the picnic lunch they had eaten on the mountain just before the avalanche. What a long time ago that seemed to be now! So much had happened since that fateful day.

Guy helped Amelie to her feet while Lizzy packed the food away, before turning to harness the horse again. The cold water had done its work to cool the animal down, which was just as well because the sun was now high in the sky. Amelie and Lizzy had found their parasols, and Guy was pleased to sit under the circles of shade cast by them as he pushed the horse on over the last mile or so to the summit.

How many times had he drawn the cart to a stop at that summit, he wondered? How the place had grown too, since his original visit, not knowing, that first time, what kind of welcome he would receive. Then there was the day he brought that dreadful Drummond fellow to see Lucy. Even he had been impressed by the view from the top. This time, he noticed more buildings had been constructed around both homesteads. The community seemed to be growing faster than he expected.

He automatically pulled the horse to a halt at the very top, just before they began the downward descent into the farm. Jumping down, he reached to hand Lizzy down, and then his wife.

From down below, standing at the door of Applecross Station, Sophia saw three silhouettes against the skyline. She knew it was Guy immediately, and her heart leapt at seeing him again. She was so excited to meet the ladies too. She just knew they would all be friends immediately. Nancy Lawton joined her in coming up the path to meet them, James, Edmund and the older boys could be seen downing their tools in the field and walking in the same direction, the working dogs milling around their masters. Guy could hear their urgent barks from where he stood. Then, the door of the schoolroom burst open, all the children of the basin tipping out into the sunshine, followed by their teacher. Guy thought it looked like Lucy Cartwright and wondered if Clara Nicol, the vicar's wife, would join the throng too. Others came from the fields and from the barns and stables to join them, some Guy recognised, some were new to him.

Standing on the crest, Amelie and Lizzy looked down on a scene that had been described many times before as paradise. Green pastures lay before them, everywhere dotted with sheep. In the distance they could see a lake of deep, deep blue, and beyond that a line of snow capped mountains, more beautiful than anything they had seen in the Swiss Alps. The flat land in front of them was surrounded by mountains, covered in snow, even in summer, and it did indeed give the impression of a basin, just as Guy had described it to them.

Closer by, they could see two homes, matching pairs on either side of a stream, both surrounded by orchards and vegetable gardens, both had a yard full of dogs and chickens. But what took them by surprise was the crowd of people coming up the hill to greet them, the numbers growing by the minute. Neither Lizzy nor Amelie had realised just how many people had made this place their home, but they could both see why you would never want to go anywhere else once you had reached this corner of paradise.

Lizzy stood, deep in thought, imagining where she and Samuel would make their home together. Would it be here, she wondered to herself, or would Samuel make room for them to live next to his workshop in Marytown? She wondered if Samuel's children were amongst the group of youngsters heading up the hill towards them. She was excited but quite nervous about meeting them. She didn't much mind where she ended up living, to be honest, as long as it was with Samuel Morling and his family.

Meanwhile, Guy took Amelie in his arms. "My darling, we have reached paradise at last," he whispered.

"And now I understand," Amelie replied. "I understand why you wanted to come home."

About the Author

Amanda Giorgis was born in Somerset, England. After a career in education and computer systems, she emigrated to New Zealand in 2008 and moved to Canterbury in the beautiful South Island.

Amanda writes while looking out across the flat Canterbury Plains with the snow-capped mountains of the Southern Alps beyond. It is a place where it is easy to find inspiration for stories of the early pioneers, who made this unique land their home.

She shares her home with her husband, Terry and three rescued huntaway dogs, Nemo, Jess and Ted, some chickens, who are as ornamental as they are productive, ten acres of wild garden and the dark skies of the Southern Hemisphere.

More about Amanda can be found on her Facebook page at www.facebook.com/Amanda-Giorgis/ and in her blog at amandagiorgis.com

Printed in Great Britain
by Amazon